A.N. VEREBES

You Can't Hurry Love

Jukebox Collection Book 2

For my parents, because the last book was for my husband and kids.
Sorry I'm a writer and not a doctor. And again I beg you: please don't read the sex scenes.

Contents

Preface

Firstly, this book contains explicit content not suitable for persons under 18 years of age.

Secondly, while *You Can't Hurry Love* is technically a sequel to *Handle With Care*, both can be read as standalone novels.

However, if you would like an ebook copy of *Handle With Care* for free, you can sign up to my newsletter* via https://anverebesauthor.wordpress.com/newsletter_signup and receive a copy in pdf, mobi or epub, distributed via Dropbox (for which you don't need an account).

*Obviously, you're welcome to unsubscribe at any time, but I promise I don't send spam (I send a single newsletter on the first of the month, Aussie time.)

Acknowledgement

Less blabbing this time, I swear!

Huge heartfelt 'thank you's again to my husband, Adam, for supporting my writing and being there to push me along whenever I get too far into my own head. You're so understanding of my need to use writing as an escape mechanism, and I can't express just how much I appreciate that you do everything in your power to allow that to happen. I love you.

Once again, thanks to my bestie, Mark, for letting me vent all manner of authorly concerns at you, and for helping me rethink the whole publishing/marketing process this time around. I'm still pretending that you might actually read this one. LOL

BIG hugs and declarations of eternal gratitude to my proofreader/editor, Tanya Tanaka. Your feedback and guidance helped shape this book into what it is now, and I can't put into words how lovely it has been making a new friend in this big, scary world of writing. I've tweaked it some more since you last saw it, though. I can't help myself!

To my other bestie, Claire, I don't think a simple 'thank you' will cut it here. You talked me down from episodes of self-doubt, imposter syndrome, and writer's block. You helped me settle on the cover, edited the blurb, and listened to me go back and forth a thousand times on every little issue. You read the first unedited draft and gave me the confidence to send it on for unbiased feedback. I'm beyond lucky to call you my friend. You're the Gemma to my Sara. So, even though the words don't come close to covering it, thank you.

Finally, as always, thank you to anyone reading this. I might write primarily for my own enjoyment, but being able to provide entertainment to other people gives me a thrill unlike anything else, and I genuinely hope you enjoy reading this one. (I'm also always looking to make new pen-pals and friends, so feel free to get in contact via email or social media - all the links are at the back of this book. Yes, that was a shameless plug. Sorry not sorry and all that jazz.)

Oh, and I don't think I have to beg any celebrities not to sue me with this one.

Chapter One

The first time Sara Carlisle heard the name 'Charlie Rhodes' it was as her best friend tearfully recounted her unpleasant meeting with the man in question.

"Who the fuck does he think he is?" Sara seethed into the phone. "Tell me your boy toy put him in his damn place, Gems, *please.*" She stretched her long legs out in front of her on her grey linen couch. "What a dick."

Down the line, Gemma snorted. It made Sara smile to know that she'd cheered her friend up a measure.

Things had been a bit rough for Gemma, what with the unplanned pregnancy and the baby's somewhat famous father making his sudden reappearance in her life just in time to watch their gorgeous daughter enter the world. But Everett –or, as Sara liked to think of him, Gemma's Baby Daddy– was now also responsible for introducing Gemma to Charlie, his older brother, who was apparently a disapproving, grumpy, arrogant twit, from what Sara had gathered from the brief phone call so far.

"He's not my boy toy…or toy boy…or whatever," Gemma argued, sounding fondly exasperated as she cut off Sara's trail of thought, "but, yeah, Everett took him outside and they had a chat. And Beatrice –their mum– made him apologise when they came back, which was ten different kinds of awkward."

In Sara's opinion, Gemma was far too sweet and too concerned about what other people thought of her. Had she planned to get pregnant? No.

1

Had she planned for her one-night stand to go AWOL? Also no. If *anyone* had the right to be sanctimonious about their situation, it was Gemma and not the dillweed brother of the guy who had knocked her up and shattered her confidence all in one sitting.

But Sara kept that to herself, knowing that it wasn't what her bestie needed from her right then. Instead, she made a sound of agreement. "I can imagine," she offered gently before asking, "did you need me to come over?"

"Nah, it's fine," Gemma assured her, then yawned. "Everett's gonna take Zoe and I'm going to nap for a bit." She paused. "But thank you. I know you've got my back."

"Damn straight. Now go snuggle that gorgeous honorary niece of mine for me and then get yourself some rest."

They ended the call and Sara tossed her phone aside. It bounced lightly on the couch beside her. Alone in her little brick and tile home -the same one she'd lived in since birth, though she had renovated and repainted over the years, preferring a sleek, modern palette of greys and whites over her mother's terracotta shades- she had time to muse over her best friend's situation.

Sara was genuinely concerned for her sister from another mister. She had been for months, really. Ever since Gemma had dropped the 'I-had-a-one-night-stand-with-my-favourite-actor-and-now-I'm-pregnant' bomb. If Sara had been fiercely protective of her bestie before it was nothing compared to now. Gemma was the only family she had.

They had met at university studying nursing and had clicked instantly.

Well, that wasn't entirely true. Sara was far more extroverted than Gemma, and she wasn't ashamed to admit that she'd sort of strong-armed her way into becoming the other girl's friend. They'd both been lost souls in their respective ways. And, despite their differences, it turned out that they genuinely understood each other. Over a decade later found them as close as actual sisters, if not closer.

They were deeply protective of one another, and Gemma's adoptive family had also taken Sara under their wing once her tragic story was out in the open. For a girl who had grown up with only her mum, having a large, loving family claim her as their own was something she truly cherished.

The sudden change in Gemma's circumstances, and therefore in her family's entire dynamic, was unsettling. None of them had anticipated that Everett Rhodes would react the way he had to becoming a parent so unexpectedly. While Sara was happy for her best friend, she was also afraid it would all fall apart.

Who wouldn't be?

Added to that was the conversation she and Gemma had just shared. Everett had brought his family over from the UK to introduce them to his daughter and, while his mother sounded supportive, his brother Charlie had undermined Gemma's confidence in herself and in whatever co-parenting relationship she was developing with Everett. Charlie Rhodes had all but called Gemma a gold digger!

If I ever meet the bastard, Sara thought to herself with a scowl, *I'll castrate him with the nearest sharp object.*

Fortuitously (*Though, potentially not for old Charlie boy,* she mused wickedly), Brennan rang to invite her to an extended family barbecue for the next evening. Everett apparently wanted their families to get to know one another, given that they'd be connected through Zoe forever. It was a sweet sentiment, but Sara suspected it was all going to end in tears.

At least, if she had it her way, those tears would belong to Everett's dick of a brother.

* * *

Unsurprisingly, Sara despised Charlie on sight. Oh, sure, he was tall and broad shouldered and insanely muscular with captivating green eyes, sandy-blonde coloured hair, and an English accent to swoon over...but he was an arrogant arse.

He had pushed all her buttons during that first barbecue. Gemma had asked her to behave, and she truly had tried, but Everett's brother had known exactly how to get under her skin. Anything she said, he disagreed with. She could have told him the grass was green and he'd have argued it was turquoise with the pure purpose of fucking with her. He clearly thought he was amusing, and she wanted desperately to knock him down a peg or two. *Or ten.*

"If you keep glaring at him like that, your face will set," Gemma chuckled as she took Charlie's vacated seat at the table under the patio. The meal had been delicious, as was to be expected when Gemma's brothers hosted, but Sara had spent a lot of it considering how best to dispose of Everett's brother while making it look like an accident. The thoughts had been therapeutic.

The men were across the yard, each clutching a beer (or wine, in Jeff's case) and discussing Brennan's desire to build a little pergola with a hot tub in it. The men gestured, or pointed, or paced out space on the patch of grass, and they were clearly absorbed in trying to work out the best position and plan of attack for the project. Charlie had boasted that he was a builder –which didn't surprise Sara at all, given the man's frame, or his tan, though Sara unkindly wondered how much sun there actually was to bask in in London– and was loudly explaining the way he would approach the task.

Sara huffed and turned her attention back to her friend. "At least he's not treating you like shit anymore," she acknowledged, before jutting her chin towards the end of the table. "Reckon his mummy gave him a talking to?"

"Probably," the other woman agreed with a nod, completely serious in the face of Sara's semi-joking tone, "Everett thought she might."

Sara reached primly for her wine. "Hmmph," she huffed, nose in the air, "as she should have."

Gemma was staring at Sara's glass wistfully but shook herself out of it. "He's not that bad. He was only looking out for Everett. Bren does the same for me."

"Yeah, but you're the one who was left heartbroken and pregnant." Sara wasn't about to give Charlie Rhodes any sort of leeway. She set down her drink and poked a finger in Gemma's direction. "You even told the Abstastic Wonder over there that you didn't want anything from him. He would have told his dickwad brother that."

Her best friend only shook her head. "Come on, Sarz, you're going to have to let it go. I mean, I have, and I'm the one he was a jerk to. If I can smooth things over with him, there's no reason you can't."

Sara's expression turned pinched and she childishly repeated, "There's no reason you can't," in a high pitched, whiny voice.

"Stop it," Gemma laughed and smacked her arm. "I'm serious."

With a long-suffering sigh, Sara gave in. "Fine. I'll try. For you."

"That's all I ask."

* * *

"Hey, babe," Roger greeted Sara outside the restaurant he'd chosen with a quick kiss to her lips.

They were currently 'on again' in their dating cycle. Given that they'd been casually dating again for a few weeks, the cynical part of Sara was waiting for the inevitable break up. Roger was a nice guy –he was an endocrinologist at the hospital where she worked– but he wasn't looking for a serious relationship.

For the most part, Sara was on the same page. She wasn't looking to settle down just yet, but she was thirty-one and she knew she would have to think about her options at some point. Her bestie suddenly becoming a mum had given Sara a tiny internal jolt that she had shoved right down under an imaginary rug in her subconscious, then dragged a metaphorical couch over the top of it for good measure.

She wasn't ready to have those thoughts. She was still in her prime, and she was enjoying dressing up in figure-hugging dresses and being taken out to dinner in upscale restaurants by her wealthy –wannabe playboy– current boyfriend.

But, despite her resolve, it niggled at the back of her brain. Roger was a good guy, and dating him was fun, but he wasn't going to be her Happily Ever After. They both knew it.

His voice shook her from her thoughts. "How are Gemma and...what'd she name the kid again?"

"Zoe," Sara answered, refraining from rolling her eyes. She allowed him to lead her towards their reserved table with a hand at her back, gracefully weaving through tables of other couples. He pulled out her chair for her and she nodded in thanks. "And they're good. They've just spent most of the week getting to know Everett's mum and brother, and I think Gems might actually miss them when they leave."

Roger made a non-committal sound to acknowledge that he had been half-listening while he perused the wine list. The warm yellow lighting bounced off his light brown hair, giving him a sort of halo effect. "Didn't you hate the brother?"

She shrugged, though he wasn't looking. "Yeah, well, I'm not the one who has to get along with him, I guess."

"Really?" her boyfriend finally looked up and across the table, arching a bushy eyebrow at her. "You and Gemma are practically attached at the hip. You're stuck with this guy in your life too, you realise."

She couldn't prevent her eyes from rolling. "Ugh," she huffed, "don't remind me."

He chuckled, flashing his perfectly straight pearly white teeth at her and, not for the first time, she was struck by how handsome he was when he smiled. "Well," he set the wine list down on the white linen tablecloth, "it probably is a bit strange to talk about other men while you're on a date."

Sara snorted inelegantly. "You're the one who asked about him."

"Point," he ceded, still smiling. "But maybe I'm the jealous type."

That almost had her laughing. Roger was many things, but jealous was not one of them. Still, she played along. Batting her lashes with exaggerated coquettishness, she asked, "So, you're just making sure I only have eyes for you?"

"Maybe I am."

Sara could feel her lips twitching with amusement. She shook her head. "Trust me, babe," she assured him, "Charlie –I'm an absolute wank-stain of a person– Rhodes is not my type."

"I'm glad to hear it," he answered, then raised his hand to hail a passing waiter. "Now, do you feel like red wine or white?"

"White," was her response.

He requested a bottle of something that sounded obnoxious and fancy, and then went ahead and ordered their meals for them as well. When they'd first started dating, Sara had considered the action of him ordering for her somewhat condescending and controlling —and it still was both of those things, to an extent— but she'd come to realise that he meant well by it. Roger truly wanted to share the best things in life with her, but he just never stopped to consider that her tastes might be different to his own.

"So, how was your day?" Sara asked him after the waiter left their table. She poured them each a glass from the carafe of sparkling water on the table. "No dramas at work?"

Given that he was a specialist, he had his own suite of offices in the hospital and mostly managed patients with ongoing endocrine disorders or chronic diseases. Roger rarely ever dealt with emergencies. Occasionally he was called in to consult with other specialists in order to diagnose what he referred to as 'curly' cases, but his job wasn't particularly stressful…even if he did consider himself the next *Gregory House M.D.* The biggest drama he'd had recently was his fight to reserve a better parking space.

"It was good," he answered, sipping at the drink she had poured him, "all ongoing patients for standard reviews. Nothing out of the ordinary." He set his glass down and cocked his head at her. "Yours?"

"Fairly standard for me, too," she replied with a half-shrug and fiddled with the corner of the linen napkin in front of her, idly musing that it practically blended into the tablecloth. This place was very on brand for Roger. Modern, sleek, a little pretentious. It didn't have a lot of character, but the food was rumoured to be amazing. (It would want to be for the price.) "Had a kid with a broken arm, and a tradie who had an unfortunate accident with a nail gun, but nothing too out there for me, either. Then I caught up with Gems after my shift, which you already know."

The waiter returned with the wine, pouring a mouthful into a glass for Roger, which he then made a show of sniffing and tasting before inclining his head in approval and gesturing for the other man to pour two proper glasses. Idly, Sara couldn't help but wonder whether her beau could truthfully tell the difference between the ridiculously priced beverage he'd just sampled, or the eight-dollar bottle in the bottom of her fridge at home. Her money was on 'not a chance'.

"And have you given any more thought to going back to uni?" he prodded, taking a sip of his wine after once again dismissing the poor waiter.

Fighting the urge to roll her eyes, she shook her head. "I'm happy working the E.D." Sara informed him, primly sipping from her own glass. *Yeah,* she thought, *the stuff at home's nicer.* "I don't really want to be a doctor."

She wondered if his 'encouragement' for the idea of her furthering her qualifications was all part of his weird superiority complex. After all, he'd love to tell people he was dating another doctor instead of a lowly nurse. Secretly, though, she felt the nurse suited his convertible driving cliché a bit more.

At least he knew to drop the issue, though he was determined to have the last word on the subject, "Of course it's up to you, but you can never have too many qualifications, you know."

Instead of continuing to argue with him, Sara made a noncommittal sound and changed the topic. She had always been good at deflection and had no qualms playing dirty.

Leaning forward to give him an impressive view of her cleavage, she pouted, "Don't you wanna see me in my naughty nurse getup anymore?"

She knew she'd been successful as Roger cleared his throat, his pupils dilating.

At least she knew she'd have some fun tonight. Once the meal was over, at any rate.

* * *

"Tell me, love, does that rod up your arse ever come out, or are you stuck like this permanently?"

Sara rolled her eyes at Charlie's ham-handed attempt at getting under her skin. "When are you leaving again?" Before he could open his mouth, she clarified, "The country, not the restaurant."

She couldn't believe that she would have to put up with this meathead for the rest of her life. Couldn't Gemma have vetted her boy toy's family before he accidentally knocked her up?

"Settle petal," Charlie's smug retort grated on her nerves, "I like your presence here about as much as you like mine."

Despite how well Gemma had taken to Charlie since the barbecue at Brennan's place, Sara couldn't see what was so likable about the man. But she'd come along to the farewell meal, this one held in public at Gemma's favourite Thai restaurant, because Gemma had practically begged her to. At least Beatrice was lovely.

"Charlie," as if to illustrate Sara's mental point, Charlie's mother scolded him like a toddler as she sat between the two of them, "I thought we'd discussed this?"

Sara valiantly fought the urge to lean back in her seat and poke her tongue out at him behind his mother's back.

Across from them, Brennan and Jeff cooed over Zoe, who was staring around at all the bright colours and gold accents with her usual unfocused gaze. It was a conversation between the two men and Sara which had set the elder Rhodes brother off to begin with, butting in to offer his opinion as though Sara had cared to hear it.

When she'd told him that she hadn't, he had bitten back with that lame attempt at an insult.

Now cowed by his mother, Charlie was silent. Sara much preferred him that way. Sitting up a little straighter, she smirked to herself and reached for the menu, catching a glimpse of the disapproving glare on her bestie's face from her seat beside her brother.

Damn it.

Sara feigned innocence. "What?"

Gemma cocked her head to the side with an eyebrow raised. "I think you know what."

Sara had promised to try to be civil, hadn't she? *Ugh.* It was harder than she thought it would be. Jutting her chin higher, she held on to her pride. "Nope," she responded lightly, "no idea."

"Sara…"

Not lifting her eyes from the page in front of her, Sara sassed, "You've really got that cranky mum tone down pat. Bravo."

There was a sigh. "Sarz. Come on."

Fuck it. She hated the defeat in her best friend's voice. "Fine," she exhaled, lowering the menu to glower over the top of it. "But I want it noted that I object. A lot."

"When don't you?" Gemma teased, but her shoulders drooped with obvious relief at the same time as Everett returned from the bar with their drinks.

"I think you'll find there are plenty of things I don't object to," Sara winked at Gemma's baby daddy as he took his seat at the end of the table just offside to Gemma, then laughed as he awkwardly deflected. Her BFF told her to knock it off while fighting off her own amusement. "Alright, alright," Sara took a sip of her wine. "I'll behave."

Even though Sara didn't like Charlie, it was good to see Gems much more at ease than she had been when Everett's family had first entered the country. She had worried for Gemma when Everett had so suddenly burst back onto the scene, especially when it seemed he wanted to be active in the baby's life. The man had a lot more money –and some might argue this meant more stability– to offer a child, and there had been a moment where Sara had been terrified that his family would demand he apply for custody, potentially whisking Zoe out of the country and out of Gemma's reach.

She thanked all the deities she could think of that Everett had proven her wrong. It would have broken Gemma if he'd been that guy.

"So, tell me," Charlie directed the question her way once she'd made her promise to Gemma, the glint in his eye seemingly payback for her smugness at his own telling off, "why doesn't your boyfriend ever attend these family get-togethers?"

"Roger marches to the beat of his own drum," she answered easily with a shrug. "Sometimes he comes along, other times he doesn't. We don't need to live in each other's pockets."

After a couple of years of doing the whole on-and-off/casual relationship thing, she was used to it. Besides, Roger didn't pressure her to attend events with him, either. Which was a good thing, because his snobby parents couldn't stand her, and vice versa.

Sara felt as though things were pretty equal in that way.

"I couldn't imagine him in a low-key restaurant like this, to be honest," Jeff chimed in, chuckling. He stuck his nose in the air and assumed a haughty tone as he looked down at his menu, "Sara, darling, I don't see a single main here over twenty-five dollars. Outrageous! We're truly dining with the commoners tonight."

Balling up a purple paper napkin, she threw it at her friend, even while she smothered her own giggles. "Stop it," she chastened, "he's not that bad."

Gemma snorted. Sara levelled her with a glare, but all Gemma did was raise her glass of water to her twitching lips and sip primly. "Sorry," she said, sounding anything but apologetic, "but that impression was spot on."

"You both suck," Sara sighed, shaking her head.

"Sounds like you could do with a real man in your life," Charlie was having far too much fun at her expense, and it ruffled her feathers the wrong way.

It was one thing for her friends –who also worked with Roger in the hospital– to playfully tease Sara about him, but altogether different for this random English wanker to do so.

"I hope you're not suggesting you're a viable option," she sassed back, "because I don't think you fall into that category either."

Okay, so it was a bit flat and ridiculous as far as comebacks went, but he scowled back at her, so she took it as a win, nonetheless.

"Don't flatter yourself, love."

"*Aww*, diddums, did I hurt your feelings?"

They were interrupted by their names being snapped on either side of them. He was cowed by his mother's frown, while Sara sighed and apologised to Gemma.

This really was going to be much more difficult than she'd initially thought.

Chapter Two

"Oh, darling, look at this one!"

Sitting in his mother's modest living room, surrounded by floral prints and walls that were too peachy in colour for his liking, Charlie bit back a sigh as she thrust yet another photo of his niece under his nose. The kid was only a few months old and, to him, looked exactly the same in every single one. He didn't deny Zoe was cute, but he drew the line at *aww*-ing and *ahh*-ing over six hundred identical pictures. "Yes, Mum."

Beatrice slapped his bicep with more force than he personally thought was necessary.

"Ow!" With his hand covering the stinging spot, he glowered at her. "What was that for?"

"You need to watch your tone," she sniffed, "giving me cheek like that. I don't care how old you are, Charles Michael Rhodes, I'll bring out the wooden spoon again if I have to."

Considering he was forty-two, he couldn't imagine anything more ridiculous. But, given the verbal lashing his petite mother had served him back when he'd been less than friendly to Gemma, he was almost convinced that she might actually follow through on her threat.

Hoping he sounded contrite enough, he offered, "Sorry, Mum." It struck him that his mother was probably missing her first –and only– grandchild terribly, which made him feel genuinely guilty. "It won't be too long 'til you get to see her again."

They'd gone back to Australia and spent a week over Christmas with Everett, Zoe, Gemma, and Gemma's extended family. His mum had been beyond ecstatic to celebrate Zoe's first Christmas with her, and he knew it had upset her awfully when they had returned to the UK again.

"We'll stay a bit longer over Easter, yeah?" he suggested. "I'll see if I can get a little more time off work."

It might be a little strange staying with Gemma if Everett was still overseas filming, but if it would make his mother happy, Charlie would suffer through it. Besides, he and Rhett's lady love got along alright these days, despite their rough start.

They'd talked it out eventually. Gemma seemed to genuinely understand Charlie was simply being protective of his little brother. And, if Charlie was being honest, he felt a bit shitty for the attitude he'd given her when he'd suspected that she was little more than a gold-digging trollop.

"Are you sure?" his mum asked, hope already blossoming in her green eyes as she clutched the photo close to her chest. He wondered if his own eyes –inherited directly from her– ever looked like that, or if it was a trick that only she could pull off, because it got him right in his guilt reflex. "You won't be missed?"

"Maybe by the boys for my shout down at the pub on a Friday night," he answered honestly, "but I've got loads of leave racked up, and we've not had a lot of work on lately."

It wasn't as though he had much of a social life to speak of, anyhow. He enjoyed his job as a builder, and it paid well, but he often pulled long hours and, outside of his casual football games and the weekly drinks with his workmates, he was usually too exhausted to do much else.

Speaking of which, his mother hadn't nagged him about his non-existent dating life in a while. Charlie assumed she was distracted by Rhett accidentally landing himself an instant family. If he was still being honest, he thought her distraction was an unexpected boon to come from the whole situation. But it was only a matter of time before she started up again.

Therefore, distracting her with Rhett's kid was the best plan of action.

"So, what do you reckon?" he prodded. "Should I line it up?"

Beatrice bobbed her head, a grateful smile spreading across her face. He knew he was a bit of a 'mummy's boy', but he did truly enjoy seeing her happy.

It had been over thirty years, but Beatrice's misery when his and Everett's dad had shot through was burned into his brain. As a kid, he'd vowed to never let his mum feel that way again. And if taking her to her granddaughter was the key to keeping her happy, Charlie would gladly accommodate her. Anyway, visiting Australia wasn't exactly a chore –outside of the lengthy flight– and he'd enjoyed their last two trips.

Well, perhaps that wasn't entirely true. The Australian summer heat and humidity had been a shock to his system. However, Rhett and Gemma's house had air conditioning and a pool, which had negated most of his whinging.

"You're going to be nicer to that lovely girl, though," his mum's voice interrupted his musings.

"Are you finally going senile?" Charlie teased, ducking as she motioned to hit him again. "Gemma and I are all good now, remember?" She'd even called him during Rhett's first trip back to LA when things had begun falling apart. He'd felt quite chuffed that she'd turned to him for help at the time.

Rolling her eyes, his mother shook her head. "Not Gemma. Her friend. Sara."

Oh. Her.

"Well, if *Her Royal Highness* deigned to treat me civilly, we wouldn't have an issue." His reply was curt. She was a bitchy little thing. Gorgeous –with legs for days– and she knew it, but she refused to forgive him for upsetting Gemma during their first meeting.

Hell, even Gemma had forgiven him, so why on earth couldn't Sara let it go?

After packing her photos back away, his mother rose from her seat next to him on the sofa to go check on the roast in the oven. The flat was a tiny one-bedder, and the kitchen was all of five steps away. An enormous, oval shaped oak dining table took up much of the space beside the kitchen, situated in front of the large window that looked out onto the street. Honestly, why did his mother need a six-seater table?

Squeezing past the item in question, Beatrice shot him a narrow-eyed glare over her shoulder. "She's as protective of Gemma as you are of Everett," she admonished. "And let's not forget the fact that you were deliberately argumentative."

"Once." Charlie huffed. "One time, and I'm tarnished with that brush forever, eh? Is that how it goes?"

From the kitchen of her little flat, Beatrice made a dismissive '*pffft*' sound. He heard the oven door creak and then clank shut. "You stir that poor girl up every time you're in a room with her."

"That *poor girl*," he informed his mother with liberal sarcasm, heaving himself from the sofa to go and set the table for lunch, "gives as good as she gets, and then some. We just don't get along," he shrugged.

It was a bit of an understatement at this point. And, yes, he enjoyed getting under her skin, because seeing her frustrated eased some of his own irritation. As far as he was concerned, he and Sara were oil and water.

"Well, she's practically Gemma's sister," his mum said as she pulled the roast from the oven and set it on the chopping board to rest. She turned and planted her hands on her hips, giving him the same stare down that had cowed him as a child. It still had a similar effect, despite the fact that he now towered over her. "So you're likely stuck with her for life." She ignored his groan. "Best get used to being civil now."

He hated to acknowledge that she was right.

Taking the steaming platter of roast vegetables to the table, he muttered under his breath, "I will if she will."

Behind him, carrying a pitcher of gravy, Beatrice snorted affectionately. "Oh, grow up, Charlie."

* * *

Easter came quickly. Everett had warned Charlie not to buy chocolates

15

for Zoe (when Charlie had asked what kind of gifts to bring, Rhett's exact words had been 'She's barely six months old, you twit') so he'd bought an obnoxiously oversized plush rabbit toy instead. His brother rolled his eyes as Charlie attempted to sneak the gift into the house.

"Gemma's going to kill you," was all Everett said on the matter, though.

Charlie grinned, stashing the toy in the guestroom before shutting the door behind him. "Ah, Rhett," he shook his head, patting his brother on the shoulder as they meandered back down the hallway towards the main living area, "your little firecracker loves me these days. I'll take my chances."

Everett was only able to stay a week over Easter and would have to return to LA to continue filming whatever role he'd most recently landed. It was good to see him in person again, and Charlie had to admit that staying in the man's Brisbane home was a little less awkward when Everett was actually there.

That wasn't to say Gemma wasn't welcoming. However, Charlie definitely felt like an outsider when he was surrounded by Gemma's family with only his mum as a buffer. Gemma's brother, Brennan, was also a nice enough bloke –as was his partner, Jeff– but they were relative strangers to him. Having his own brother there filled the clumsy gaps in conversation.

"You're a braver man than me," Everett shrugged. "I've been learning when to pick my battles."

It was still a bit weird seeing his brother all settled down and domesticated, but there was no denying that Rhett's unexpected foray into fatherhood was good for him. Additionally, the whole situation had brought the two of them closer again. Charlie knew that this last part made their mum particularly happy, too.

Speaking of... he wondered to himself, asking out loud, "Where'd Mum run off to?"

Everett arched a dark eyebrow at him. "There's nothing but air between your ears, is there?" He sighed, then explained, "The ladies and Jeff have all gone off on a spa day."

"Ah," Charlie bobbed his head, "that's what they were rabbiting on about at breakfast." He'd been distracted with his plan to get his Easter gift shopping done as quickly as possible. As a self-confessed walking, talking cliché of a man, he absolutely detested shopping. Having a plan of attack meant he'd been able to knock the whole lot over in one go.

He cocked his head as he followed his brother into the kitchen. It was a bright, modern space, with granite benchtops and brand-new appliances. Charlie thought they could probably fit both his own kitchen and his mum's inside this one. "Where's the sprog, then?"

"Your niece," his little brother answered pointedly as he opened the large stainless-steel fridge and pulled out two bottles of beer, "is napping in her cot."

"Ta," Charlie accepted one of the beers, twisting the top and relishing the hissing sound as the cap released. He took a swig and leaned against the counter. "No wonder it's quiet." Zoe was a generally happy baby, but she was loud about it.

She was *definitely* his brother's kid.

"Enjoy it while it lasts," Everett responded, clinking their bottles together before taking his own mouthful of beer. He rounded the bench, crossed the room, and slumped down on the couch situated on the other side of the open plan dining and living area.

Not for the first time, Charlie considered just how much things had changed. For example, their mum's entire flat probably spanned the whole kitchen-dining-living space of Everett's house. The little council flat he and Rhett had grown up in hadn't been much bigger. While this house was perfect for a growing family, it was still strange to think that his brother lived in it...when he wasn't off working, anyway.

The space in front of the couch was filled with an assortment of brightly coloured baby toys. Charlie picked his way past it all to sit down on the two-seater beside his brother. "I don't know how you do it," he confessed into the comfortable silence that had descended. At Rhett's raised brow, he extrapolated, waving his free arm over the space in front of them. "This daddy business. Nappies, bottles, toys, constant noise...ugh." He took another generous draw from his beer. "No offence, little brother, but this is how I imagine Hell."

Everett chuckled. "Good thing you're an atheist, then, eh?" He set his drink down on the side table. "Besides," he pinned Charlie with a bland look, "it's nothing you've got to worry about when you're perpetually celibate."

"Oi!" Charlie rolled his eyes, then sighed. "Yeah, alright, fair point."

Rhett continued to look at him expectantly.

"Oh no; don't you start."

"I had my reasons for avoiding serious relationships," it seemed Everett wasn't going to be discouraged, "but what's stopping you?"

Charlie cast his gaze to the ceiling. "For fuck's sake."

"I watched at least five women attempt to get your attention at the airport the other day, so it's not your looks."

He knew Everett had always been a little jealous of his taller, broader physique and his naturally golden coloured hair, so he snorted. "Thanks, Rhett."

"I'm serious, Charlie. You're forty-two-"

"Please don't remind me."

"-and I can't remember the last time you were seeing someone."

It was Charlie's turn to throw his brother a flat look. "One: we've not really had the sort of relationship where we talked about this stuff until recently," he began, counting on his fingers for emphasis, "and two...well, alright, look, I've had a bit of a dry spell, but, like you, casual was always my thing. *Is* my thing."

"Uh huh." He hated that Everett didn't sound convinced.

Scowling, Charlie demanded, "Did Mum put you up to this?"

He knew he was onto something when Everett shifted his gaze.

"I knew it!" Downing the last of his beer, Charlie stood up to deposit the bottle into the recycling bin in the kitchen.

"Shh!" Everett was frowning at him now. "Do you want to wake the baby?"

"If it'll get you and Mum off my back about fucking settling down?" Charlie asked rhetorically as he ambled back to the couch and dropped down heavily. "Yes."

"You wake her, you get to look after her." The other man shot back, before asking, "Is it so wrong that we want you to be happy?"

Charlie blinked back at him, dumbstruck. "Who *are* you?"

"Oh, shove off."

"No, I'm serious – you should know better than anyone that I don't need to be in a relationship or have kids to be happy."

"I never said you had to have kids." Everett was standing firm. "You're getting a bit old for it anyway."

Despite himself, Charlie cracked a grin at the unexpected ribbing. "Piss off."

His brother's expression softened. "Look, I get it. Being alone's easier, right? Nobody to hurt you or get hurt by, nobody to nag you or whatever. But," he raised his hand as Charlie moved to interrupt, "and hear me out, alright?" Charlie shut his mouth and nodded defeatedly. "It's going to sound ridiculous, but you just need the right person."

Given that he'd already heard all about how *effortless* and *easy* Everett thought being with Gemma was, Charlie decided he didn't need to hear him wax poetic any longer. "That's probably true," he acknowledged, "but I am happy as I am right now, Rhett. So lay off, alright?"

His brother pursed his lips and looked as though he wanted to belabor the point, but after another moment conceded, "Alright."

"Thank you."

"But–"

"Oh, Christ…"

"Just know that you can change your mind about it at any time, yeah?" Everett nudged his shoulder. "It won't make you any less of a man, you stubborn git."

Before Charlie could respond, a familiar, obnoxious voice cut in with a laugh. "That's assuming he's man enough to begin with." Sara sauntered into the room, dropping a handful of shopping bags onto the floor beside the kitchen bench. She hopped up to sit on the granite surface, crossing her long legs at the ankle and chirping, "What are we talking about, anyway?"

From between gritted teeth, Charlie responded, "Nothing that concerns you, princess." His spirits rose at the expression of distaste which flitted across her face. For some reason she despised the moniker, and so he used it frequently.

"Alright children," Everett interrupted, narrowing his gaze at Charlie, "behave." He stood up and crossed the room to greet Gemma with a kiss. "Did you lovely ladies enjoy your day?"

It was Jeff who answered, striding in arm-in-arm with their mother. "We did, thanks. It was just what the doctor ordered."

"That massage was heavenly," Beatrice agreed. "Worked out all the kinks from that Godawful flight."

Charlie stretched his neck from side to side at the reminder. "I shoulda' gone with you, then."

Sara muttered something that was likely uncomplimentary under her breath, but, at Everett's disapproving glower, Charlie bit his tongue. He was unused to this dynamic: previously, he'd been the one delivering looks like that in response to Rhett's antics. He didn't particularly appreciate being on the receiving end.

"How'd Zoe go?" Gemma asked. Charlie could tell she was attempting to change the topic, too, if the glare she'd sent Sara was anything to go by.

It was still strange to watch his brother switch completely into daddy mode. Everett grinned at his girlfriend. "We went to the park, came home and she tried some pureed sweet potato – she's a fan, by the way." At six months old, they were starting to introduce solids. How did Charlie know this? They'd regaled him and his mother with the information over dinner the previous night. His mum had lapped it up. Charlie had been bored as fuck. "And then she had a bottle and went down for her nap without any issues."

With his mother cooing at his brother, Charlie did his best not to roll his eyes, but let his mind drift. He loved his niece, but he wasn't all that concerned by the minutiae of dealing with an infant. Glancing around the room, his gaze landed on Sara. Still perched on the kitchen bench, she was examining her fingernails, clearly just as interested in the conversation taking place as he was.

Look at that, he thought to himself with droll amusement, *we've got something in common after all.*

The moment was broken as she sensed his stare and looked up to catch him observing her. Her eyes rolled and she made a shooing motion with her perfectly manicured talons, which, he noted, were painted a vivid, cherry red. He flipped her off and looked away, wishing he could point out what a cliché she was.

Vapid cow.

* * *

Sara's doctor boyfriend, it turned out, was even more of a pain in the arse than she was. He'd been invited to the family Easter lunch held on Easter Sunday, and had come along mostly, Charlie suspected, to brown nose with Everett.

From the moment he'd waltzed through the front door, he'd been beyond obnoxious and snooty. Wearing a casual outfit that Charlie was certain was designer but looked utterly ridiculous, the guy had sidled up alongside Everett and attempted to name drop and brand drop in conversation.

Seated across from Roger at the dining table with his back to the kitchen, Charlie had wanted to snigger. Roger (*Christ*, even his name was affectatious and stupid) seemed oblivious to the fact that –despite his posh accent– Everett Rhodes had grown up dirt poor in a council estate and didn't give a rat's arse about status or wealth. Yes, he was somewhat of a celebrity, but he hadn't forgotten his roots, and he'd never been big on flashing his cash about.

Charlie had always been proud of his brother for keeping his head when the fame and money had started rolling in. A bit narcissistically, Charlie liked to think he was responsible for that. After all, he'd been Rhett's male role model after their dad up and left.

At this point, Roger was pontificating about which luxury cars he thought Gemma and Everett should investigate buying. While Gemma had essentially employed the 'smile and nod' tactic, clearly ignoring everything being said, and Everett excused himself to change the baby, Charlie felt as though he couldn't keep his mouth shut any longer. However, just as he began to speak,

21

so did Sara.

"You're being a dick," she said, taking Charlie completely by surprise. He almost thought that she was addressing him, but, no, she was definitely speaking to her boyfriend. "Gem's already told you she's happy with her car. Not everyone needs a status symbol to feel good about themselves."

The doctor sat back in his seat, blinking in surprise. "It's not a status symbol…" he attempted to argue, but she cut him off, scoffing.

"Then why not buy a Toyota? Or a Hyundai or something?"

It was kind of fun not to be on the receiving end of Sara's protective streak. It was even a little admirable that she'd rounded on her boyfriend when Charlie would have otherwise assumed that she enjoyed the benefits of the doctor's lavish lifestyle.

"I mean, there's nothing wrong with those makes, babe, but…" Roger shrugged.

Gemma excused herself to 'go help Everett', leaving the man to deliver his lecture to Sara and Charlie.

Feeling stuck, Charlie looked down the table to see if any of the others could rescue him, but they were all involved in their own conversation. No help there, then.

Roger continued, "I'm just saying that if they can afford luxury, they should indulge. The guy's a celebrity, for crying out loud, but he's living in a fairly standard house out in the suburbs instead of a mansion in Ascot, and he's driving a plain old soccer-mum-mobile. It's a little weird."

Charlie bristled on Everett's behalf, but apparently so did Sara. She set her cutlery down with more force than necessary and, with exaggerated patience, responded, "Again: not everyone feels the need to blatantly splash their cash around." She looked up and across the table at Charlie, demanding, "Back me up here."

Roger spoke before Charlie could. "No offence," (With that, Charlie knew that he would very much take offence to the next words that came out of the man's mouth.) "but Old Mate here's a builder, right? That's not exactly on the same level."

The sound of frustration Sara made at the back of her throat almost had Charlie chuckling. "Maybe not the same as Everett, no," she argued –bizarrely– on Charlie's behalf, now folding her arms across her chest as she stared down her boyfriend, "but I'm willing to bet he's just as financially comfortable as you are. Possibly even more. But that shouldn't change how valid his opinion on the topic is either way."

Her tone was heated now. Charlie felt a little badly for Roger, who probably began the whole conversation with good, if misguided, intentions.

"Look," Charlie said diplomatically, attempting to ease the tension, "I can see both sides here. As a kid, I always thought if I had the dosh, I'd live the high life. But that's not actually me, and it's not Rhett, either. But it doesn't make enjoying your money wrong if that's what make you happy."

"That's the point I was trying to make," Sara huffed. Charlie was almost worried that Sara would lecture him about mansplaining the topic –which he suspected that he might have done a little– but her boyfriend, for all his book smarts, seemed a bit thick witted, so putting it into different words might have helped.

Roger was silent for a moment. "Well, yeah, alright," he finally acknowledged, reaching for his glass of wine. "I won't pretend to understand it, but I see what you're saying."

As he raised his drink to his mouth, Sara rolled her eyes and mouthed 'No he doesn't' across the table at Charlie, who snorted and then covered the sound with a cough.

"You alright there, Charlie?" Everett asked, giving him a thump to his back as he reclaimed his seat beside his brother. In a lower voice he added, "Don't tell me you've been arguing again."

"I have been on my best behaviour," Charlie assured him, catching Sara's gaze and nodding in acknowledgement.

Perhaps, he thought to himself, being civil wasn't completely out of their reach.

Chapter Three

"I can't believe," Sara puffed as she pummelled the punching bag swinging in front of her, "that fucking douche dumped me." She paused to swipe at the line of sweat on her forehead with the back of her hand. "*He* dumped *me*. That fucker."

"Language," Gemma half-heartedly scolded from the exercise bike before she attempted to sound empathetic. "You did say you didn't see a future with him. And this is, what, the fourth time you've broken up now?"

"Fifth."

They were in Gemma and Everett's home gym (a space the latter had spent a fortune on setting up for his fitness regime) with the now two-year-old Zoe occupied with her toys in the playpen at the far corner of the room. They were able to keep an eye on her through the mirror taking up the entire wall in front of them.

Sara grabbed the punching bag with both hands and brought her knee up to it almost viciously. She imagined it was Roger. "And this time it's for good. He said I was getting too old."

Gemma panted, pushing her legs to work her through the incline setting on the bike. "So you've said. Eight times now."

"The bastard is forty, Gemma! I'm barely thirty-three!"

"The bah-tad," a little voice repeated from across the room.

"Thanks for that," the toddler's mother replied dryly, "we've been working on her vocabulary."

Sara had the grace to appear sheepish. "Sorry," she apologised, pummelling the bag again. "I'm just so mad! I mean, the gall of him!"

What upset her the most was that she hadn't seen it coming this time. She and Roger had had a fairly good streak for their relationship —just over eighteen months this time, not counting the break-up after Christmas— and she'd gotten comfortable in their routine. She might have even started to convince herself that she'd originally been wrong; that there might have been a future with him after all.

Then his convertible driving, fake tan wearing, Rogaine using, mid-life crisis having self had gone and dumped her out of nowhere.

Arsehole.

"Too *old*, Gems! *Me!*"

And, yeah, alright, that had stung a bit, too. She wasn't old. She was *barely* thirty-three. Still well and truly in her prime. She was tall and slim with long legs and an hourglass figure she was extremely proud of. She was hot, God damn it, and he was an idiot for letting her go simply because her age didn't begin with a '2'.

Disgusting. She took back any kind thought she'd ever had about the man.

"You knew he was vain the first time you hooked up with him," her friend reminded her, now sitting back and pedalling at a more relaxed pace. "What makes this breakup different to all the others? You know, outside of the fact that *he* broke up with *you.*"

Having exhausted herself, Sara dropped her hands from the punching bag and shrugged. "I thought maybe we might actually have had something, I guess." She felt silly putting the words out there now. Her throat tightened and she grit her teeth, refusing to give Roger the satisfaction of making her cry. "Maybe he had a point. I'm not getting younger."

"Sarz, don't be stupid. You look like a supermodel." Gemma slowed the bike and turned it off, reaching for her water bottle. "And you know I hate you a bit for that."

Snorting as she patted herself down with her towel, Sara shook her head.

"Not like that. I mean…I'm at that point where most women my age are getting married, or," she jutted her chin towards Zoe, "having kids. Now I have to start all over again with someone else? Time is kind of running out, isn't it?"

Understanding dawned in her friend's hazel eyes. "That's not true. You've got plenty of time. There aren't any rules for this sort of thing."

"Except for my actual biological clock." It terrified her that her time was starting to run out and she could feel it.

Gemma regarded her seriously. "Do you want kids?"

"Not right this second, but…well, I always thought I'd have at least one one day, I guess." She'd been an only child and had been very close to her mum, and some part of her had always secretly hoped to have a similar relationship with her own kid. "And I know there's always fostering and adoption, or even using a surrogate, but…" she trailed off, sighing. "I kind of want to do things the same way as you, y'know?"

"Get accidentally pregnant from a one-night stand with your favourite actor?" her bestie asked sardonically.

"No, you idiot," Sara scrunched up her towel and lobbed it at Gemma. It missed. "I want to find someone I have this amazing connection with. I want to fall stupidly in love. I want to be trusted and respected and supported and be able to offer him the same in return."

These feelings were at war with her equal desire to be as strong and independent as her mum had been. After Sara's father's unexpected death, her mum hadn't sought out another partner. Sara had asked her once why she'd chosen to remain single. Her mother had held her close and said that she couldn't bear losing anyone else.

To that very day, her mother's response had stuck with Sara.

While she understood that her heartbroken mum had been guarding herself from further heartache –and, hell, she even felt as though she could relate now– Sara couldn't help but think that it was a lonely path to have chosen.

Bringing herself back to the conversation at hand, Sara shook her head and a few locks of her sweaty dark hair fell loose from her ponytail. She smoothed them back with a grimace. "You lucked out with Everett. Where do I find one of those?"

A wicked expression flitted across Gemma's face. She threw her own towel over her shoulder and planted a hand on her hip. "Well, you know he has a brother."

That caused Sara to burst into loud peals of laughter. "You can fuck right on off with that idea," she managed between cackles, once more forgetting to censor herself. "Just consider yourself lucky that Charlie boy and I have learned how to be civil."

Ever since that first Easter, they seemed to have reached a silent truce. She was fairly certain he still hated her –and she couldn't say she had particularly warmed to him, either– but they didn't go out of their way to argue anymore. What few conversations they shared were stilted and stiff, but she knew that Everett and Gemma were grateful for their efforts. And, she had to admit, it did make their family get-togethers more comfortable all around.

Gemma continued to tease her, though, as she picked up Zoe from the playpen and settled her neatly on her hip. "You're actually pretty similar. You might get friendly yet."

"Ugh." Euphemism or not, Sara wasn't at all on board with that suggestion. It was time to get a little payback at the playful ribbing. Her lips twisted into a mocking grin. "You know what I'd rather know? When's Wonder Boy going to put a ring on your finger already?"

Her best friend groaned and rolled her eyes. "Will you give it a rest? We don't need to get married-"

"Because you have a house and a kid together and these are big enough commitments... Blah blah blahdy blah." Sara pushed a bit further, having heard this argument before. She knew it drove Gemma crazy when she teased her about the possibility of her boyfriend proposing. "Lover boy popping a ring on it is basically a formality at this point."

Sharp as ever, Gemma was quick to divert the taunting back onto Sara. "So's giving Charlie a chance. He might surprise you."

"Sure. And pigs will fly."

"Piggy!" In Gemma's hold, Zoe's bright blue eyes widened, and she clapped her hands. "Say oink oink!"

"That's right, missy moo," Sara praised as they left the gym and closed the door behind them, "pigs say oink. And they will *never* fly."

She pointedly ignored Gemma's muttered, "You never know…"

* * *

"Wow, you look smokin' hot," Sara's date greeted her as she approached the table at the restaurant he'd chosen. He stayed seated and looked her up and down in the same way she imagined a captive lion eyed a steak. She felt a little gross. "Hotter than your profile pic and everything."

Make that very gross.

The dress she'd worn was demurer than her usual fare: a fitted and flared 50s inspired tea dress with teardrop cut outs at the chest. In soft pink, she felt young and feminine. It was a striking juxtaposition from the sexy and powerful feeling she got from the femme fatale getups which she was more known for. And, considering this guy's leer, she was glad she hadn't worn anything more seductive in nature.

So this is going to go well. She internally rolled her eyes, wondering if she shouldn't just turn around and leave.

"Thank you," she responded a little coldly, pulling out her seat and settling into it.

He'd asked her to meet him at a cute little Indian restaurant in the middle of the city. It was warm and inviting, decorated in burnt orange with gold accents. And the smell of the other diners' dishes had her salivating. If nothing else, she knew that she'd enjoy her meal.

"What's good here?" she asked, picking up her menu to peruse it.

Thankfully, he copied her actions. "I dunno," he answered. "I usually just get Butter Chicken."

Ah, and he's worldly, too, she mused with heavy sarcasm. Not that there was anything wrong with Butter Chicken –it was a staple for a reason– but there was something to be said for being adventurous, wasn't there? Or did these thoughts make her just as snobby as Roger? *Oh, God, don't let me be like*

Roger.

"Butter Chicken is always good," she agreed upon her final thought, closing the menu and setting it back down.

Immediately she felt awkward again.

"So, Josh, what was it you do again?"

She hated small talk. Hated the whole song and dance of getting to know a complete stranger who she already knew she wouldn't see again. But this was what she'd signed up for when she −after a few glasses of wine with Gemma− had set up a Tinder profile.

Ugh. Was it too late to join a convent? No, wait, she wasn't religious in the least. Maybe she should just buy a handful of cats and resign herself to spinsterhood. She liked cats.

Josh gave his answer and she nodded and asked a follow up question, already forgetting whatever it was he'd said. There was no spark here. None of the instant connection Gemma had recounted (at length) about her first meeting with Everett. Not even any of the 'damn, he's handsome' feelings that she had experienced when she had first met Roger. Nothing.

But she had wanted to try. She had wanted to put herself back out there. To prove she could date and be happy with whatever came her way. Unfortunately −at least in this case− it didn't look like that was going to happen.

Over the course of their meal, her companion made crude jokes, talked over her, and even requested that she pay for her share. It wasn't that she had any issues doing so, but the way he'd demanded it left a sour taste in her mouth.

But the cherry on top was his expectation that she would come home with him.

"But…it's Tinder," he complained as she turned him down politely, but firmly. They were still standing in the doorway of the crowded restaurant. "You know that Tinder's all about hook-ups, right?"

She straightened her back and finally rolled her eyes at him. "Listen, Jason−"

"Josh."

"Whatever." If he wasn't going to respect her right to turn him down, she wasn't going to remember his name. "I'm gonna say this louder for the people in the back. No means no." He shrank back, clearly embarrassed as eyes turned their way. "You can't just expect someone is going to fall into bed with you for any reason, do you hear me? Hook up culture or not, not every Tinder date has to end in sex. A mentality like that's going to get you into a world of trouble."

A part of her ached as she wondered how many women had actually gone home with this guy because they'd felt guilted into it. It was incredibly wrong, and it made her feel as though she was going to bring the Butter Chicken right back up over his shiny –but cheap– shoes.

"Jesus," his lip curled with derision as his humiliation brought out his fight reflex, "who woulda' thought you were a stuck-up feminist when your profile pic is so slutty?"

Sara hated that she missed Roger in this moment. He'd been an elitist, ageist prick, but he'd had enough of a moral code that he'd never call a woman names (except for 'old' when he was dumping them) or just expect that they owed him something for giving them a sliver of his attention.

Incensed, she widened her eyes and raised her voice, bitterly declaring, "Wow! I'm sorry. You're right! That *really* makes me want to take you home now and find out what you're trying to compensate for."

Somewhere behind her, someone applauded. But she was shaking with anger now, and she just wanted to curl up in her bed –alone– and cry.

"Fuck you," he snapped before he turned and stormed out.

Her shoulders sagged in relief. "You wish," she muttered at his retreating form.

Had she mentioned how much she hated dating?

* * *

It took Sara a couple more months before she braved another Tinder date at Gemma's urging. This time, the guy was friendly and open, and Sara found herself relaxing enough to tell him the whole sad story of her previous disaster of a date.

"Shit," the guy –Max– said as Sara concluded her narrative with the admission that she'd been nervous to try again. "What a wanker." He sounded genuinely upset for her, and this eased something inside her. "For what it's worth," he added, his dark brown eyes meeting hers earnestly, "I don't want to sleep with you."

She blinked, not having expected that. "Uh…"

He facepalmed and cringed, staring upwards at the ceiling of the trendy diner at Southbank where they'd agreed to meet. "That came out wrong."

"No, no," she taunted playfully as she leaned back in her booth seat, snagging up one of her remaining fries and drawing it through her pool of tomato sauce, "please tell me how very undesirable I am. I enjoy that," she smirked.

Max laughed; the sound was deep and rich. It sent a pleasant shiver up Sara's spine, which was an impressive feat for a man who had just told her that he wasn't interested. "If it weren't for my complexion," he informed her, "you'd be able to tell how badly I'm blushing right now." He shook his head and ran his hand through his dark hair. "No; you're gorgeous and I hope you know it. I'm just…*ugh*, I'm messing this date up is what I'm doing."

"You're still doing better than the last guy," she quipped lightly.

That earned her another laugh.

"Admittedly, I don't think the bar's set that high." He drummed his fingers on the Formica tabletop between them. "Okay. Confession time. This is going to sound all sorts of pathetic, but I was in a long-term relationship… until I wasn't anymore…and my sister forced me to put myself back out there, but…" he lifted one shoulder and dropped it in a half-shrug.

Sara's expression smoothed out into understanding. "You're not ready."

"I'm really not."

Some part of her sank. Their date had been everything her first Tinder date hadn't. Max had been sweet, conversation had come easily, and he was an extremely attractive man with a bright smile which made her go a little weak in the knees. But she understood exactly how he felt, and she couldn't begrudge him that.

"I get it," she nodded, "and I appreciate you being honest." She held out her hand. "Friends?"

There went that smile of his. "Friends," he agreed, shaking on it.

* * *

By her third Tinder date, Sara had a bit more confidence. This guy, Cameron ("Call me Cam"), reminded her a little of Roger. Though he was a handful of years younger than Roger, he had chosen a posh restaurant and had met her at the door in a suit which was clearly tailored to his tall, lean body.

He was charming and attentive, and seemed a little horrified when, while perusing the menu, she informed him that her last boyfriend had insisted he order for her. It felt a little sad that she gave him brownie points for that.

Their conversation was a bit awkward at first –he was the CEO of a rapidly expanding tech company and, outside of her phone and laptop, she knew nothing about technology– but he seemed genuinely interested in her work as a nurse, asking all sorts of questions until she realised that they had exchanged the bigger details of their life stories.

"I travelled a lot in my late teens and very early twenties," he confessed over their main meal. "I was lucky my parents had a fair amount of cash, but Dad made me get a job when I was fifteen to teach me the importance of working for and saving my own money."

Sara smiled and chewed her steak, then swallowed and responded, "That's respectable. He sounds like a great dad."

"He is," Cam nodded back at her as he speared a piece of asparagus with his fork, his expression tender. "He hated the fact that I refused to go to uni, but I used my own money to start up my business and, when it took off, he helped teach me the practical stuff about management I didn't know about."

"Mum was my mentor," she found herself telling him. "My dad died in an accident when I was little, so it was just the two of us, for the most part. She was a doctor: a G.P. I kind of wanted to follow in her footsteps, but…nursing called out to me, I guess."

That was the shorter version of the story. When her mum had passed away unexpectedly from a brain aneurysm during Sara's senior year of high school, Sara had gone off the rails a bit. Studying medicine lost its appeal, as did getting the grades required to get into the right university courses straight out of school. She'd already turned eighteen, had inherited the house, and had mostly focused on keeping herself alive instead.

Eventually, after a gap year, she got into nursing and had intended on getting enough credits and high enough grades to switch degrees, but she'd unexpectedly discovered that she loved nursing and everything it involved. From then on, she had never looked back.

"You said she was a G.P. Did she retire?" Cam inquired, carrying the conversation forward.

This was the part of the 'getting to know you' dialogue about family that she always hated. Nothing brought down the mood more than adding more death into the equation. "She died." There wasn't an easier way to deliver the information – she knew that from experience. "I was eighteen. It's been a bit rough not having my parents around, but..." her lips curled upwards as she recalled Gemma's family's insistence that she was now one of them, "I've kind of been unofficially adopted into my bestie's family."

"Oh." He set his cutlery down, staring at her with genuine compassion. "I'm sorry."

Yep, there went the vibe.

"Really, it's okay," Sara smiled, hoping to reassure him and get the date back on track. She popped the last bite of her potato au gratin into her mouth, chewed it, and then changed the subject, "You said you've travelled?"

Cam's expression smoothed out as the discussion moved back into more comfortable terrain. She learned that he'd backpacked through Europe –she teased him that he didn't strike her as the backpacking kind– and had spent a while in Asia as well. He was down to earth and she liked that he'd experienced 'roughing it' as well as living the high life.

After splitting a sinfully decadent chocolate mousse between them for dessert, she was vaguely disappointed to find the date was coming to an end.

"Thank you for dinner," she said, slipping her cardigan back on while he paid the bill, "it was lovely."

"It's my pleasure," he smiled back and folded his jacket over his arm, opting to carry it rather than wear it. "I'm glad you enjoyed it."

"I really did."

They fell into step beside each other as they left the restaurant, and it seemed to be some unspoken agreement that they continue to walk aimlessly through the city while they chatted.

After a little while more of wandering, Cam exhaled and said, "It's late. I should let you get home."

Sara bit her lip and nodded. "Yeah. I have work tomorrow."

"Let me order you an Uber?"

"Nah," she pulled out her own phone, "I've got it, but thank you."

"I'll wait with you, then. Make sure you get in safe."

She accepted the offer; they sat down on a nearby bench seat while they waited.

As the Uber pulled up, Sara pressed a kiss to Cam's cheek, feeling the beginnings of stubble beneath her lips. She caught a whiff of his aftershave –spicy and a tiny bit floral– and then he was kissing her lips, his tongue begging entrance to which she happily obliged.

Separating with reluctance as the driver beeped his horn, she blurted, "Come back to my place?"

"I thought you'd never ask."

Sara giggled as they both climbed into the car. She tipped the driver handsomely via her app for having to deal with the pair of them making out like teenagers in the backseat. She giggled some more as she fumbled with her keys, struggling to unlock the front door to her house.

Once inside, they were back to behaving like a couple of horny adolescents. Cam pressed Sara up against the wall of the hallway. It felt as though his hands were everywhere. His kisses were hot and insistent. It seemed like forever since someone had ravished her this way.

"Bedroom?" he asked, his voice strained.

"Two doors down, to the left."

As she led the way, she discovered that he'd managed to unlatch her bra with startling precision. Her lips –now complete with smeared remnants of her lipstick– curled upwards into a grin. This one knew what he was doing.

She felt him tug at her zip and felt the material slacken but had little time to concentrate on that because his mouth was on the back of her neck and shoulders creating a trail of warm, wet kisses across her skin. His hands came around to fondle her breasts. He pressed his erection into the small of her back.

Cam was fully clothed, while all Sara wore was a scrap of black lace masquerading as a g-string. And by now it was damp as hell. This wouldn't do at all.

She spun around, turned him and then directed him to sit on the edge of the bed. His hands went back to cupping her breasts while she straddled his lap, grinding down as she captured his lips with her own again.

Just as she was undoing the first of his buttons, his phone rang, the shrill sound cutting through their mutual panting and whispers.

"Ignore it," she urged, rotating her hips against him as extra incentive.

He obeyed with a groan but pulled away from her next kiss when the ringing started up again.

Understanding that it must be something important, she climbed off his lap and allowed him to dig into his hip pocket in order to extricate the source of the interruption.

Cam raised it to his ear and answered with obvious irritation, "What?"

While Cam listened to whoever had ruined their moment, Sara spread herself out on the bed and waited as patiently as possible for the call to be over. Unfortunately, from what she could hear, it sounded like their evening was coming to an end.

"For fuck's sake," he seethed, running his hand through his already messed-up hair. "Yeah, yeah, I'm going in. Fucking hell."

He hung up and turned to her, apology written all over his face. "Work emergency," he explained, pushing himself to his feet and doing his best to smooth out his hair and his shirt. "Something has tripped the alarm and they need the master code. It's probably just a fucking possum, but…"

Disappointment and sexual frustration filled Sara in equal measures, but the look on his face told her where he'd rather be. "It's fine," she replied, covering herself with her discarded dress as she stood up to escort him to the door. "Maybe call me again some time?"

"Yeah." Cam sounded distracted, already fiddling with his phone to get an Uber back to his offices in the city. "Definitely."

She kissed him goodbye as she let him out, then locked the door behind him and sighed deeply.

"Am I cursed or something?" she asked aloud into the silence of her home.

Settling herself back in her bedroom, she reached into her bedside drawer, consoling herself with the knowledge that at least Bob (her Battery-Operated Boyfriend) was always there for her.

Unsurprisingly – but still disappointingly – she didn't hear from Cam again.

Chapter Four

Time moved on as it was wont to do. Charlie wanted to say that he had no complaints in life. He enjoyed his job, had a group of mates, played rugby and football –and continued to playfully argue with Gemma via Facebook that, no, it wasn't called *soccer*– and felt closer than ever with his family, even if more than half of them lived across the pond and sometimes even beyond it, depending on wherever Rhett was filming. However, as his forty-fifth (fuck, he was getting old) birthday came and went, he started to feel restless.

He wasn't quite sure how to explain it.

"Men have a biological clock too, y'know," his mate, Jim, told him as they nursed a couple of pints down at their local pub. It was a real old school joint – dimly lit, full of worn timber, the walls lined by booths, the floor scuffed from years of people walking and dancing over it. It had been there for what felt like forever, and it felt comforting and inviting. As the area around it developed, the clientele changed, but the pub itself stayed the same. "You've done well to last as long as you have, but maybe your mum's on to somethin'? Maybe you're lonely?"

In the hazy lighting, Charlie ran his index finger through the puddle of condensation left behind from his glass and contemplated Jim's hypothesis. Rhett had said the same thing recently, too, but he'd brushed his brother off. Jim, however, was an unbiased party. Was it possible that he actually might

–somewhere deep in his subconscious– want to settle down?

"Or maybe," Jim continued after another mouthful of beer, "you just need to get laid." He chortled after this final assessment and clapped Charlie on the back. "I dunno how you're survivin' with just your hand, mate."

"Piss off," Charlie gave him a good-natured nudge with his shoulder. "It's not been that long."

"Really?" The other man raised both eyebrows in challenge, propping his elbow on the worn, water-stained timber of the bar. "When was the last time, then?"

"Well, I guess it would be…" *Shit. Before my birthday.* He fell silent, hanging his head while Jim smirked knowingly.

"Bingo. Months, right?"

"Sod off."

Jim laid his callused hand on Charlie's back and patted it consolingly. "So, you've pro'lly got a massive case of blue balls, eh?"

Charlie grunted and took a generous mouthful of beer.

Still clearly amused, Jim straightened his back and began scanning the crowd. It was a Friday night, so the place was filling up quickly, all the booths along the walls taken, and plenty of the standing tables full now, too. The place was primarily filled with office workers from nearby businesses, all dressed in corporate attire. He and Jim stood out like sore thumbs, but nobody paid them any mind. This was their local, and many of the faces around them were familiar.

"Should find you a nice bird to take home tonight, then," Jim muttered while he looked around.

"Don't be daft." The barkeep interrupted as he wiped down the worn timber surface in front of them. He didn't even pretend he hadn't been eavesdropping.

Charlie offered the man a grateful nod and raised his glass in appreciation. "Cheers, Sam."

Sam smirked back. "This isn't the place to pick up." He tilted his head to the left, blonde dreadlocks swaying with the movement. "You want the club on the high street. Much better pickings."

Charlie groaned while Jim laughed and slammed a tenner down on the bar. "Keep the tip, Sam," he instructed gleefully, "you've earned it."

"Oh, fuck off, the both of you." Charlie shook his head, clutching his beer a little tighter. "We're not going clubbing. I'm too old for that shit." And not dressed for it, either, considering he was perched on the stool wearing his filthy work clothes.

"Spoil my fun," Jim sniffed, polishing off the last of his drink and gesturing for another. "You'll just have to join the tech-age, then. Get yourself a Tinder or whatever if you're not willing to look for dates the old-fashioned way."

Charlie nodded in resignation. He already had a Tinder profile, but he didn't need to tell his mate that. "Yeah," he agreed, though he didn't sound at all enthusiastic about it. "Yeah, I guess you're right."

* * *

"Online dating is awful," Charlie complained to his brother a few weeks later, during one of their spontaneous Facetime calls. He flopped back against the black leather of his couch, pinching the bridge of his nose. "Why am I doing this to myself?"

Via the tiny screen propped up on the coffee table, Everett offered him an empathetic shrug. "Because you've finally admitted you don't want to be alone anymore?" He smiled. "It'll be worth it eventually."

"Steady on," Charlie shook his head, "I'm not looking for a wife, mate. Just some casual fun."

His brother's expression fell. "You're still on that, then?"

"I'm not the settling down type, Rhett."

"Yeah, and neither was I."

Here we go again. Charlie knew he'd walked himself right into it this time. But he wasn't going down this path without a fight. Not this time. Rolling his eyes, he said, "Until you fucked up and knocked a one-night stand up like a right git."

"Not my finest moment," Everett responded smoothly, no longer biting at the reminder of his 'mistake' – though neither of them would *ever* describe

Zoe as a mistake, "but…yeah. Best thing that's ever happened to me."

Charlie honestly couldn't argue with that. His mind flashed back to the day Rhett had called him and their mum, red-eyed and almost manic, confessing he'd become a father overnight. Charlie had thought –and had all but told him– that he'd ruined everything he'd worked for.

Charlie had been wrong.

He'd never been happier to admit it.

The unexpected addition of Zoe to their family seemed to completely transform his brother. Prior to her birth, Everett had been distant and lonely. Conversations with him had felt forced, and Charlie had always felt as though he was lecturing his brother rather than talking with him. Since becoming a father, Everett had gentled, become more open and focused on maintaining familial relationships for the enjoyment of being together, instead of doing so out of some sense of obligation.

Certainly, there had been bumps along the road, especially as Zoe had entered the *terrible twos*, and he knew that Everett struggled sometimes to balance his career with his personal life. But it was more than obvious to Charlie that forming a family with Zoe and Gemma had filled a hole in his brother's life that Everett had never previously acknowledged was there.

However, it didn't mean that Charlie was cut from the same cloth, even if they were brothers.

"I'm glad you feel that way," he replied, "but I'm not about to go get some woman up the duff to see if that's the right path for me."

Everett's response was droll. "You're a regular comedian."

"What did you want me to say, then?"

There was a pause while his brother seemed to carefully consider his next words. "Just…I don't know…promise me you won't give up on the prospect of a real relationship if the right girl comes along, alright?" There was a knowing glint in Rhett's blue eyes, visible even on the little phone screen. "Neither one of us is going to repeat Dad's mistakes."

Not certain that he appreciated his little brother psychoanalysing him, Charlie shook his head. "Stick with your day job."

Everett fell silent, and Charlie figured that was as good as he was going to get. Unfortunately, they were as stubborn as each other, and he knew his brother wouldn't let go that easily. Especially not with their mother in his ear.

Charlie supposed it would have to do.

* * *

Despite disliking everything about online dating −from the swiping based on aesthetics, to the texting back and forth as they each tried to work out what, exactly, the other person was looking to achieve from their potential 'match'− Charlie still found himself going out every Friday night.

Unfortunately, despite some of the women being lovely, he had to admit that his heart just wasn't in it. He wondered if maybe he was just getting old and bitter and boring. In his twenties, he never would have imagined that he'd ever feel blasé about sex, but, outside of the momentary enjoyment, he was starting to feel like it wasn't worth the effort.

These feelings were compounded by his slowly growing resentment of his brother's relationship.

Perhaps resentment wasn't quite the right word.

Everett was ridiculously happy. He'd found a match in Gemma that was, in Charlie's estimation, almost unheard of. They genuinely did seem to fit together like two pieces of a puzzle. That wasn't to say that the couple didn't have their own issues to work out on occasion, but the fact that they continued to resolve them and fall back into their usual lovey-dovey connection prickled under Charlie's skin, even though he was pleased for them.

Jealousy. This was a better way to phrase the way he felt. Charlie didn't want to admit it, not even to himself, but it was the best way to describe the feeling.

Worse than admitting his jealousy, though, was the realisation that perhaps Everett had been right all along: Charlie was lonely. It wasn't just about sex; it was about companionship.

He might actually desire what Everett had.

Someone he could have effortless conversations with. Someone who shared his interests, but who also knew when to give him space or let him live his own life, and for whom he'd happily do the same. Someone whose company he enjoyed and looked forward to sharing.

Damn it, he actually wanted a relationship after all.

Charlie silently cursed his brother for putting the notion in his head to begin with. He'd been perfectly fine the way he was…until he wasn't anymore. And that, he decided, was Everett's fault. Somehow.

"What's got you looking like you've just sucked a lemon?" his mother's voice startled him from his musings. It was Sunday again, and he was at her flat for their usual roast lunch.

Beatrice wiped her hands on her apron as she wandered out from the kitchen and sat down in her favourite armchair, which was bedecked in floral print. Regarding him with concern, she asked more gently, "Is everything alright, darling?"

"I'm fine," he brushed her off, not wanting to go into his unexpected new feelings with her. He'd never hear the end of it if he did.

Unbidden, he recalled an old girlfriend complaining that his relationship with his mother was off-putting. 'Nobody finds a mummy's boy sexy,' she'd said. He'd broken up with her shortly afterwards for various reasons – that assessment being one of them.

Roughly twenty years later, would women still feel the same way? He refused to apologise for being close to his mum. She and Everett were all he'd had in this world, and he didn't think that having a standing lunch date and sharing the odd phone call during the week was particularly strange. If they were living in each other's pockets, however, he'd rightfully understand.

"Have you forgotten that I raised you? I can tell when you're being untruthful." She reached across to where he was seated on the end seat of the sofa –a faded purple monstrosity that was irritatingly comfortable– and patted his knee. "Is it work?"

He shook his head. "No. Work's fine."

"Then what?"

"Mum," he felt a little like a moody teenager, which was absurd, "just leave it. Please."

She arched her eyebrows but nodded, raising her hands in surrender as she sat back in her floral seat. "Alright, alright. I'll drop it."

He snorted and shook his head. "I find that hard to believe."

"For now," she clarified, "I'll drop it for now."

As far as promises went, it would have to do. Charlie gratefully accepted the declaration. "Thanks."

Throughout their lunch, Charlie continued to mull over his feelings, knowing that his half-arsed participation during the conversation was only worrying his mother more. But what could he say? 'Sorry, Mum, I've just realised that I'm lonely after all and have no idea how to go about fixing this mess'? Absolutely not.

It felt so silly to be in his mid-forties and not know how to date seriously. It felt sillier still that he was almost afraid to put himself out there and try. He knew he was an attractive man. He had a stable career, made good money, and didn't think his personality was abhorrent…even if he was prone to being a bit gruff and moody. He was a pretty good catch, if he did say so himself.

But there was a niggling fear that he'd left it too late, or that he wouldn't find someone with whom he was compatible. He hadn't felt an immediate connection with any of the women he'd been out with recently, and he was starting to suspect that the problem was him.

Was he being too picky? Expecting too much? Not enough?

It wasn't as though wanting to explore a more serious relationship meant that he wanted to settle down immediately and have a horde of children. Hell, he wasn't sure he ever wanted children at all, and for many women that was a deal-breaker. Not to mention his age – he was on the downward slope to fifty now. He felt too old to be starting from scratch.

"You know what might help get you out of this funk of yours," his mother interrupted his musings.

Charlie looked up from pushing his peas around in a puddle of gravy to watch her wipe her mouth with her napkin, fold it and set it down beside her empty plate. Opting to humour her –because he felt as though he owed her as much, given his abysmal mood during the visit– he asked, "What's that, Mum?"

"We're due to return to Brisbane for Zoe's third birthday in a couple of months." Her response was bubbly, her eyes lighting up with the prospect. "Surely a change of scenery will help."

He wasn't so sure about that. Having to sit through *The Everett and Gemma Show* in person was even more nauseating than over the occasional Facetime call. But he could see just how excited his mum was, and that brought a small smile to his face.

"Yeah," Charlie nodded, "a holiday's always nice."

Something appearing a lot like guilt seemed to flit across her face. "Yes," she agreed with a bit too much enthusiasm, "a holiday."

Her sudden awkwardness set him right back on edge. "Mum," he began cautiously, abandoning his meal altogether, "what's going on?"

His eyes narrowed as she fidgeted with the corner of her napkin and glanced away. "I don't know what you mean."

"Mum."

Shoulders slumping, she sighed and said, "I'd hoped to tell you when you were in better spirits…"

"Tell me what?"

Her confession shouldn't have surprised him, but it did. "I'm thinking about staying in Australia. You know…permanently."

"What?" Charlie blinked, dumbfounded. He knew his mother had found it more and more difficult to return to the UK after each visit, but he'd never expected her to make that particular decision. A very juvenile part of him felt as though she was choosing Everett over him –just one more thing to be envious of– but he knew the notion was ridiculous. They weren't children anymore.

If anything, Beatrice Rhodes was putting herself first for the first time that Charlie could remember, and he knew she would be much happier being closer to Zoe. Shifting in his seat, he unfolded his arms and asked with measured calm, "When did you decide this?"

"If I'm being honest," her response was gentle, as though she knew how brittle he felt right now; and she was his mum, so she probably did, "from the very first moment I held my grandchild."

Almost three years, then.

"Doesn't the whole process take a while?"

The guilt was back on her face. "I applied last year."

Of course she did.

Charlie didn't bother asking about the cost: he knew Everett would have covered it without her having to ask. He didn't begrudge his mother that, or his brother for that matter. Not with the life they'd shared prior to Everett's fame, or Charlie's successful career. Both men would bend over backwards to help their mum.

However, it hurt that this plan had been in the making for a year and neither his mother nor Everett had said a word about it.

"Because of my age, I didn't know whether they'd let me in," she tried to explain, and he realised with a start that he'd admitted the last bit out loud. "Darling, I didn't want to upset you if it wasn't going to work out."

He understood. He did. But it still hurt.

He'd feel even lonelier with the last of his family living abroad.

He attempted to shake off the melancholy the realisation evoked. "So, that's it, then? You'll be staying there after this trip?"

She bobbed her head, her blonde hair swaying with the movement. Excitement sparkled in her eyes again. "Everett will sell this flat once I've left. I'll be staying with him and Gemma until I can find a little place nearby to theirs."

"Does Gemma know what she's gotten herself into there?" Charlie teased.

"I beg your pardon?" His mother responded, affronted. "Gemma and I get along swimmingly."

"I'm aware. She's the daughter you never had. Etcetera, etcetera." He leaned his elbow on the dark wood of the tabletop and she glared across at him. "But you've only ever been for short visits. You're going to have to try not to smother the poor woman with your affection."

Beatrice rolled her eyes. "Thankfully, I trust Gemma will set me straight if I do tread on her toes."

It would be highly entertaining from an outside perspective, Charlie realised. Both women were feisty when they wanted to be. Perhaps it was actually Everett who had no idea what he'd gotten himself into.

That thought, at least, was amusing, but Charlie wisely kept it to himself.

* * *

Charlie felt bittersweet getting on the plane to Brisbane with his mum for what would be the last time. He'd be returning on his own in just over a week, and the next time he flew back to Brisbane –which would be for Christmas– he would be travelling alone for both legs of the journey.

For her part, his mother was a ball of nerves. She was excitable one moment and anxious the next. He understood, though. She was uprooting her life, leaving everything she'd ever known behind, and he knew that she worried about him, too.

Over the course of the past few months, he'd helped his mum pack her most meaningful possessions and had watched as she cleared out the flat that Everett had talked her into letting him buy for her when he'd first started to climb to fame. At the time, Charlie had offered to assist with the purchase, but Rhett had convinced him to provide renovations instead. His mum had loved that, not least because it had caused them to spend even more time together.

It was strange to think that he and his mum wouldn't have their Sunday lunches in the little dining area –seated around the too-large dark oak table– anymore. It was stranger still to think that she'd be practically on the other side of the planet rather than a short drive away.

However, he knew this would be good for her. While Beatrice had a small social group in the UK, she had a ready-made extended family in Australia. She got along like a house on fire with Marcus, Gemma's dad, and Charlie knew Beatrice Rhodes would be more than comfortable slotting herself into his social circle or finding a new one of her own. Everett had inherited his extroverted nature from her, after all, while Charlie himself was a bit more withdrawn, like his father had been.

46

For his part, to make the transition as easy as possible for his mother, Charlie had tried not to let his growing sense of loneliness show. She'd pushed him to open up a few times during his piques of melancholy, but he'd continued to brush off her concerns. Dating still hadn't progressed beyond a few dates here and there with a couple of women, and he was beginning to suspect his heart just wasn't in it.

Maybe his mum was right: maybe a change of scenery would reinvigorate him. It would be better than moping around at home.

So, when they finally landed in Brisbane a few days shy of Zoe's third birthday, he pasted on his customary grin and forced himself to appear jovial for his brother and his family. It wasn't hard to laugh at and tease his younger brother, and as long as he didn't ruminate too long on the way Rhett and Gemma had started finishing each other's sentences, he was genuinely happy to spend time with them.

"Uncle Charlie!" Zoe raced towards him on legs which seemed longer than the last time he'd seen her. Her dark hair was longer, too, and whipped around her face, though she didn't seem to care.

He dropped his bag and kneeled down in the middle of the fluorescently lit Arrivals Hall just in time for the blur of his practically-three-year-old niece to barrel into him. She wrapped her arms around his neck and giggled madly as he peppered kisses on her face. "Excuse me, young lady," he asked with affected solemnity, "but have you seen my niece? Her name is Zoe."

"That's me, silly," she laughed at him, and it suddenly struck him –as he realised just how much more grown up she was since he'd last seen her at Easter– that he'd missed a lot. Facetime calls hadn't prepared him at all.

He'd theoretically understood why his mother was moving here, but now he grasped the emotional gravity of it as well.

Swallowing, and avoiding the knowing look Everett was pinning him with, Charlie shook his head. "No. You can't be *my* Zoe. You're too grown up!"

"It is me," she insisted, now tugging at his arm. "My birthday," here he bit his lip to prevent his laughter, because she still pronounced the 'th' sound with an 'f' and it was adorable with the amount of sass she was giving him, "is soon. Right, Daddy? Tell him!"

"I'm afraid she's right," Everett played along, his lips twitching as Zoe folded her arms across her chest and glared imperiously.

"Told 'ya."

Her accent was also hilarious. It was a strange mixture of her mother's Australian and her father's middle-class RP English. Charlie couldn't help but notice that she had definitely become her own person in the months since he'd last seen her. He grinned. "I stand corrected."

"Good." Zoe nodded, still amusingly haughty, before she caught sight of her grandmother coming to join them.

Beatrice and Charlie had been separated at Customs –he assumed because she was emigrating to the country– and she'd informed him that she would catch him up in Arrivals. He honestly couldn't say which of the two were more excited to land eyes on each other.

Dropping her bags, Beatrice held her arms open wide as the little girl flew into her embrace, crying, "Grandma!"

"My little poppet," his mum greeted warmly, and the joy on her face was further confirmation to Charlie that her moving across the world was a good idea. "Oh, my darling, I've missed you terribly."

Charlie stepped away to collect his mother's bags and handed her suitcase off to Everett who had also moved to help. "Where's Gemma?" he asked as he slung his mum's carry on over his free shoulder. It was unusual that she hadn't come along to greet them at the airport. "You're not arguing again, are you?"

Everett shook his head and attempted to reach for Charlie's suitcase with his spare hand but was batted away. "No. She's at work. Couldn't get tonight off, but she's taken leave for the next two weeks."

"Ah, pity," Charlie knew Everett would support Gemma completely if she wanted to stop work, but he was proud of his little brother for respecting her wishes. She loved being a nurse, so her decision to keep working despite her partner's wealth wasn't entirely due to her pride or determination, either. "She's on night shift, then?"

"No, thankfully. She should be home by nine." They fell into step beside each other, and Everett grinned at their mum. "Shall we?"

Zoe gripped Beatrice's hand and continued to babble at her excitedly during the walk to the car.

"When'd she start talking like an actual person?" Charlie found himself asking, still surprised that the chubby-legged toddler who could barely string three words together was now this talkative little girl.

Everett chuckled. "It wasn't like it happened overnight," he answered, sounding somewhere between exasperated and fond. "She surprises us with something new every day."

They'd reached Everett's car, which was an SUV similar to Gemma's, and Charlie put the bags in the boot while Everett got Zoe situated in her car seat.

"I want Grandma with me," she declared.

Naturally, Beatrice was thrilled to oblige.

"And what am I?" Charlie asked playfully after shutting the boot and sliding into the passenger seat. "Chopped liver?"

Zoe blinked her big, blue eyes back at him. "What's that?"

"Just an expression," Everett answered for him. As an aside to Charlie, he explained, "Trust me, it's not worth going down that rabbit hole."

"I like rabbits!" The chirpy little voice from the backseat interjected.

Charlie snorted. "Me too, love." Under his breath he added, "Particularly in a good stew."

Everett shot him a warning glance while his mum reminded him to behave himself.

As he smothered his laughter, he had to admit that being with his family again actually did feel good.

Perhaps the change of scenery would help him, after all.

Chapter Five

"Are you sure I can't help with anything?" Sara asked her sister from another mister for the fifth time.

It was Zoe's third birthday and, for the first time in the little girl's life, Gemma and Everett were throwing an actual birthday party. Captain Abtastic had, naturally, suggested hiring a team of professionals to cater the event, but Gemma had stood her ground and insisted that this was something she had to do herself. A rite of passage or whatever. At the time, Sara had sat back with Brennan and Jeff and watched the debate with amusement, knowing the actor would cave and give in to his girlfriend's wishes. He was a real pushover.

Also predictable was Gemma biting off slightly more than she could chew. So, by the actual day of the party, Sara had arrived to find her friend in a fluster. Unexpectedly, though, Gemma had given in and allowed Everett's brother and mother to assist her in setting up for the big event, while Everett chased the Guest of Honour around the yard.

Beatrice was organising party foods on the large trestle tables set out under the marquee in the backyard, and Charlie was inflating balloons with a small helium tank. Sara watched as he carefully tied off a balloon, secured it with string and then tied it to a leg of the table with a cluster of others that he'd already finished. She hated to admit it, but what he'd completed looked

50

good.

"I told you," Gemma huffed in response to her question, shaking her from her observations, "it's pretty under control now." She glanced up at the clock on the wall and frowned. "Except the petting zoo people were due here fifteen minutes ago."

Sara blinked. "Petting zoo?" She couldn't help the lilt of surprise in her voice. "That's one spoilt kid you've got there."

"Shut up," Gemma tossed a packet of rainbow coloured paper napkins at her and Sara deftly caught it. "I might have gotten carried away."

Shaking her head, Sara softened her tone to understanding. "Hey, I get it. You just want to give her what you never got. Plus, Sir Abs-A-Lot lives to spoil you both and he can afford it, so…" she shrugged as another packet of napkins was hurled at her.

"Would you stop calling him that?" Gemma sounded annoyed, but she was struggling to hide her smirk.

"Never!" Sara chortled, this time catching a packet of plastic spoons –bright pink in colour– as they sailed her way. She held up her collection. "I'll take these outside and then call the zoo people for you. When are Bren and Jeff getting here?"

"I think they're waiting on Dad. He said he was going to park at their place, then they'd walk over together."

It made sense, really. Gemma's home was situated in a little suburban street, and it sounded as though Gemma had invited half of Zoe's day care centre to celebrate with them. Parking was going to be insane. Everett had apparently smoothed it over with the neighbours by offering them all an open invitation as well. Sara had found that tidbit amusing – she didn't think she'd ever so much as nodded to her own neighbours, and she'd lived in her house her entire life. She continued to muse on this as she headed outside.

It was a perfect September day. Warm, but not insanely humid, with a light breeze to soften the heat from the sun, which bore down on the backyard from a bright blue, cloudless sky. On the other side of the large space, behind secure fencing, the crystal blue swimming pool sparkled invitingly. Sadly,

Sara knew that it was not yet warm enough to take a dip. In a few more weeks, when summer's higher temperatures began to creep in, she'd be visiting more often to take advantage of the cool water. Well, when the summer storms weren't keeping everyone trapped inside, anyway.

"Hey," she greeted Everett's family as she placed the packets down on the table.

"Hello, Sara darling," Beatrice welcomed her with a big smile, reaching for the packets she'd just set down. "How are you? We've missed you the last few nights."

"Yeah, sorry – I've been stuck on night shift." Sara replied. She watched as Beatrice carefully laid out the napkins and then placed a decorative paperweight on top of them. "Spent yesterday recalibrating so I could fully enjoy today."

"Recalibrating, eh?" Charlie asked with a knowing smirk. He sat back on his haunches, a bright orange balloon in his hand. "Meaning you slept the whole day?"

"There was some Netflix in there," she defended herself lightly, and he chuckled.

"More power to you, I say," he inclined his head, and she couldn't help but notice he was actually quite handsome, backlit by the sun as he was. His green eyes seemed to glimmer at her as he added, "I'd be useless working nights, then going back to days."

"Big on routine, huh?" This was perhaps the most casual conversation they'd shared in the three years they'd known each other. Considering he only visited a few times a year, and their truce was unspoken, they generally stayed out of one another's way.

Beatrice snickered lightly. "Does that come as a surprise to you, love?"

Given everything that she'd known about Charlie Rhodes, Sara had to admit that, no, his being a creature of habit was hardly unexpected. She shook her head, the corners of her lips lifting. "No," she answered honestly, "I guess not."

"Mum," Charlie sighed and rolled his eyes, but his affection for his mother was obvious, "don't you have something better to do than try and wind me up?"

Sara laughed and left them to their bickering, smiling to herself at the relationship that Everett and Charlie shared with their mother. It was endearing; however, she couldn't help but miss her own mum as she intruded on those moments.

"Still need me to call the zoo peeps?" she asked Gemma as she stepped back into the house, distracting herself from the sudden pangs of melancholy.

Her friend shook her head. "No, I've just let them in the gate, and they'll be setting up on the small patch of lawn on the other side of the driveway."

"Makes sense to keep them away from the main party," Sara thought aloud. "All those kids sugared up and running around would scare the animals. Plus, it'd make your yard pretty cramped."

"Bingo."

"B.I...um...B.O!" Zoe's voice rang out as she bounded through the door from the patio with Everett hot on her heels.

Sara laughed and swept her up into her arms, settling her on her hip. "Close, but no cigar, kiddo."

Zoe had already moved on to a new topic. "It's my birthday!"

"It sure is," Sara grinned and bounced her. "Happy Birthday, ZoZo."

"Do I get presents?"

"Not until later," Everett answered. Sara pouted right alongside her honorary niece: she'd been looking forward to giving the little girl her gift. Spoiling her rotten was something she genuinely enjoyed, even though Gemma tried to discourage her from doing so.

A split second later, though, Zoe was grinning again. "Party first?"

"Party first," Everett agreed with a nod.

The toddler cheered, and Sara was swept up in her childish enthusiasm, finding herself looking forward to the party, too.

* * *

There were children everywhere. Hordes of small human torpedoes powered by sugar and adrenaline. They were loud, and sticky, and messy. But, despite all of that, Sara loved watching them. They had wide eyes, and big grins, and seemingly boundless energy. They were all fascinated by everything new they came across, wonder and delight painting their expressions and infusing their high-pitched little voices.

As the guests had filtered into the party, though, Sara had found herself inching into the background. These were all families. Couples with children. Or, in the case of some of the neighbours, couples without kids. Groups of people with whom she shared very little in common.

Gemma had been swept up in hostess duties, while Everett had maintained a close eye on Zoe as he chatted casually with her little friends' parents. Even though Sara teased her best friend about Everett proposing to make their relationship official, watching them now only highlighted the truth underpinning the joke. They were essentially an old married couple as it was. The loving looks they kept exchanging were just further proof that they were perfect for each other. Sara's heart gave a squeeze; she looked away, surveying the other guests.

Marcus had thrown himself into 'uber Grandpa mode' and was entertaining a group of children on the lawn, and Beatrice flitted between following Zoe's adventures and helping Gemma. Even Brennan and Jeff had become part of a little clique formed by the neighbour couples – which shouldn't have surprised Sara too much because they only lived a few streets away.

Sara knew she could have wandered over and joined any one of the huddles of people scattered across the backyard, but the fact that she didn't really fit in niggled at the back of her brain.

She tried not to be jealous.

After all, it wasn't lack of trying that saw her perpetually single. And, sure, she'd love a kid of her own, but she had no intention of rushing into parenthood, regardless of how clucky her biological clock was making her. She needed to find the right partner first and she knew it.

Unfortunately, that seemed like a pipe dream at this point.

As if taunting her, the stereo that was set to play a random assortment of songs switched to The Supremes' *'You Can't Hurry Love'*. Sara closed her eyes and groaned.

"Not enjoying yourself, then?" Charlie's voice startled her. In response, she jumped a little in her seat.

She glared up at him. "I just have a personal vendetta against this song."

He surprised her by pulling up a chair beside her. They were the only two people at the glass table under the patio. "It is annoyingly optimistic," he acknowledged.

"And it's too catchy. I won't be able to shake it for days now."

"At least it isn't a *Wiggles* tune." Out of the corner of her eye she watched him shaking his head ruefully. "I've had that bloody '*Hot Potato*' racket stuck in my head since we drove back from the airport the other night."

This confession took her off guard and she found herself laughing genuinely at the thought of the big, muscular man stuck singing a kid's tune to himself for days on end. "That is pure gold," she chuckled, catching her breath and wiping her eyes. "Thank you."

Two seconds later, though, the aforementioned song itself was in her head. She caught herself humming it as her gaze drifted back over the yard, watching a group of kids playing chasey. "Ah, fuck."

This time it was his turn to laugh, the sound deep, and warm and rich. "Sorry." He didn't seem at all apologetic.

Reaching out to slap at him playfully, she called him out on it. "Bullshit."

"What can I say?" he asked, grinning unrepentantly. "I needed to share my pain."

Her intended reply was cut off as one of the kids' mothers came to stand under the patio, eyeing Sara warily before turning a megawatt smile towards Charlie. "Charlie," she said imploringly, "aren't you going to come back and join us for Pass the Parcel?"

"Ah, sorry...er...Jen?"

The poor woman's expression fell. Sara felt for her. "Jess."

"Jess. Right. Sorry." Once again, Sara didn't think the apology was at all genuine. "I'm actually going to rest here for a bit longer. I'm still kind of jet-lagged, and I'm not yet used to being in the Australian sun for extended periods of time, you know?"

Jess was clearly disappointed but nodded and mustered another smile.

"Right. Yeah. Of course. Well," she slid her glance back over Sara, then looked at Charlie again, "if you change your mind, you know where to find me. Us."

"I do," he agreed with a nod, before he softened the blatant rejection with a smile of his own, "tell Zoe to play fair. That niece of mine's a bit sneaky."

"Hey, I taught her those mad skills." Sara affected offense, but the upwards curl of her lips gave her amusement away. "Girl's gotta look out for number one."

He shook his head, and Sara felt a little sorry for poor Jess who backed out of both the conversation and the patio.

"Single mums not your thing?" Sara couldn't help but ask Charlie once Jess was out of earshot. He groaned.

"I don't know what Rhett was thinking there," he admitted, "she's nice enough, but we've nothing in common. And yet that pair…" he gestured to Gemma and his brother, who had their arms around each other's waists as they watched Zoe and her friends settle into a circle on the ground "…have been pushing me towards her all day."

Sara's lips curled upwards again. "Maybe she just had an itch to scratch."

"I'm not going there." Once again he surprised her, this time by turning serious. "And Rhett knows better than to try and set me up."

"To be fair, it's probably more Gem's doing," Sara shrugged. "She's found eternal happiness and wants everyone else to experience the same." Her sigh escaped her before she could reel it in, and she smiled softly as Zoe attempted to keep a hold on the parcel instead of passing it to the next kid. "Unfortunately, it doesn't work like that for everyone."

"No, it doesn't," Charlie agreed quietly at her side. There was a moment of awkward silence before he added, "I'm sorry things didn't work out with whatshisname. The doctor."

Behind her sunglasses, her eyes widened with surprise. She turned her attention back to him and shook her head. "Don't be. It was ages ago and he was an epic dick, which would have been more bearable if he'd also *had* an epic dick, but…" she trailed off and shrugged, while her unexpected companion choked on his spit. She grinned knowingly. "You right there?"

"Fine," he wheezed, then managed, "I *knew* that fancy car of his was compensating for something."

"Oh, it definitely was!"

They laughed together and Sara felt some of the tension she'd been carrying unwinding. She was surprised to think that it was a conversation with Charlie Rhodes –of all people– providing that sense of relief. But she supposed that was the case because he was also single and child free – sticking out like a sore thumb at this particular party.

"Want a drink?" He asked as he pushed himself to his feet. "I wasn't lying about being unused to the heat here."

"Please." She inclined her head as he walked over to the esky which had been set out for the adults. "You realise it's not even summer yet?"

"Yeah, well, this is as hot as it gets back home. I'd be down at the beach with my mates on a day like this." He handed her a can of beer dripping with condensation and melted ice.

"Cheers," she said, clinking it against the one in his hand.

He settled back in his seat and cracked the can open, slurping at the foam pouring out of the top before he sighed in contentment. "That hits the spot."

She was a bit demurer with her own, tapping at the bottom of her can with a bright red fingernail (for some reason this always seemed to settle the liquid inside) before cautiously popping it open. There was no spillage. She sipped at it happily. "Yeah," she agreed, "it does."

Their conversation appeared to fizzle out, but it didn't feel awkward to sit there in silence beside him. She tried to focus on the children as the rest of Pass the Parcel played out –and, unsurprisingly, every kid got a little treat from it before a little boy from Zoe's day care won a small stuffed toy– but her attention continued to drift back to Charlie every so often.

Out of the corner of her eye, she watched him surveying the goings on. He seemed just as amused by the kids' antics as she felt, but his expression seemed to inexplicably shutter now and then. Following his gaze, her own landed on Gemma and Everett.

Her eyebrows drew into a frown of her own. Why would Charlie be looking at them like they'd kicked his puppy?

Oh, God, he's not into Gemma, is he?

The thought came unbidden to her, and her frown deepened.

It couldn't be the case, could it? Sara studied him a bit more closely, but couldn't read his expression, even though she was certain it was jealousy she'd seen.

She hoped that if that was his issue, he'd leave well enough alone. Gemma and Everett were perfect together, and anyone could see that they were it for one another. Knowing her best friend as well as she did, Sara was confident Gemma would never give Charlie the time of day, especially not while she was so happily –almost sickeningly– in love with his brother. But should Charlie act on these clearly misguided feelings, it would make things awkward, potentially ruin his relationship with his brother, and would also then impact his relationship with his mother and his niece. It wasn't just him who would get hurt if it all came to a head.

His voice startled her out of her thoughts. "When's this thing scheduled to end?"

Raising her left wrist to check out her watch, she scrunched up her nose. "About an hour. Why?" She cocked her head to the side, "Not enjoying yourself?"

"Eh. I'm not a huge fan of small humans I'm not related to."

Now *that* was hardly a shock to hear. "Pretty sure you're not in the minority there."

"Why aren't you over there, anyway?" He took another mouthful from his drink before gesturing towards the group of adults and children still sprawled out on the grass. "You seem to love the little tykes."

"I wouldn't say *love*." Her correction was light and deflective. "I just…well, kids can be fun."

There was no way she was going to tell this man that she could literally feel her biological clock ticking away at hyper speed. She didn't think their truce would extend so far that he wouldn't mock her insane cluckiness. Hell, even she thought it was ridiculous. She'd been perfectly happy the way she was…and then *bam!* She wanted a family of her own.

"Uh huh." Charlie didn't sound convinced. He tilted his own head, his blonde hair taking on a golden hue as the sun hit it at just the right angle. With his squared jawline –wider and more pronounced than his brother's– she couldn't help but think how handsome he was.

She immediately berated herself for that thought.

Being clucky was one thing. Being lonely was another. But getting the hots for her best friend's formerly dickish brother-in-law? *Nope.* Not happening. That development could fuck right off. *Especially* if he was potentially harbouring feelings for that same aforementioned best friend.

Thankfully, he was oblivious to everything going on inside her head because he continued talking. "What's so fun about them, then? They're loud and sticky and annoying." She resolutely did not watch him lick his lips after he took another long drag of his beer. "Princess Zoe excluded, of course."

Sara begrudgingly approved of his caveat.

Realising that he was actually waiting for an answer, she tilted her head from side to side, thinking out loud, "I mean, they're cute. The way they try to pronounce things, or their excitement for stuff that we take for granted. They're also free with their affection, and their chubby little arms hugging you is just the best feeling…" Dear God, she was tearing up. Fuck, could she blame that on the beer? Hormones? *Ugh.* Swallowing roughly, she tried to discreetly blink the sudden onset of complicated feelings away. "I know they're hard work –some of Zoe's tantrums have been insane– but they can also be kind of amazing."

Charlie was quiet for a few beats. She hoped that he hadn't noticed her random bout of emotion. She didn't think she'd live that down if he had. Thankfully, he eventually said, "Alright, yeah, I s'pose they have some redeeming features." His lips shifted into a crooked grin. "I still don't like them en masse."

Raising her beer to him in salute, she acknowledged, "I can respect that." And then the companionable silence was back.

* * *

Charlie sent Sara a friend request on Facebook later that afternoon. After blinking at it for a few moments, she shrugged and accepted it. Their conversations during the party had been the longest they'd ever shared, and had been...pleasant, for lack of a better word.

They'd made each other laugh, and the urge to slap him stupid hadn't reared up once. She figured that she must have mellowed over the years without realising it. Or perhaps he wasn't as much of an arse as he had been three years earlier. Or some combination of both things was at play. Any which way, their truce was now Facebook official.

She had mixed feelings about this new development. On the one hand, it would make Gemma and Everett happy to see the two of them actively getting along. On the other, she would miss the tiny little jabs they made at each other when nobody was around.

'*So the lady deigns to add me after all,*' was the first message she received from him.

Or, she smirked as she read the words on her screen, *the jabs have just moved to a more private arena.*

'*After three years, I've come to terms with the fact that I'm stuck with you in my life,*' she wrote back, adding the emoji poking its tongue out.

She didn't hear much from him over the next few days. She hadn't really expected to, not only because they weren't exactly what she'd call friends, either. Everett had planned to spend as much time as possible with his family while they were all in the same country, so he had arranged a few little side-trips with his mother and brother –taking Gemma and Zoe along, too, of course– and Sara imagined that all the excursions and exploring up and down the coastline would be far more entertaining than messaging her.

Besides, Sara had her own life to lead. Gemma wasn't her only friend –though she was definitely her closest– and she rarely had much time off work, so she took advantage of her own small break, catching up with some other friends for lunches, and even went on a couple of lukewarm dates in the evenings.

"Still on the hunt for Mister Right?"

Sara was jarred from her musings by the question and frowned across the café table at her friend, Eve.

Eve was a former colleague who also knew Gemma, but who had bonded more with Sara, given their personalities were so similar at times. She had gone on maternity leave the previous year and had decided that being a stay-at-home mum was much more rewarding than working. It didn't hurt, either, that Eve's husband had a high-paying job and was very supportive of whatever she wanted to do. Sara thought her friend had lucked out with that one.

With her blonde hair now in a pixie cut, and a cheeky grin on her face, Eve looked as impish as she sounded.

"We can't all meet our Prince Charming right out of high school." Sara tried to sound playful and not defensive. "Some of us have to kiss a few frogs first, or whatever."

Eve shook her head. "Unfortunately, you've mostly gone for toads." She had never made any secret of her dislike for Roger and had absolutely lost the plot when Sara had described her first disastrous Tinder date. Eve used the side of her fork to cut herself a corner from the caramel slice she had ordered and then pecked at for the last twenty minutes before waving that very utensil at Sara. "I just want you to be happy."

Though she and Eve were the same age, and were both extroverted, her friend had a maternal streak a mile wide, and often said things that were very mum-like. This, Sara felt, was one of those times.

With a fond smile, Sara shrugged. "It's not as though I'm not looking."

"But are you looking hard enough?"

Laughter bubbled up Sara's chest and out through her lips, and she set down the cup of coffee she'd been attempting to sip at. "What else do you expect me to do? Put out an ad in the paper? That's pretty old school. I might get lucky and snag someone's Grandpa." The face she made expressed exactly how she felt about that idea.

"I dunno...Richard Gere's still kinda' hot." Eve shrugged and took another small section off her caramel slice.

"Who even are you anymore?"

Eve laughed and pushed her seat back, excusing herself to the bathroom.

Sara sipped at her coffee and let her gaze wander around the café.

For the middle of the day on a weekday, the cosy little suburban café was bustling and busy. The few tables around them were occupied, and the few set outside on the footpath were taken, too. The rich brown and gold colour scheme gave it a traditional coffee shop kind of vibe; the sort you'd see in any Hallmark Christmas movie, and the scents coming from the kitchen were intoxicating. It was a perfect, intimate venue for a catch up with an old friend. Plus, it was nice to be out and about and not moping around her house alone.

On the table, Sara's phone lit up with an incoming Facebook message.

'This is the sort of rubbish I have to put up with.' Charlie had written, followed by a photo of Everett and Gemma feeding each other cake. *'Send help!'*

Her fingers flew across the little keyboard on her screen. *'Aww, are they being too cutesy for you?'*

'Yes.' The one-word reply was almost instant, but the ellipsis animation denoting that he was typing popped up immediately afterwards. *'We're in public. There are children present. And little old ladies.'*

Sara snorted. *'And weirdly repressed men in their forties.'*

"Oooh," she wasn't sure she liked the teasing lilt in Eve's voice as her friend returned to the table and dropped back down in her seat, "who's put that silly little grin on your face, then?"

Tucking her phone back into her handbag, Sara rolled her eyes. "It's definitely not like that."

With an arched eyebrow, Eve argued, "Yeah, protesting like you're thirteen and being asked if you *like*-like him makes me think otherwise."

"I didn't say it was a him."

"Or her, then," Eve waved her hand dismissively. "Either way, it was cute."

The look Sara shot her in return was flat. "It's not like that," she repeated firmly.

"Sure," Eve snickered as Sara wadded up her napkin and tossed it at her. "I just want to know more about this person who put such a goofy expression on your face."

"It's nobody," Sara insisted. She didn't know why she was so determined to keep it a secret. After all, if there honestly wasn't anything going on –and there wasn't!– there was no reason to be so mysterious about it. And yet there she was, herself digging a deeper hole by lying. "It was just Jeff being his usual ludicrous self."

"Oh," Eve's hopeful expression fell, and she slumped back in her chair. "Damn. I really thought you'd found that spark again." She sighed and turned apologetic. "I'm sorry, Sarz."

Sara pasted on a smile and dismissed the apology easily. However, for the rest of their catch up, Eve's assessment played at the back of her brain, along with her own reaction.

Why had she kept it to herself if she had nothing to hide?

Or had Eve picked up on something that she, herself, had missed?

But that was impossible. She didn't feel that sort of connection with Charlie Rhodes. She couldn't.

Could she?

Surely not.

Maybe she just *really* needed to get laid. That had to be it.

There was no other option.

There couldn't be.

Chapter Six

Charlie was bored out of his brain. For the days following Zoe's party, his brother had graciously arranged to play tour guide. His grand idea had been born when their mother had mentioned that she was looking forward to seeing a little more of the country –or at least the cities nearest to Brisbane– as all of their visits for the last few years had been spent altogether stationary at Gemma and Everett's home and the surrounding suburbs. So, Everett and Gemma had arranged accommodations in Hervey Bay, a few hours' drive from Brisbane, and off they'd set as a group.

They'd made stops along the way for Zoe's sake –allowing the three-year-old to stretch her legs and go to the bathroom– and had made it to Hervey Bay just after noon. To Charlie, it seemed much like the other coastal towns they'd visited for day trips on the Gold and Sunshine coasts, if a little less tourist driven. It felt sleepier, somehow, and also slightly more dated. There were certainly far fewer skyscrapers or large hotels than the other coastal cities, and he appreciated that it wasn't overbuilt or overpopulated. But, as Gemma informed him, Hervey Bay's main claim to fame was its whale watching.

Every year from July until late October, tourists would arrive in droves to take part in the whale watching tours in the hopes they'd get up close and personal with the gentle giants that were humpback whales.

Naturally, being that their trip was during peak whale season, Everett had booked them a private charter for their visit. Charlie wasn't certain who was more excited by that revelation: Zoe or his mother.

To be honest, he suspected his mum exaggerated her excitement for Zoe's sake, but even though she was a convincing actress, he did wonder if maybe some of her childlike glee was genuine. However, this only served to amuse him, even if he pretended otherwise. It was good to see her happy and exuberant. After the life she'd led, Beatrice Rhodes deserved to have fun now.

Their first day, though, was written off with a stop for fish and chips for lunch, which they ate in an oceanside park. The weather was perfect, the ocean breeze preventing Charlie from complaining about the heat of the day, and the glistening blue water seemed incredibly inviting. They weren't in a rush to eat. Knowing that they had to wait a little while longer before they could check in to their Airbnb, Zoe was set loose on the little playground to work off some of her pent-up energy from the long drive.

Not wanting to sit and watch Gemma and Everett behaving like besotted teenagers, Charlie chased after his niece, much to her delight. He pushed her on the swings and pretended that he was an ogre and she was a princess –to which she giggled and told him that in *Shrek* the princess was also an ogre– and startled as his brother approached and took photos of their playing.

"Mum made me," Everett informed him as he tucked his phone back into his pocket.

Charlie raised an eyebrow. "Really, mate?"

The corner of Everett's lips lifted. "It's my story and I'm sticking with it."

"Uh huh." Charlie couldn't find it in himself to be annoyed. He didn't have many photos of himself and his niece together, let alone any candid shots. "Just send the best of them through to me, yeah?"

Everett grinned and agreed, slapping him on the shoulder as he called for Zoe to start wrapping up her playtime. "You can go down the slide three more times," he bargained patiently, "but then we're going to go and see our home for the next few nights."

Zoe had already expressed her excitement for the holiday house, so she wasn't at all disappointed to stop playing if it meant she'd get to finally see it. Charlie laughed at the way she cheered and threw her little fist into the air. She had spunk, his niece.

Not unlike her honorary Aunt, said a little voice in his head which, all too annoyingly, sounded like his brother. *You do like them feisty.*

He had no idea where that had come from. Certainly, he and Sara had been civil over the course of the last couple of years, on the few occasions where they'd actually spoken at all, but Zoe's birthday had been the first time they'd shared a genuine conversation. They still teased each other, but the fight wasn't there anymore. It had been pleasant, for lack of a better word, but that didn't mean he would automatically switch to fancying her. That just seemed ridiculous.

But she was stunning. With her long, dark hair and model's physique, he was surprised Sara was still single. Certainly, she could be a pain in the arse, but she had character and that was far more valuable than how attractive she was. After all, beauty could fade, but her fire…well, he hoped that would remain forever.

Shit.

He fancied her, didn't he?

Of –bloody– course.

Trust him to feel a spark of interest in a woman who a) couldn't stand him and b) lived halfway around the world.

What the hell was wrong with him? Did he want to spend the rest of his life alone? Because that was exactly where this would lead to. He needed to get this entire notion out of his head now, before things got complicated.

* * *

Charlie ignored his instincts and pressed 'send' on his message to Sara. He'd been forced to watch Gemma and Everett sharing dessert after their lunch and, in a pique of jealous irritation, had pulled out his phone and shot her a complaint. Her response was quick, igniting hope within him. For what, though, he wasn't completely certain.

A little bit of that hope withered and died as she deemed him repressed. He knew she was teasing him —bickering and bantering had become their 'thing'— but the assessment still stung.

He wasn't repressed! He had a healthy libido and was usually fine with public displays of affection…but he couldn't exactly tell her that he was jealous of the relationship his brother had found, could he?

Wanting to slap himself, he realised that he was being a prat. Unfortunately, this just made his mood worsen. Charlie hated feeling stupid. And, in that moment, he felt incredibly stupid.

He sent Sara a gif of some kid rolling their eyes, but she didn't respond. This also didn't help his disposition.

"What's got your knickers in a twist?" his brother asked as Charlie stuffed his phone back into his pocket with a huff.

Their mother beat him to answering. "He's been in a right mood for months," she told his brother, before casting a soft look his way. "I'm a mite bit concerned."

"I'm fine," Charlie insisted, but even he knew he'd overused this response. Shoulders slumping, he shrugged, "I've just got a bit on my mind, alright?"

As the words left his lips, he realised that all he'd managed to do was increase their worry, if their matching expressions were anything to go by.

"What's going on, darling?" his mum asked, leaning across the table to grasp at his forearm. "We can't help if you don't tell us."

At this point, he felt as though they'd had this conversation a thousand times.

Taking a deep breath, he turned to look out across the water. They were all seated around the outdoor table on the second storey veranda of their holiday home. It was right on the esplanade and looked out over the ocean which, at any other time, would have felt idyllic and relaxing, but right then and there, Charlie felt trapped. Still, he knew better than to snap at his mother when she was attempting to comfort him.

With a gentled tone, he shrugged off her hand. "It's nothing you can help with," he said, ignoring the instinct to tell her that he wasn't a child.

"Uncle Charlie, what about me?" Zoe asked, squirming away from

Gemma's attempts to wipe her face clean of the spread of ice cream she'd managed to create. "Can I help?"

Well, damn it. He couldn't exactly be shirty with a three-year-old, could he? Especially when she was looking at him with such a wide-eyed, earnest expression on her face.

"Ah, little love, you already have," he told her with a big grin, which was only mildly forced.

The words weren't entirely a lie, either. He actually had been enjoying himself for the last few days, almost forgetting his woes. The change of scenery had helped, but he was coming to realise that a lot of that was due to the distraction that Zoe provided, rather than the actual holiday he was on.

And, alright, bantering with Sara had helped, too…but now that he'd realised why he had enjoyed it so much, he was berating himself for it.

After all, he'd still be lonely when he returned to the UK. Compounding upon that was the realisation that he would be trying to get over his attraction to her. He was self-aware enough to know that attempting to date other women during that process would be a terrible idea.

"Then we have to play more," Zoe chirped happily, thankfully oblivious to his musings.

Charlie smiled warmly at the way she spoke, pronouncing 'have to' as 'haffta', and the 'r' of 'more' sounding a bit closer to a 'w'. Aside from his love life, he was slowly coming to realise that he was going to miss his family more than he'd anticipated, too. Particularly his niece.

If the melancholy he was suddenly experiencing was a fraction of how his mum had been feeling, he definitely couldn't blame her for moving to Australia.

He responded in the affirmative and glanced around the table, averting his gaze from his brother's when their eyes met. It was obvious Rhett wanted to say more, but Charlie wasn't going to budge.

He was supposed to be the adult –the older brother– giving life advice and leading by example. A little bit of his ego felt crushed simply by admitting to himself that, at least where romance was concerned, Everett had made the better life choices. To admit aloud to his kid brother that he was jealous of him? That might actually break him.

Thankfully, Gemma broke the awkward moment which had been building and suggested that they go for a walk down the esplanade to explore their surroundings some more. His mum begged off, opting to take a nap instead, and Everett also sighed and admitted that he had a few contracts he needed to look over and discuss with his agent.

On that note, it still astounded Charlie that, following Zoe's birth, Rhett's career seemed only to have blossomed rather than stagnated from the potential controversy. Yet another reason to be jealous. It truly seemed as though his brother was able to have his cake and eat it, too.

Nevertheless, Charlie was glad Everett had found the balance between his two lives and was happy and thriving. He acknowledged that his younger brother worked hard at it and that it wasn't always sunshine and roses for the younger man, no matter how it might seem on the surface. And he was genuinely proud of Rhett for sticking it out for the long haul where lesser men might have crumpled.

Once again, he reminded himself that he was made of the same stock as his brother. He, too, could suck it up and sort out his life. If Everett had managed, there was no reason why he couldn't. Even if he was seven years older and felt as though he'd blown his chances.

"You know you can talk to me if you don't want to talk to Everett or Beatrice, right?" Gemma's voice cut into his thoughts as they walked along the esplanade, each of them holding one of Zoe's hands while she skipped happily between them.

Passers-by smiled and nodded, and it struck him that they probably looked like a happy family unit. And, not for the first time since he'd arrived in Brisbane for this trip, he couldn't help but think that maybe it wouldn't be so bad if he did settle down and start a family of his own. But he was forty-five. Surely, at this point, he'd left it too late?

"Charlie?" Gemma prompted.

"I know," he finally answered her, hoping he sounded appreciative enough of the offer as he turned it down, "but I'm fine. I swear."

She nodded and they walked a bit further, reaching a stretch of little shopfronts across the other side of the road with the ocean still on their left. Zoe entertained herself by pointing things out to them as they went: discarded shells on the footpath, a seagull begging for hot chips at a nearby picnic table, boats on the horizon.

Between that and the calming sounds of the ocean, Charlie felt himself unwinding.

"Is this a mid-life crisis sort of deal?"

Comically, he swivelled his neck quickly to stare at his brother's girlfriend with an incredulous expression. "Oi!" He complained. "Steady on there. I'm not that old yet."

Gemma was unable to prevent the smirk that twisted her lips. "You're five years off fifty, bud."

"You know, I used to like you."

She tossed her head back as she laughed. "Well, come on," she urged as they swung Zoe between them and she giggled with delight, "what else could be bugging you, then?"

Why on earth had he thought that escaping the house with Gemma was the safe option?

"Nothing." Alright; now he even sounded petulant to his own ears. That sucked.

As did the little voice, again sounding irritatingly like Everett, that asked him whether Gemma hadn't made a point just now. What if his loneliness and these random desires to settle down were actually born of some sort of mid-life crisis?

Gemma snorted. "Pull the other one," she wasn't dropping the subject, even as she finally released Zoe to go play in a little oceanfront playground they had come across, "it plays *Jingle Bells*."

With his eyes glued on the three-year-old climbing up a structure that had clearly seen better days, Charlie exhaled. "I'm just working through some shit, okay? And I appreciate the fact that you and Rhett care, I really do, but I'm not exactly the '*kumbaya*, talking it out' type." Surely, after three years, she'd have worked that much out by now.

He could feel her gaze boring into him as he kept his own aimed towards the playground where Zoe had befriended another little girl. "I don't think you're as gruff and tough as you think you are," she said when he refused to turn and acknowledge her stare. "It's okay to feel emotions."

"Yeah, well, that's always been more Everett's scene than mine." He finally glanced away from Zoe to glower at his brother's girlfriend. "He's the lovey-dovey feely type. Not me."

She rolled her hazel eyes. "Sure. That's why you're the one who's had the best emotional advice for him over the last few years." Shifting so their positions were reversed, now seeking out her daughter while he stared incredulously at her, she added, "You're more emotive than you want to admit, Charlie. It's time you started giving yourself the same advice you've been giving your brother for years."

He had nothing to say to that. Especially not when Gemma's tone was so final. She had some spine; there was a reason he'd nicknamed her 'firecracker' after their first meetings. And, he mused on their walk back to the holiday house after Zoe had tired herself out on the swing and slide, it was possible she was right. He had been able to counsel Rhett through some of his darker moments over the course of the last few years, so why couldn't he apply some of the same strategies to himself?

However, Charlie knew the answer to that, too.

Most of the advice he'd given his brother over the years had been common sense. He'd urged Rhett to talk through his feelings with Gemma, especially when he was feeling doubtful or resentful. The conversations would have been difficult –even for someone as open and honest as Everett– but the key to those issues was, at their core, communication.

And Charlie had absolutely zero desire to communicate with anyone about his current feelings.

So back he went to square one.

When they arrived back at the holiday house, Charlie dutifully ignored the way Everett raised an eyebrow in Gemma's direction, as well as the tiny shake of her head in response. Instead, he carried Zoe –now snoring quietly into the crook of his neck– to the bedroom she was sharing with his mum and carefully laid her down on the bed she'd chosen herself.

She grizzled and rolled over onto her side before succumbing to sleep again, and he smoothed his hand over her hair.

"Want one of your own yet?"

"Jesus Christ," he hissed, jumping at his mum's voice. He turned around to glare at her as she came and sat down on the edge of her own single bed. "Could you not?" Whether he was referring to her startling him or the subject of her question was anyone's guess.

Unrepentant, she shrugged. "You're good with her."

"Yeah, because I get to do all the fun stuff and then give her back." And only for a few weeks a year, at that. He was a novelty to his niece, and, on some level, she was a novelty to him.

Beatrice shook her head, and he wondered if she could still see right through him as she had when he'd been a child. "I think you'd be a natural father, just like Everett."

"For fuck's sake," he tilted his head back and glowered at the ceiling. "I wish people would stop comparing me to my little brother." That was twice in one day now. Like the whole lot of them were in on it.

Come to think of it, they probably were.

"Darling," his mother patted the spot beside her, "I didn't mean it like that."

Despite his better instincts, he complied and sat down, spreading his legs enough to lean forward and rest his elbows on his knees, his hands hanging loosely between them. He was the picture of calm when he felt anything but. "Then what, pray tell, *did* you mean?"

Her hand settled on his forearm, and she squeezed. "Just that he had no desire to have children, either. However," she turned her head to smile softly at Zoe, "he adores being a dad. And I think you would, too."

If it had been anyone other than his mother, he would have told them to mind their own business and stop doubting his life choices. It was the twenty-first century, and it was totally fine if grown adults chose not to have children, or get married, or both. But this was his mum, and, as much as the line of questioning frustrated him, he thought he could see where she was coming from.

For most of her life, her entire identity had been wrapped up in being a single mother. Her children were her life. They were all she'd had in the world. And, as rough as being a single mum had been when they were kids, she had enjoyed being their mum. They would be forever connected as a family. She probably just wanted the same for him, especially now that Everett had fallen into it, however accidentally.

"I'm already forty-five," he reminded her, and she scrunched up her nose, "and even if I wanted to, there's the rather significant issue of needing someone to settle down and start a family with. Which takes time that I don't think I have."

Charlie didn't know where the confession had come from. He'd honestly wanted to calmly explain that not everyone had to have children to feel content or fulfilled. And, damn it, but it did actually sound –when he said it out loud– like he was having a mid-life crisis!

"Forty-five is hardly ancient," she refuted, before gently asking, "is this what you've been struggling with?"

Coward that he was, he decided it was easier to admit that he was having some sort of age-related meltdown rather than admit he was actually lonely. "Yeah," he shrugged, feeling awkward and embarrassed for admitting any weakness at all, even to his mum.

She removed her hand from his arm and wrapped him in a sideways hug. A sound of complaint left him at her sympathetic sigh. "Oh, sweetheart…"

Extricating himself from her embrace, he pushed himself to his feet. "It's fine. I'm being ridiculous."

"You're not–"

"I am. People age. It's not a surprise to me."

He hated the pity on her face.

"Stop it," he demanded, once again hearing petulance in his own voice and hating it. He pointed towards the doorway. "And not one word to them, alright?"

He stared her down until she nodded reluctantly. "But–" she tried, only for him to cut her off again.

"Good. It's settled. Not a word." Now he pointed at his chest. "I'm being an idiot and I'll get over myself eventually."

Of course, he knew it was unlikely that his mum would refrain from telling his brother and Gemma about their conversation. She couldn't help herself, and deep down he knew that they were only concerned because they cared. But he felt even more foolish now than he had when he'd started harbouring these feelings, so he hoped that they'd know him well enough to give him some space while he tried to process them.

But he also knew his family, and they could be meddlesome. His mother particularly.

Forcing himself to drop his shoulders, he mellowed his tone and attempted to change the subject. "Now, let's enjoy the rest of this little holiday, yeah?"

He wasn't oblivious to her pursed lips or frown as he left the room.

* * *

The whale watching charter that Everett had booked turned out to be a phenomenal experience. Charlie had to admit that he'd thought it might be somewhat boring being stuck out on the ocean with only the possibility of catching sight of a whale or two. He was glad to be proven wrong.

Their tour guide was knowledgeable and witty, telling them about the history of the area and about the whales' migration patterns as he directed their boat (a rather fancy catamaran) to spots he believed would guarantee them a whale sighting or two.

Charlie had also been a little concerned that his niece would lose interest, but she was fascinated just being on the boat. As they travelled, their vessel bobbing up and over slightly choppy seas, she peppered their tour guide –who she solemnly referred to as 'Captain No Sword', having decided that a Captain was defined by his weapon, or lack thereof– with hundreds of questions.

The Captain, as he would forever be dubbed, answered each one with patience and good cheer. He was in the middle of explaining how the marine radar system worked when he slowed the boat and pointed out toward the horizon. "And there are our first whales," he declared, having previously explained that it was illegal to deliberately approach within one hundred metres of the majestic creatures, or three hundred metres if there were three or more vessels already within that distance of the whales.

"And if the whales come to you?" Charlie had asked, genuinely curious.

"Well, they're wild and free," the man had shrugged and smiled, "and we won't get in any trouble for that."

"Fair point," Charlie had acknowledged, before wondering, "but how can you prove you didn't do the wrong thing?"

The Captain quirked an eyebrow, "You mean, aside from being seen on marine radars and by all the other tour boat operators around?" He'd followed this up by gesturing around them, where a number of other boats could be seen floating various distances away. "Honestly, I guess it's pretty well known that whales are curious – especially when a vessel's stationary – and we're all licensed operators who do the right thing because we're passionate about conservation and the whales themselves, so it's an honour code thing."

It had made sense, and Charlie reflected on those words as their boat came to a stop, the motors turned off. It felt instantly relaxing to listen to the sounds of the ocean lapping at the sides of the boat. He watched the horizon as a whale leaped from the water and appeared to belly flop, landing with a spray of water.

"Was that a whale?" Zoe asked excitedly, leaning forward over the bow of the ship. Both Everett and Gemma were quick to grasp her hands. She bounced up and down and beamed up at her parents, declaring, "I saw it jump!"

"It looked like a calf," The Captain informed them, squinting as he peered towards where the whale had landed, "a baby. So, its mum and her escort are probably nearby, too. They travel in pods."

No sooner had he said that when a much larger tail broke the surface of the water, closer to their boat than the jumping whale had been. Zoe cheered and begged for more, and Charlie couldn't blame her, though he did feel a little uneasy about the comparative size of that tail to the vessel they were standing on. While it was a large catamaran, a big enough whale could probably capsize them with the right intentions or could do some hefty damage if it misjudged its landing.

Charlie suspected he was being mildly paranoid, but he'd never really been out to sea before.

Nobody else on their vessel seemed to share his concerns, though. Instead, they all *ooh*-ed and *ahh*-ed as the pod of whales appeared to put on a show for them. And, alright, he had to concede that there was something magical about the experience. Reassured by their tour guide's easy demeanour and lack of concern for his boat, Charlie was able to set aside his fear for the most part. Especially when the whales stayed about the length of a football field away from them.

Charlie didn't know whether it was their size, or the fact that there was no other way he'd ever get to see whales like this, but the experience inspired a quiet awe inside him. However, it wasn't until later, when they came across their second pod of their day, that he was truly blown away.

The whales in the second pod were much more curious than the first lot.

The calf swam right up alongside them, followed by its much larger mother.

"Holy shit," Charlie breathed, the uneasiness from earlier on coming back with a vengeance. As the larger of the two whales rolled onto its side and seemed to smack the water with a very large, barnacle laden fin, he took a step back into the centre of the catamaran. He was suddenly more than aware of how insignificant a creature he was in comparison. The fin on its own seemed taller and much, much broader than he was. It was mind-blowing to make that comparison in person.

He wondered if anyone else was now experiencing an existential crisis. Glancing around, all he saw was awe on his family's faces.

"She's saying hello," The Captain told Zoe, whose eyes were now as big as saucers. She was gripping Everett's hand tightly but didn't seem bothered that even the calf was the size of a small car.

Instead, the little girl beamed and yelled "Hello!" back at the whale in question.

Beatrice, who had been quietly taking in the whole experience, seemed almost brought to tears. "They are beautiful, aren't they, Zoe?" she asked with wonder colouring her tone as she bent beside her granddaughter to also peer down at the whale calf through the wire of the boat's rails.

"Very bumpy," was Zoe's assessment.

Charlie couldn't help chuckling at her brutal honesty, while their guide attempted to explain the creatures' tubercles to the three-year-old. As bright as she was, Charlie thought the man might have bitten off a little more than he could chew. Hell, even Charlie couldn't really bring himself to listen. Especially not with the massive animals splashing about right in front of him.

The mother whale breached and then dove before bringing up her huge tail and smacking the water with it, not unlike the action she'd completed earlier with her fin. The boat rocked over the disturbed water she'd created. Her calf moved away from the boat and towards her, leaping out of the water and landing on its side before repeating the manoeuvre. Spy hopping, their guide called it.

Charlie barely registered Gemma's exclamations, or Everett's filming of the event. He was entranced. He couldn't properly verbalise it. Certainly, their sheer enormity had him realising just how small humans were –especially out here in the seemingly endless, vast expanse of the ocean– but it was more than that. There was genuine majesty to these creatures that sent a tingle up his spine. A natural magic which lifted his spirits and distracted him from his petty concerns.

Watching the calf and its mother frolic and put on a show wasn't an experience he would soon forget. However, as Charlie turned his head to see his brother wrapping his arm around his girlfriend's shoulders, a sliver of jealousy came creeping back in.

He rather hated himself a little for it. Here he was, in the whale-watching capital of the world, experiencing a once-in-a-lifetime event, and he couldn't fully enjoy the moment because he wanted to share it with someone, just like Gemma and Rhett were sharing it with each other. Even Zoe and his mum were hugging as the whales played for them. But he was alone.

Well, alone unless he wanted to snuggle up with The Captain.

It wasn't an appealing thought, but it did make him chuckle to himself and provided the impetus to give himself an internal shake.

He was a grown man. If he was lonely, he was the only person who could fix that. And, for the moment, he shouldn't let it stand between him and a magical experience like this one.

Pulling out his phone, he took a couple of photos of the scene in front of him. He was proud of his timing on one of them, having managed to capture the calf mid-leap with its mother's tail standing almost vertical in the water beside it. He sent the picture to Sara without a second thought.

'*You're missing out,*' he wrote beneath it.

'*Wow!*' Came her response shortly afterwards, followed by, '*I'm so jealous!*' While he contemplated how to reply to that, she asked, '*Is Zoe loving it?*'

'*I think she wants to become a marine biologist at this point.*'

'*Haha. That's impressive! Can she even pronounce that?*'

Snorting, he typed, '*Alright. I might've paraphrased...and exaggerated. But she's having the time of her life. Rhett and Gemma have had to hold her back from leaping into the water a couple of times.*'

'*That's my girl!*' Sara replied, adding a gif of a cheerleader for good measure.

"Are you seriously texting someone instead of paying attention to the natural wonder happening in front of you right now?" Everett's voice, full of incredulity, interrupted the playful reply Charlie had been formulating; he looked up from his phone with a frown.

"I took some photos and sent them to a friend," he justified grouchily, tucking his phone back into his hip pocket. "Terribly sorry for turning my attention away for just a moment."

"A friend, eh?" His brother's questioning turned playful.

Charlie didn't know what possessed him, but he lied. "Yeah. Jim."

As Everett's expression fell, Charlie wondered why he'd kept the truth from his brother. It wasn't as though his messages to Sara were untoward or even suspicious. But the fact that he fancied her...well, that was probably what he was trying to keep under wraps. He would never hear the end of it if Rhett was to work that out. Not to mention whatever Gemma would say. Considering the hell he and Sara had given each other, he assumed that Everett's firecracker of a girlfriend would not find his sudden change of heart −or certain appendages− amusing.

"Right," Everett shook his head, "well, I reckon Jim can wait, yeah? Luis," he jutted his head towards their guide, "says we'll be returning to shore soon."

"Alright, alright, point taken," Charlie let out a long-suffering sigh. "Since when'd we switch roles, eh?" He asked, casting his gaze back out to the whales, which had stopped leaping about, but were still visible. "I could have sworn I was the older, more responsible one. But here you are, treating me like a recalcitrant teenager."

Everett bumped his shoulder with his own and grinned. "Well, if you'd refrain from behaving like one..." he trailed off, laughing as Charlie threw a light punch to his upper arm.

As Charlie stood beside his family and watched the whales perform, he tried to shake off the thought that next time he'd be sure Sara was invited along, too.

He was far too old to indulge in those sorts of daydreams, and he knew it.

* * *

The rest of their little getaway was uneventful. Charlie didn't share his mother and Gemma's excitement of all the P.L. Travers memorabilia when they stopped in Maryborough, though he thought the little city was quaint. And, he supposed, seeing Zoe pose with statues and murals of Mary Poppins was quite cute.

"Pretty sure Travers decided she was British after she moved across the pond," he teased Gemma during the drive back to Brisbane.

In her spot in the front passenger seat, his brother's girlfriend folded her arms. "She was born in Maryborough. She was Australian."

He had pulled out his phone at this point and Googled. "Wikipedia says she believed her birth was 'misplaced' –whatever the hell that means– and she considered herself Irish, so...on a technicality, we're both wrong, but I'm closer to being right."

Gemma laughed, shaking her head. She turned around in her seat to face him, and her hazel eyes sparkled with mirth. "You just can't stand to be wrong, can you?"

"I can't help it if I'm usually right is all I'm saying."

Her gaze switched to his mother, but she was still grinning as she teased, "Where'd you go wrong with this one? Mine is much more charismatic."

Beatrice laughed while Charlie checked his other side. And how had he wound up sandwiched between the toddler seat and his mother, anyhow? Oh, yeah, chivalry. He'd sacrificed his own comfort for his mother's for the three hour drive, and this was how she repaid him? With a complete lack of defence? The traitor!

Redirecting his thoughts, he ascertained Zoe was asleep. Certain that she was, he said, "Well, of course Rhett's going to be charming: you're sleeping with him."

"Oi," Everett cut in, his tone a bizarre mix of amusement and warning while he drove. "Careful, mate, or I'll pull over and you can walk back."

"Not denying it, though, are you?"

"Oh, leave your brother alone," Beatrice interjected, patting his knee consolingly. "I think you're both charming."

"Great. My Mummy says I'm charming," he muttered with self-deprecation, catching Gemma's gaze in the rear-view mirror. "I blame you for this delightful new low."

She cackled, not at all repentant.

"Right, well, I've had it with you lot," he declared playfully, waving his left hand over his niece's snoozing form. "Zoe's got the right idea. I'm going to nap. Wake me up when we're back at your place." To illustrate his point, he closed his eyes and leaned his head back against the headrest. It wasn't particularly comfortable, but he had no other option.

"You're really selling me on your charm," Gemma snarked, and he opened one eye and gave her the finger, before shutting his eye again to the sound of her snickers of amusement.

Actually drifting off, he woke to his mum shaking him. "Come on, then, we're home," she told him, and he groaned and yawned widely.

He always felt a bit groggy after a midday nap, and this time was no different. If anything, it was worse, because his right leg had fallen asleep –cue the pins and needles– and his neck ached from the awkward angle he'd had it in.

Charlie grabbed his bag and hobbled inside the house, ignoring his brother's jokes about his old age beginning to show. He could hear Beatrice hushing Everett as he popped his bag back into the guest room and he sighed. "I can hear you," he called out to them, and the whispered conversation stopped.

He had known that his mum wouldn't be able to keep his impending mid-life crisis to herself, but he would have liked it if she could have at least waited until he had flown back to the UK before she spilled the beans. Casting his gaze to the ceiling and begging a power he didn't believe in to "Give me strength", he plastered on a cocky grin and made his way back down the short hallway and into the open-plan living area.

"Alright, Charlie?" Everett asked, to which Charlie nodded.

"Go on," he encouraged, rolling his eyes and also his wrist, "out with it. I'm not fragile. You're not going to break me by saying whatever it is you're itching to say."

Everett tilted his head towards the door leading to the patio. "Let's grab a beer, then, eh?"

It was mid-afternoon, so Charlie agreed with a nod and followed his brother outside. Everett grabbed two amber bottles from the fridge beside the barbecue and handed one to Charlie, and they sat side by side at the outdoor table. Charlie couldn't help but recall being seated here next to Sara, flirting –though he hadn't realised it at the time– and enjoying her company.

"Mum said you're having second thoughts about being a bachelor forever?" Everett leapt right on into the conversation without preamble, leaving his beer untouched and dripping condensation onto the tabletop.

Charlie itched to mop the mess up, but bit back that surge of minor anal-retentiveness. Instead, he stalled for time by taking a generous swig of his own beverage. Everett waited patiently for his response. Charlie didn't think his knee-jerk reaction to say 'Mum says a lot of things' would deter him.

"Yeah, well, it turns out I'm not as immune to ageing as I thought I was," he confessed awkwardly, picking at the label of his bottle. "And I let you both get into my head, which didn't help."

His brother made a dismissive sound and shook his head. "You've never let anything I've said get to you before."

"I know," Charlie sighed and looked out across the lawn –perfectly manicured, because his anal-retentive brother paid a landscaping service to keep it to his standards– and shrugged. "And I don't know why all your nagging to settle down finally got to me, but it did. For a minute."

Out of the corner of his eye, he watched Everett's dark eyebrows wing upwards. "For a minute?" he echoed, sounding sceptical.

"Yeah. I think there was a whole lot of stuff going on in my head –I turned forty-five, Mum said she was moving across the world– and I got a bit turned about. But," he forced himself to turn his attention back to his brother and smile, "turns out a holiday's all I needed." He raised his drink. "So cheers to that, eh?"

Everett didn't respond. He narrowed his gaze and stared back at him intently, trying to weigh the honesty in Charlie's words.

Charlie had never considered himself an actor –that was always Rhett's forte– but he'd sounded convincing enough to himself. He tried to gentle his smile and lowered his bottle. "I'm serious, Rhett. I'm fine. I had a moment, but I'm good now."

It wasn't entirely a lie. Not really. Something inside him *had* shifted during their time in Hervey Bay. It was as though he'd come to terms with his life choices. He refused to mope about it any longer. And even though he fancied Sara, he was resolved to keep that in a little box in his head for fantasy only. There was no way she'd return his feelings, after all. And that was okay.

It wasn't as though he was unhappy as a perpetual bachelor. He earned a fair amount of money and knew he was attractive enough, so he knew he could seek out romantic company when he felt the itch needed to be scratched. And he didn't need children. Not when he had Zoe in his life.

Of course, now he understood his mother's need to be closer to her, Charlie wished that he could stick around and watch the kid grow up, too. But he would settle with Facetime and quarterly visits to the country. He would make it work.

"Are you sure?" Everett asked him, slowly reaching for his own drink.

Having convinced himself now, too, Charlie grinned more sincerely and clinked their bottles together. "Yeah," he answered, "I am."

* * *

Charlie genuinely believed that everything would be fine, right up until he was seated beside Sara in a posh waterfront restaurant in the city on his second-last night in Australia. The farewell dinner was organised for that evening as Everett was scheduled to fly back to LA the next day, so it would be the last night that the entire extended family, including Gemma's father, brother and brother-in-law, would be able to get together.

The restaurant itself was perched in front of the Brisbane River, on the tail end of the bustling Central Business District. It was decorated in a very modern, minimalist style, with pressed white linen tablecloths and chrome accents everywhere. Fairy lights hung above their heads where they were seated out on the dining deck overlooking the river. The Story Bridge lit up against the night sky a short distance away.

The evening was warm, but there was enough of a breeze that it was comfortable, and the low murmur of noise from the other diners conversing around them, in combination with the general clinking of glassware and cutlery, added to the relaxed atmosphere. It was upscale but not stuffy, and it was obviously a favourite venue for Gemma's family, as the servers had greeted them all by name.

The meal was wonderful. It had been a long time since Charlie had been out somewhere this fancy, and it had felt good to wear the suit Everett had procured for him specifically for the occasion. It had felt even better to catch a number of women –and even some men– eyeing him hungrily in it. Including Sara, whose appraising stare he was almost certain he hadn't imagined.

He was seated at the end of the table, directly across from Brennan, with Sara on his left. His mother and Zoe were down the opposite end of the table, unable to provide any distraction from the woman he fancied. Conversation around him flowed easily, especially when he talked shop with Brennan, who owned his own business in the construction industry, supplying trusses and frames and the like to builders.

And then Sara had turned away from her own discussion with Gemma on her other side and had joined in on theirs. It wouldn't have been an issue, but she was breathtakingly beautiful in her chosen dress, which clung to her like a second skin and shimmered under the soft lighting of the restaurant. Charlie had to shift in his seat when his gaze had dipped too low into the deep 'V' cut of her décolletage. She'd smiled like she had known exactly where his thoughts had gone, her bright red lips pulling upwards coyly, and she'd teased him in the way they'd been wont to do since they'd met.

"My eyes are up here, buddy."

Banter. He could banter with her. He knew he could. But his tongue felt tied, and he was suddenly glad that it was Brennan and Jeff witnessing his fumble and not his brother. Everett would read into the behaviour instantly, but these men didn't know him as well.

"Sorry," he recovered as smoothly as possible, "I was momentarily blinded by your dress. How many fairies had to die to glitter that thing?"

As far as comebacks went, it was lame, but they eased into their usual bickering –without animosity– from there. Except it didn't feel right.

Like his brother, he was a bit of a flirt himself. In the right setting, with the right woman, he knew that he could turn on the charm and smarm as though it came naturally. Whenever he'd done this with Sara previously, it had been exaggerated and pointed, determined to rile her up and get under her skin, and she'd never disappointed him. But now he was more subtle, not wanting to anger or fluster her, and it startled him to find that she seemed to be flirting right back.

Was he misreading the signs in his old age? Had he turned forty-five and lost his touch?

When Brennan changed the subject, asking Sara what she intended to do with the last of her time off work, Charlie could have sworn that she batted her lashes coquettishly at him before turning back to Brennan and answering, "Nothing much. Just laying around the house, I guess."

"You haven't given up on dating already, have you?" Jeff asked her with obvious concern. "A couple of bad Tinder dates doesn't mean there aren't viable men out there."

Charlie hoped his expression gave none of his inner turmoil at the question away. Was he jealous of other men taking her out? Damn straight he was. But could he do anything about that when he lived on the other side of the world? No. So he bit his tongue and waited on her reply.

Once again, she seemed to cast him a sideways glance before she said, "I wouldn't say I've given up. I'm just…" she brought her hands up and held them with palms facing the ceiling, shifting them in a weighing motion, "taking a break from Tinder."

Was it just him, or did her last statement sound pointed?

It was probably just him.

God, he'd never been this insane over a woman before. It wasn't anything she had done or said, either. This was all a mess of his own making and he needed to snap out of it before he humiliated himself.

Coming back to the conversation, he had a witty response on his lips, but it died as her hand landed on his thigh. He jumped in his seat –glad, at least, that he'd kept any sounds of shock internal– and eyed her in surprise as she continued chatting with Jeff confidently, as if nothing was amiss.

Alright, he considered as he willed his heart rate back to normal, *maybe she's not aware of it.* Maybe she'd been making some sort of point, or had needed to steady herself, or…something.

Charlie had almost managed to convince himself that he had overreacted, and then her thumb, high up on his thigh, started *stroking*.

Still, she continued talking to Brennan and Jeff as though everything was normal.

Charlie swallowed roughly. *What the actual fuck?*

She wasn't in the right position to feel how he was physically reacting to her actions, but all she had to do was move her hand a fraction and…well, he didn't know what would happen then. He didn't want to know. Well, some part of him did. And not just the part currently rising to attention, as it were.

Christ, he was confused.

Was she drunk? That could definitely explain it.

However, he knew that she wasn't. She'd had half a glass of wine over the course of the evening, having previously declared that she had to drive home and was going to be sensible.

But if that wasn't it, what was it? Charlie couldn't quite fathom why she'd be touching him –*definitely* flirting with him– the way she had been.

Suddenly she gasped, and he wondered if perhaps her touch had been an unconscious action after all. Maybe she'd finally realised what she was doing and felt embarrassed? But, no: she only squeezed down harder on his thigh. He also noticed her left hand had flown to splay across her chest while she made the strangest, choked "Aww" sound.

The restaurant seemed to have fallen silent around them and it was then that he observed the couple across from him. In his haze of distraction, he hadn't paid any attention to Brennan leaving his seat to get down on one knee in front of Jeff, but he watched on now.

It felt odd to be witnessing a proposal in such proximity, but it was a welcome diversion from the bewildering moments beforehand. He'd missed the majority of whatever Brennan had said, too wrapped up in his own drama to focus, but it was obvious the words were emotional and genuine. Beside him, Sara was sniffling and grinning, and across from him, both men were teary-eyed while Jeff beamed and accepted the proposal with a loud, "It's about freaking time!"

Their entire table erupted in cheers and applause. In fact, many of the patrons at surrounding tables were also clapping as the two men embraced and kissed in celebration. Pulling away, but still holding his new fiancé close, Brennan had turned red in the face, but was grinning from ear to ear. Gemma had abandoned her seat and raced to hug her brother and brother-in-law, with her dad, Marcus, following closely. Even Everett was up and clapping Brennan on the back, while Zoe clutched his hand and loudly asked them what was going on.

It was chaos. Wonderful, happy chaos, but chaos nonetheless.

In the bedlam of everyone suddenly hugging and babbling, Charlie almost didn't register Sara excusing herself to go fix her makeup. In a split-second decision, he followed her towards the bathrooms, determined to get some answers.

The hallway to the bathrooms was dimly lit –carrying the mood lighting from the main restaurant– and thankfully empty of other people.

"Sara," he reached out to grasp her upper arm gently, stilling her escape before she could make it into the ladies' room. "What the hell was that?"

In another uncharacteristic move, she played dumb. "Brennan finally got his act together and proposed."

Despite himself, Charlie's lips curled upwards into an amused smirk. "You know that's not what I was referring to." Feeling bold, he stepped closer into her personal space, backing her up against the wall. "What were you doing before that?"

She straightened her shoulders and met his challenging gaze head on. "Getting your attention."

He searched her brown eyes for any hint of her motivation but couldn't get a read on her. "Why?"

Her laugh was loud and unexpected, but her expression gentled into something fonder than the defensive one she'd been wearing. "Why?" she echoed, incredulous. "You need to ask why a woman would be throwing herself at you?"

"Under normal circumstances, no…" he pulled out of her space a fraction to scratch the back of his neck. "But it's you."

"Oh." Her cheeks reddened and her expression was once again guarded, and he realised too late that she had misinterpreted his words.

"No, wait!" He prevented her from abandoning the conversation by planting his hands on either side of her. However, despite the brutish action of practically boxing her in place, his words were soft and vulnerable. "I just meant…well, I didn't think you'd be interested in me, considering our history."

It was her turn to search his gaze for honesty. After a few moments, she rolled her eyes and reeled him in by his tie. "You're an idiot," she declared, before capturing his lips in a searing kiss.

He could taste the remnants of the last sips of her wine as their tongues met, and he couldn't stop himself from deepening the kiss, his hands slipping from the wall to travel down her sides, landing at her hips. Immediately, he recalled the feel of her hand on his thigh, taunting him, and he pressed the evidence of his growing arousal into her, causing her to gasp.

She took control, sidestepping and fumblingly guiding them towards the accessible bathroom. They parted as she got the door open and they tumbled inside the tiled room, shutting and locking the door behind them. Then she was on him again, mouthing at his neck, up near his ear, while her nimble, long fingers moved to his belt buckle.

"You…in this suit…" Sara murmured against his neck, her 's's turning sibilant with her whispering, "so hot. You need to wear suits more often."

"I'll make a note of that," he agreed, now taking fistfuls of the material of her dress –thankfully stretchy and flexible– on either side of her hips, pulling it upwards.

Charlie didn't stop to think too hard on where they were or what they were doing, or that someone in their party might come looking for them if they were gone too long. He was far too invested in pursuing this completely unexpected side of Sara and their connection. He hadn't felt chemistry like this with anyone in years.

And now was certainly not the time to ponder whether his subconscious had been ahead of the program, or if that might have been a contributing factor to his less than stellar love life.

Having unbuckled his belt, she'd moved on to popping the button above his fly, and it wasn't long before his pants were completely undone and around his ankles.

At least the tiles at his feet were clean. Thank God this was an upscale restaurant and not some dingy pub!

"Well, hello," she purred, wrapping her hand around his still clothed erection. He sucked in a breath. "You know, if your brother is half as gifted in this department as you are, I can see why Gemma's always so keen to spend time with him."

He snorted, squeezing the top of her ass beneath his fistfuls of fabric. "Could we not mention my brother or his cock right now? You're kind of killing the mood here, love."

She rolled her eyes, undeterred. "I was giving you a compliment."

He decided he wasn't going to belabor the point. Not with her hand wrapped around him, stroking him through his boxer briefs. Instead, he dipped his head, muttering, "You're a bloody tease," with warmth before their lips reconnected. He wanted to complain when her hand released him, but she brought both of her arms around his neck as the kiss intensified.

Knowing they had limited time, he shuffled her towards the basin, thanking as many deities as he could imagine that there was a proper built-in marble vanity unit on the wall instead of a plain sink. Another upside to being in a posh restaurant.

Sara squealed into his mouth as he lifted her with ease and set her down on the bench. "It's cold," she complained as he hushed her.

Arching an eyebrow, he released the bunched-up material of her dress and slid his hands under her to encounter smooth skin.

"No underwear?" he asked in a voice tighter than he'd have liked.

She smirked. "G-string. This dress clings a bit."

Biting back a groan of appreciation, Charlie nodded, "I'd noticed." He slipped his hands further under her, squeezing as he shifted his hips forward, "It's my new favourite."

"I'll make a note of that," she echoed his earlier words back at him, drawing her arms back down from around his neck to tug at the band of his underwear, releasing him completely.

He retaliated by bringing his right hand around to slide aside the tiny scrap of lace masquerading as the front of her panties. He was beyond delighted to find her wet for him, and eagerly slid two fingers inside her, eliciting a moan that reverberated off the tiles surrounding them.

He chuckled. "Shush, or we'll be caught."

Charlie couldn't help but feel like a teenager as he said the words. This wasn't like anything he'd done before. Generally, he was rather straitlaced. Rhett had been the scoundrel, and he'd been the 'by the book' kid. The thrill of potentially getting caught was an aphrodisiac on its own.

The thought of being arrested for public indecency, though? Not so much.

"Then fuck me already," Sara didn't appear to share any of his concerns.

Speaking of concerns... "Shit. Condom." He pulled back slightly, his fingers still inside her, wondering if he might be lucky enough to have one in the wallet in his pants –which were still around his ankles– but she moved with him, shaking her head.

"It's fine as long as you're clean." She let go of him to touch her left bicep. "I've got an implant."

Her declaration had him torn. Ever a boy scout, prophylactics were something he'd always insisted upon. *Always.* It was a personal mandate. Even in the few long-term relationships he'd had in his lifetime. One might argue he was paranoid, but it was a rule that had served him well to this point. Besides, it wasn't just an unplanned pregnancy that terrified him, either. STIs worried him. And, if he was being completely honest, wearing a condom made clean-up a hell of a lot easier.

But Sara was so tight and wet around his fingers, like a siren's call directly to his cock. And, despite the years spent sniping at each other, he trusted her. At that moment, though, he didn't want to look too deeply into why she was any different to his previous lovers.

Knowing the clock was ticking, and unsure as to whether he even had a condom in his wallet at all, Charlie swallowed roughly and broke his number one rule. "Okay," he acknowledged quietly, bobbing his head, "I'm clean."

"Thank fuck," she breathed, grabbing his lapels and yanking him in for another intense kiss. She squirmed on the countertop, shifting her hips towards him, and he manoeuvred awkwardly until she'd arched her back at just the right angle for him to slide home, the scrap of her panties still pushed to one side.

"Jesus," he cursed, unable to properly describe the sensation of her wrapped around him. Even with the mildly uncomfortable position, he couldn't ever recall sex feeling so good...and it had been all of a couple of seconds so far, which was rather pathetic, really.

Dear God, he thought with ample amounts of self-deprecation while he attempted to adjust to the new feelings, *I might as well be a forty-five-year-old virgin. Christ.*

She laughed into his mouth, the carefree sound completely bubbly and light and uplifting. "It's Sara, actually." She tried to thrust up against him, hampered by her position. "Now *move*. This time's gotta be quick."

"As much as I'd love to argue," he responded, picking up the pace and breathing a bit more heavily, "I don't think that's going to be a problem tonight."

He didn't think he could have promised more than a few minutes at that point, even if he had wanted to. Not with how worked up he was, and how long it had been since he'd last been with a woman. And the new hyper-sensitivity he was experiencing wouldn't have helped him, either.

"Oh, right *there*," she encouraged on a shift of his hips. He endeavoured to maintain the angle she was enjoying, holding her backside in place with his left hand while his right thumb sought out her clit.

Even with the air conditioning, a light sheen of sweat formed on Charlie's forehead and his hair flopped forward from its previously styled back position, landing in his eyes. Between kisses, he attempted to blow it away, and caught a glimpse of Sara.

He did his best to memorise the image she presented. Her hair was wild, her cheeks, neck and chest flushed delightfully pink, and her lips parted in bliss as her orgasm built. He could feel her walls tightening around him, and her breathing quickened while she puffed out little emphatic 'oh's of pleasure.

With a flick of his thumb, he sent her careening over the edge. He watched raptly as she tossed her head back against the mirror and just caught herself from crying out in time, choking off the sound as best she could. The squeezing around his cock did him in, and he followed right after her, coming hard and as silently as possible.

Sara scrunched up her nose as he withdrew. He grabbed a wad of paper towels from the dispenser beside the sink, ran them under the tap and offered them to her with a sheepish smile. He averted his gaze while she cleaned up, pulling up his trousers and smoothing back his hair before he looked in the mirror.

They both looked thoroughly dishevelled, and it wouldn't take more than a single guess for their friends and family to know what they'd been up to. But she smirked at his reflection, and he grinned back at her, finding he had zero regrets.

Well, aside from it being his second-last night in the country. That part sucked.

She seemed to read his thoughts —not that he'd ever been that good at disguising his expressions anyway— and smoothed down his lapels, looking up at him with those captivating dark eyes of hers. "So, maybe make your way to my place tomorrow?" she suggested before biting her lip as she waited for his answer.

He nodded and bent to steal one last kiss. "I wouldn't be anywhere else."

Chapter Seven

Sara studied herself in her bathroom mirror the next morning. By some utter miracle –*Or, she suspected, since everyone was distracted by Brennan and Jeff's surprise engagement*– nobody had caught on to her tryst with Charlie. They'd returned to the table separately. She had touched up her makeup and combed her hair in the minutes after he left the bathroom, and not one member of their respective families had batted an eyelid.

She'd been relieved by that. Her spur of the moment decision to seduce him had taken even herself by surprise. However, he had been far too tempting in that suit of his, tailored to his measurements so it highlighted his broad shoulders, muscular chest and thighs, and squeezable butt to perfection.

Finding out that Everett had arranged the clothing for him had explained the tailoring.

Sara had just about swallowed her tongue when she'd first seen Charlie climbing out of Everett's car. He'd been clean shaven, with his sandy blonde hair swept up and coiffed in a style not dissimilar to Everett's, and his green eyes had popped against the charcoal colour of his suit.

When they had entered the restaurant as a group, she knew that she wasn't the only person there to notice him. She couldn't blame the others for staring, either. He was damn fine.

During the week that followed Zoe's party, Sara had to admit that she had enjoyed his messages. After Eve had pointed out her reaction to them, she'd tried to deny it, but with each alert on her phone, she'd felt the smile stretching her face. While she could lie to her friend, she couldn't keep the truth from herself.

She liked him.

When had that happened?

She had stopped hating him back when she'd still been dating Roger, when Zoe was still a baby, but this affection for him totally blindsided her.

But he was witty –in a dry sort of way– and funny, and surprisingly insightful and sensitive beneath the wall of muscle and stoicism. He'd had to grow up early and she could definitely relate to that, not that he knew about that part of her own childhood. When he pushed her buttons, she felt alive in a way she couldn't recall feeling with anyone else…and that scared her a little.

When she had started flirting with him, Sara hadn't given a second's thought to the fact that he lived overseas. To be honest, she had conveniently blocked the issue from her memory. Besides, Charlie had flirted back, and it had surprised her that he had been more subtle and restrained than usual. Determined to get a rise out of him, so to speak, she'd upped the ante.

All she had done was touch his thigh –a fairly innocuous act– but the solid muscle under her hand had fanned the flames of her desire for him, turning the smouldering lust to a raging fire. She wasn't unaware of the effect the action had had on him, either. His entire body had tensed, and from beneath her lash extensions she'd caught a glimpse of the flush on his neck as he'd tried valiantly to control the other physical reaction he was having.

Then Brennan had proposed, and she'd cried at his beautiful speech, and she had left the table with the genuine intention of fixing her makeup because her mascara had not been waterproof. Her heart rate had sped up when she'd realised Charlie had followed her, and she had been unable to stop herself from goading him on, issuing a silent challenge for him to follow through and act on the tension that had built between them.

Sara had been certain he would be the responsible, rule following boy scout Everett had always maintained he was. But he hadn't backed down. Instead, they'd fucked, quick and dirty, in the accessible bathroom of one of her favourite restaurants. And she hadn't been lying when she'd complimented him: Gemma really had been holding out on her if Everett was half as well-endowed as his brother.

But, standing there in her own home the following day, Sara stared her reflection down and considered what she was going to say to Charlie when he arrived.

She couldn't bring herself to apologise because she didn't believe she had anything to apologise for. They were two consenting adults, and it was obvious that each of them had wanted it. But he was more sensitive than he let on, and she wondered if he might regret having rushed whatever had been developing between them during his short return to Australia.

God, she hoped not.

Because –and she was aware her thoughts were turning circular– she liked him, and she was fairly certain that he returned her feelings.

Gemma would have a field day with this when she found out.

If she found out.

The doorbell rang and Sara shook herself from her musings, giving her reflection one last glance over. She was in casual wear, however she had been sure to choose leggings which boosted her butt, paired with a crop top that bared her toned midriff.

She wasn't above playing dirty to get what she wanted.

With renewed confidence, she left her master suite and headed for the front door.

So, he can play dirty, too, she mused as she opened the door to reveal all 6'3" of Charlie Rhodes. He was once again clean shaven, sporting the same hairstyle as the night before, wearing khaki trousers and a grey form fitting polo which seemed just a little too tight around his biceps, but really made the green of his eyes stand out. The bastard smirked as he caught her appraising him.

"Hey," she greeted, stepping aside to let him in, "come on in."

The smirk settled into a more genuine smile as he complied, wiping his shoes on the mat before he stepped through the threshold. He ducked his head to kiss her cheek. "Hi."

Sara had never truly understood what it was about Everett that had made Gemma a swooning fangirl way back in those early days, but now she got it. Only it was the other Rhodes man making her weak in the knees.

This was most certainly better than the alternative, though. Sara wouldn't do her sister from another mister dirty like that, even if she did love to tease Everett about how hot he was. It made Gemma laugh to see the actor flustered, and that was reason enough to continue.

However, Sara's attraction to Charlie was no laughing matter.

Sara led him down the hall, giving him an abridged version of what she had affectionately dubbed 'the tour', and they settled into the lounge room overlooking her small backyard.

"So," she began, then stalled. For all of her confidence, she wasn't certain how to start.

Charlie bobbed his head. "So," he repeated.

"We, uh, we should talk." No, honestly – where the hell had her bravado gone, she wondered. This was so unlike her.

The mountain of a man sitting beside her merely nodded again. "Yeah," he scratched the back of his neck. "We should."

He was being utterly unhelpful at this point.

"Last night–"

"Was out of character for me."

Sara blinked at him. What the hell did that mean? Was he regretting it? Did he think it was all a mistake? That she'd been metaphorically fucking with him through the literal action of fucking him? Because, if that was the case, she had news for him!

But, before she could channel these indignant feelings into actual words, he extrapolated.

"I'm not usually that impulsive," he admitted, his cheeks turning a little pink. It was all sorts of endearing and, in an instant, the rage she had felt at his initial declaration melted away. "That's always been more of a Rhett trait, or so I thought. But then you come along, and you're bloody stunning, and you make me crazy –in a good way– and I throw all of my usual rules and inhibitions aside."

Worrying her bottom lip between her teeth, she confirmed, "But...you don't regret it, right?" She wasn't used to feeling so unsure. It wasn't exactly insecurity, but she definitely didn't feel as confident about where they stood with each other as she would have liked.

Placing his hand over hers on her knee, his voice was calm and reassuring. "Absolutely not." His conviction settled any remaining doubts she was having. "It's not great we had to rush, but I don't regret that it happened."

He was smoothing his thumb over her hand in much the same way she'd brushed hers over his thigh the previous night. She smiled. "So, it wasn't just a one-time thing for you, then?"

What did it say about her that she found the flash of disappointment across his face comforting?

"No," he frowned, "was it for you?"

She shook her head, trying not to feel too giddy at the relief in his gaze and posture. "No. I'd like to explore this thing between us."

"Me too," Charlie squeezed her hand and released it, then cupped her face and brought their mouths together for a tender kiss.

Unlike the fiery, almost bruising kisses from the night before, this one was soft and exploratory. Despite years arguing with him, or the sex they'd had the night before, Sara realised that she didn't really know him, and he certainly didn't know that much about her, either.

While the kiss was gentle, she still felt as though he kissed with purpose. There was no hesitation, and he knew exactly what he was doing. She practically melted into it, unaware that she was reaching out to pull him in closer until he chuckled lightly and moved his hands to her waist before guiding her into his lap.

This angle was much better, she decided as she straddled him, relishing in the way he immediately shifted his hands to her butt. Spreading her legs a little wider, she ground down and smirked into their continued kissing when he bucked up to meet her.

"Should we move this to the bedroom?" he asked as they parted for air, one of his large hands now splayed across the exposed skin of her back.

Nodding, she slid off his lap, and extended her hand to him. He took it in his, and she led him back through the house to the master bedroom. There, she reluctantly let go of his hand to pull her top over her head, and he zeroed in on the black, lacy bra she wore.

Sara batted his hands away, playfully. "Nuh uh." She gestured to his shirt, "That comes off first."

He acquiesced without argument, grabbing the hem of his polo and tugging the offending item up over his head, discarding it carelessly on the carpeted floor. He allowed her a moment to ogle his toned, muscular torso, before he asked, "Better?"

"Much," she appraised, reaching out to touch the smooth, tanned skin. Where his brother was practically covered in dark hair (it was hard to avoid knowing this when she spent her summers in the man's swimming pool), Charlie had a fine smattering of light hair across his pectorals and trailing down his abdomen but was otherwise bare and smooth. Gemma might have been into the fuzz, but Sara thought Charlie's expanse of skin was much hotter.

"Am I allowed to touch if you are?" he asked teasingly.

She pretended to think if over. "Hmmm, I don't know. Maybe the pants should come off, too."

With a wicked smirk, he stepped closer into her space, so her lace covered breasts were brushing against his chest, and he bent to tuck his thumbs into the waistband of her leggings. "I agree."

Before she could protest, he'd tugged her leggings down, dropping to his knees in front of her to pull them free of her legs. "You know I meant your pants," she informed him, stepping out of the material anyway.

"You didn't specify," Charlie shrugged with one shoulder. Still on his knees, he dropped his eyes to her boy short panties and ran his index finger lightly up the front of them. His pupils had dilated, and his voice was deeper as he asked, "May I?"

"Please." Her own voice came out huskier than she'd intended, too.

She'd assumed that he would pull her underwear down immediately, but he surprised her by repeating the same motion with his index finger over the soft cotton, only he pressed harder on his upward stroke, pushing the material into the moisture that was beginning to pool between her thighs. She couldn't tear her eyes away, watching him smile to himself as he rubbed at her clit through the dampening material. She never would have thought that she'd find this as hot as she was, but there was something incredibly arousing about the anticipation he was building.

"I think we should move to the bed," he suggested, "or that wall behind you."

"The wall?" she questioned, and his expression turned mischievous.

"Wall it is," he decided, gesturing for her to back up a few paces, and he followed on his knees once her back was flush against the cool, hard surface. "Perfect."

Charlie pulled her panties down. He assisted her to step out of them and tossed them aside before he hooked one of her legs over his shoulder and leaned forward, licking the same path his finger had previously been travelling.

"Oh!" Sara cried out, the sound a mixture of pleasure and surprise, and he reached up with his left hand to steady her against the wall while he used the fingers on his right to open her up to him properly.

Her eyes almost rolled back in her head when he dove in deeper, licking and sucking, using his fingers and tongue to pleasure and taste her. He seemed to be taking note of which angles and movements earned him the biggest and loudest reactions, and then it seemed as though his actions turned tactical.

He sucked her clit and fucked her with his fingers at an angle that had her teetering on the precipice of an orgasm, but he stopped before she could go over the edge, licking gently until she squirmed and begged for release. Her legs felt wobbly, her mind hazy, and all she wanted was to come.

She didn't know whether to think he was amazing or evil at this point.

"Please," she heard herself whimper, writhing against his fingers and face, "Charlie, please."

"Please what?" His voice was tight, but he still sounded far too proud of himself.

Evil. She was going with evil.

"I need...*Charlie*...I can't...*please*..."

Instead of answering, he put his mouth back on her, repeating the motion which had driven her wild, and this time he didn't stop, not even as her release finally crashed over her, sending her nerve endings skittering, jolts of pleasure exploding inside her. She was unaware of the sounds she was making, riding his fingers and mouth for all they were worth as she squeezed every last moment of bliss from her orgasm.

She barely registered him carefully setting her leg back on the floor, or the few steps she took on legs made of jelly before she was splayed out on the bed, naked save for her bra. What she did register, though, was the sound of his belt –and the pants it was securing– hitting the carpet with a dull thud.

With hooded eyes, she craned her neck to take him in in all his glory. She'd been with a few very attractive men over the years, but nobody compared to Charlie. She recalled the ease in which he'd picked her up and deposited her on the bench the night before and could see how that was feasible. He was an Adonis. She knew he was in his mid-forties, but between his physical career and the sports he played, he was in peak shape. And, as she'd discovered the night before, he was in perfect proportion in *every* possible way.

"That looks painful," she drawled, gesturing to his straining erection, which was flushed a deep purple at the head. She wanted to reach out and feel it properly, her meeting with it the previous night much too brief, but she was still feeling far too blissed out and boneless after her epic orgasm.

With a crooked smile, he stalked towards her. "Worth it."

She laughed and beckoned him to join her with a curled finger. "We should do something about that."

"You sure you have the energy?" he teased, crawling over her and kissing a path up her body as he moved.

"Mmm," she answered as their lips met, the fogginess in her head dissipating as she felt her body responding to his proximity, "I think I can manage."

This kiss was more reminiscent of the previous night, with Charlie's restraint fading. Sara could taste herself in his mouth, but she didn't care.

She shimmied down the bed a little, reaching between them, stroking him and smearing his precum along his length. He thrust into her hand, fucking her mouth with his tongue to the same rhythm.

Impatient as she always was, she brought her legs up around his hips and guided him inside her. She loved those first moments –the stretch as she accommodated to his size, and the little sparks of pleasure that she felt as his cock brushed her sensitive spots– and knew the appreciative sounds she made gave her away.

And this time around, they had the time for him to exploit that discovery.

He pulled back out agonisingly slowly, teasing her with the tip before sinking back inside her again. Then he repeated the motion, and she squeezed around air for a moment before he once again allowed her the pleasure of the action. Her hand slid between them to rub slow circles over her clit, and he pulled the cup of her bra down so he could first fondle –then mouth at– her right breast, before moving to the left to lavish the same attention there.

Charlie nipped at her nipple, sending a jolt of pure enjoyment through her, and when he went back to the right and did the same thing, she couldn't contain the short, sharp exclamation that escaped her.

"Like that, eh?"

She nodded, already feeling the toe-curling pressure and tension of another orgasm building beneath her skin. "God, yes."

"Good."

He reclaimed her lips, and his slow thrusts sped up until he was fucking her with wild abandon, moving the bed with enough force to slam the headboard into the wall. When he propped himself on one elbow to twist her nipple, white light exploded behind her eyes and she came, keening loudly, squeezing around his cock until he cursed, and his hips faltered, and she felt him swell and empty himself inside her.

They were both panting, flushed and sweaty as they separated, with Charlie rolling onto his back at her side. After a moment, he pulled her against him and kissed the top of her head. "Tell me again why we've not been doing this for years."

She blinked back completely unexpected tears. What was that about? Clearing her throat, she answered, "Because you were an arse."

His laugh was deep and booming, and she felt it reverberate through his chest. "And you were a prissy princess."

She half-heartedly smacked him. "You deserved it."

"Alright, yeah, I'll wear that. I was a bit of a tosser."

"A bit?"

"Oi." He gave her an affectionate shake. "That's all you're getting from me."

"I'd say I've gotten more from you than that now," she snuggled up against him, kissing the top of his chest. He rubbed her back. The silence was comfortable, and she almost regretted having to ruin that. "Are we on the same page, though? I mean...what does this mean for us now?"

She could feel him tensing up. "What do you want it to mean?"

"I guess I want to date you."

"You guess?" Charlie sat up, propping himself up against the headboard, and she followed suit. "Love, I'm going to need you to be a bit more specific."

She fiddled with her sheets, starting to feel a little self-conscious. "I...Look, I want to date you, but it comes down to whether you want to give it a shot, doesn't it? Because you're flying back to the UK tomorrow, and that means—"

"Long-distance." Charlie finished for her.

She nodded. "Long-distance."

The words hung in the air between them, and she was almost certain his thoughts had turned to Everett and Gemma's relationship as much as hers had. How could they not? Not when the entire reason they were in each other's lives to begin with was their families' unorthodox constitution.

"It's not ideal," he eventually broke the silence and reached for her hand, "but I'd like to give it a go."

The mounting worry she'd been feeling began to ease away. "Really?"

"Really."

As elated as Sara was, she had to admit that he was right. It wasn't ideal. They would spend around twenty-four hours together romantically before he had to leave, and it would be months before they'd see each other in the flesh again.

"I know it won't exactly be easy," she told him, "but Gems and Everett made it work, and they had far greater odds to beat than we do."

He smiled softly at her, nodding. "Yeah, that's true."

"I mean, okay, they obviously struggled a bit," Sara continued to muse out loud, a frown creasing her forehead.

Charlie shook his head and sighed. "Yes, well, they also had the additional pressure of being relative strangers raising a baby together. We don't have either of those issues to contend with."

"At least not yet," she teased, patting her flat abdomen.

He paled and choked on air, then attempted to stammer out some sort of refutation. She thought it was impossibly British, and highly amusing.

"Relax," she soothed, smothering down a laugh, "that's not going to happen. The chances are, like, slim to none with this thing." She patted the inside of her left bicep appreciatively. "I'm just fucking with you."

Colour returned to his cheeks, and he scowled at her. "It wasn't funny."

Realising she had hit a nerve, Sara had the grace to appear apologetic. "Sorry," she rubbed her hand down his side and leaned over to kiss his shoulder. "I know you gave Everett a bit of a hard time when Zoe happened. It's a huge thing for you, isn't it?"

"Yeah," his answer was gruff and curt. She held his hand and didn't pressure him for any more information, and he eventually exhaled and extrapolated, "Our dad bolted when Rhett was little. I resented him for that, and when I was about thirteen, I found the letter he'd left Mum. He said he couldn't deal with us kids –with how rowdy and bratty and needy Everett was in particular– and that's why he left."

"What?!" Unaware that she was squeezing his hand tighter, Sara seethed, "That's awful! What an arsehole!" A lot of what she knew about Charlie suddenly seemed to make far more sense. "You poor thing! You shouldn't have *ever* had that put on your shoulders."

"Mum tore me a new one for snooping through her things," he acknowledged, "and neither of us have ever said anything to Rhett, obviously. It would have crushed him. And he was already a bit of a rulebreaker. Taking that shit into his teens would have been a right disaster."

"Well, sure, but it wasn't anything you should have had to deal with either." Her heart ached for his thirteen-year-old self, carrying those words with him his entire life. "You know it wasn't your fault, though, right? Or Everett's?"

"I do now," he nodded slowly. "It took a couple of decades to get there, but we were just kids being kids, and he was just looking for an excuse –any excuse– to fuck off and shirk his responsibilities."

"And that's why you don't want any of your own," she filled in the blanks softly. "You don't want to risk being him."

Charlie shrugged and looked away. "Yeah, well, even if I know now that he and I are very different people, and that his letter was all exaggerations and bullshit excuses, it definitely put me off the idea of having any children of my own from a young age." She watched his Adam's apple bob as he swallowed and turned his head back to meet her gaze. "Is that a deal-breaker for you? I know you want your own…and I might never come around on that."

"Hey, I seduced you knowing it's not something you want," she tried to bring the tone of the conversation back up, bumping her shoulder into his bicep. His lips twitched, but he still seemed rather morose. "No, it's not a deal-breaker. Besides, it's super early days. We've still got to give this long-distance thing a go first."

Some of the tension in his shoulders dissolved. "You really want to?"

She felt a bit guilty to find comfort in the fact that he seemed just as anxious about her interest as she had felt about his. To her, it put them on equal footing. They were both invested, so they both had something to lose if it went pear shaped. "I really want to," she confirmed with a smile. Shifting on the bed, she was starting to feel sticky and gross. "And I guess that means we need to set some ground rules, but…did you want to join me in the shower first?"

Charlie did not need to be asked twice, and she giggled as he chased her into her ensuite.

At least, she thought to herself as they stood under the spray, taking the opportunity to soap each other up and explore more thoroughly, *I'm confident that the spark is real.*

It was just the bigger picture that worried her now.

* * *

"So," Sara asked Charlie later on, setting down a plate of sandwiches on the table between them as she took her seat, "did, um, do Gems and your mum know you're here?"

Once again, it was unlike her to beat around the bush, but she wasn't sure what she wanted his answer to be. On the one hand, it would be encouraging if he'd told them, like he thought their relationship had promise, but on the other...

"No," his voice, tinged with apology, cut into her thoughts and she felt a wave of relief wash over her, "I'm sorry. It's not that I'm trying to hide it. I just wasn't sure where we stood, and the last thing I wanted to do was get either of them in a tizz over us if it was a non-event."

That, she thought warmly. *He just took the words right out of my mouth. Brain. Whatever.*

"I completely understand," she assured him, smiling and picking up a triangle of sandwich. "And I'm not gonna lie – I feel like maybe we should sort of keep this between us for a bit. Not because I want to hide it, but... well...we're going to be in each other's lives forever, so if it doesn't work out, I don't need our families knowing it, you know? Obviously, we will tell them eventually, but–"

"It's not worth getting them in a tizz," Charlie repeated. "It makes sense. I know how Mum and Rhett can get."

"Mmm." She swallowed the mouthful of chicken, lettuce and mayo that she'd taken. "I reckon Gems and Jeff could give them a run for their money. And Bren can get a bit overprotective..."

Charlie let out a short bark of laughter. "Rhett did mention something to that effect, back in the day." He plucked an egg and lettuce sandwich corner from the plate between them and held it as he asked, "So...how did you end up unofficially adopted into their family, then?"

Sara hoped that her expression didn't fall too much. She'd known that she would have to tell him her whole tragic life story at some point, but she also knew that it would once again bring down the mood. With him leaving the next day, she had selfishly wanted to maybe have this particular exchange via text or Facetime, rather than in person.

"I've, uh, well I've got a bit more in common with Gems than going to uni and then working together," she began, keeping her tone as light and airy as she could. "I wasn't in the foster system or anything, but I lost my parents when I was young." His face fell, morphing into the same sympathetic look that everyone had when she told them the story, and she shrugged. "I mean, I was three when Dad died in an accident, so I don't remember that much about him..."

Charlie set down his half-eaten sandwich and reached for her hand, and she cleared her throat of the lump which had developed in it, while he interrupted, "What happened?" Then he shook his head and a lock of his blonde hair fell into his eyes. "Sorry," he corrected himself, brushing the hair back with his spare hand. "That was insensitive. You don't have to–"

"It's fine," she assured him. It was actually sweet that he cared enough to ask for details. Most people tended to squirm away from the heavy subject. "It was a traffic accident. He was a cop, and he was stationed at some night roadworks." She repeated the story she had been told when she'd been old enough to understand what had happened. "It was raining. Some guy lost control of his car."

Charlie's shoulders slumped. "That's terrible. I'm so sorry."

"Yeah," she agreed, adding, "and from all reports the guy that hit him hadn't been speeding or anything. His car aquaplaned and...well, there was nobody to blame. It was just a freak accident."

"That must have been rough for your mum."

Warmth bubbled up inside her. Of course he'd see it from her mum's perspective, considering his own upbringing.

"It was," she and her mum had spoken about it as she'd grown up, on her birthdays, on her dad's birthdays, and on her parents' anniversary each year, "but she was relieved, I think, that it hadn't been a malicious attack. She didn't have anyone to hate or resent. Except, sometimes I think she would have preferred to be able to blame someone."

But Sara had to consider that this might have been her own projections. Knowing that she'd had a dad who had loved her and who hadn't wanted to leave her had been a bitter pill to swallow in her childhood.

"It's okay to feel that way, too," Charlie seemed to have read her mind, because she knew that he wasn't addressing her mother's hypothetical feelings, he was acknowledging hers.

How had she ever believed this man was an emotionless douche bag? She felt a little guilty for that now, but, incongruously, still felt as though he'd earned himself the assessment at the time.

Nodding, and unsure what else to say, she opted to pick up the rest of her initial story. "So, yeah. Then it was just me and Mum, for the most part, until she died from an aneurysm just after I turned eighteen. I, um, I was still in high-school, but I was legally an adult, so..."

"So you were on your own." He sounded pained, and sympathetic, and this was exactly why she'd hoped to have the conversation at a later date.

"Yeah. And I went a bit feral." It was an understatement, of course. She'd been eighteen, and had inherited the house, which had been paid off following her dad's death, and a sizeable amount of money from her mum, not to mention her mum's life insurance. So, being young and reckless, Sara had partied hard to dull the pain of her most recent loss. She regretted a lot of that now, but there was no going back and changing it.

Her downplayed confession earned her a snort of amusement. "Feral, eh?" Charlie squeezed her hand to let her know he was being playful, "I can imagine that."

With a roll of her eyes, she continued, finally answering his original question, "After that, I ended up taking a year off between school and uni. Then, at uni, I met Gemma and clung to her, I guess," because she had distanced herself from her school friends and the life she'd led before her mother's death, "and we got close. After we exchanged our tragic life stories, she dragged me along to meet her dad and brother." Her lips curled upwards, recalling their insistence that she was always welcome in their home, Gemma or no Gemma. "They pretty much demanded I consider them family, and the rest is history."

"They're good people," Charlie acknowledged.

"Yeah," she was already feeling lighter, "they are." She let go of his hand to pick up another sandwich, and cheekily added, "But we're still not telling them about us yet."

Charlie laughed and picked up his own discarded lunch. "Whatever you want, love. I'm easy."

"One of your most endearing qualities," she sassed back, ducking and squealing as he flicked a stray piece of egg from the plate towards her in retaliation.

The rest of their meal was spent exchanging playful banter, and, as he followed her into the kitchen and took the plate from her hands, washing it for her, she leaned her hip against the counter and quietly asked, "This is going to work out, isn't it?"

He licked his lips in contemplation before turning his head and looking her in the eye. "I hope so, love. I really do."

Chapter Eight

Charlie's day with Sara went by far too quickly for his liking. He felt as though he'd finally found exactly what had been missing in his life only to be forced to enjoy it from afar for the next few months. And, alright, he acknowledged that these thoughts were mildly melodramatic, but this was all very new to him.

He had learned more about Sara in twelve hours than he had over the course of the past three years, and that made him feel a little bit guilty. Learning that the reason she'd despised the way he had tauntingly dubbed her 'princess' came from the fact that it had been her mother's pet name for her made his heart ache, and he didn't think he could apologise enough for having unknowingly twisted the knife for years. Sara had assured him that he couldn't have known, but it didn't make him feel any less of a twat for it, and he vowed he would make it up to her somehow.

They had also spoken a little more about their childhoods —starting with the biggest, most traumatic parts seemed to have broken the ice very well— and Charlie had been surprised to discover they had so much in common. Obviously, he'd grown up in a much lower socio-economic setting than Sara had, but fundamentally they shared the experiences of being raised by single mothers doing their best to provide loving, stable homes for their kids.

He still couldn't believe that he'd told her about reading his dad's letter, though. Outside of his mother, he'd never told another soul what he'd read. But the words had spilled out, and there had been an instant feeling of relief as Sara had validated his bottled-up anger and pain. And, as much as he had already known that neither he nor Rhett were to blame for their father's cowardice and selfishness, hearing it from an outside party had soothed over the last vestiges of guilt which had been lurking beneath the surface.

But he would still never tell his brother about the letter – he just couldn't do that to him. Especially not now, when their own relationship had never been better.

Sara had also made him laugh harder than he'd known he could when she had asked him, seemingly seriously, whether he had a thing for Gemma. After regaining his breath, he had assured her that he did not.

He had no idea where she had gotten the idea from, and he didn't think he wanted to know.

Saying his goodbyes at the door as he waited for his Uber, Charlie lamented that she couldn't come see him off the next morning.

"How weird would that look, though?" Sara asked him, sounding fondly exasperated. She folded her arms and shook her head, leaning against the wall by the door. "As far as Gems and your mum are aware, we're not at a point where we see each other off at the airport."

Charlie was beginning to see the downside of agreeing to keep things secret while they tested the waters of their long-distance relationship. Still, he had agreed –and it did make sense to keep it quiet until they were certain it would work out– so he didn't argue the point.

Instead, he nodded and bent for a chaste kiss, resting his forehead against hers as they parted. "I'm going to miss you."

"I'm gonna miss you, too." Her reply was soft and tinged with melancholy.

"There's Facetime," he rallied, forcing a smile, "and don't they say absence makes the heart grow fonder?"

"People who say that are stupid," she pouted, "and you'll be back to dating your left hand, while I'm back to Bob."

"Right hand," he corrected mischievously, before asking, "Who the hell is *Bob?*"

Sara burst into a peal of nearly infectious giggles. "My battery-operated boyfriend."

He groaned good-naturedly. "You're ridiculous." A sly smirk pulled up the corners of his lips and he waggled his eyebrows. "But now I'm *definitely* looking forward to Facetime."

She slapped at his chest in reproof, but he noticed that she didn't actually turn down his unspoken suggestion. Even though he'd been joking, he wondered if perhaps being a bit more creative would lessen the discomfort of being half a world away from each other.

It couldn't hurt to try, could it?

"You'll message me when you land?" she asked, interrupting his thoughts and smoothing her hands down his chest.

"Care about me that much already, eh?"

Her eyes rolled. "Unfortunately."

"Good thing I return the sentiment, then." Charlie dipped his head for one last kiss, trying to memorise the feel of her lips against his and the scent of her perfume. "I'll message."

She wrapped her arms around him, resting her head beneath his chin. "Good," she declared imperiously. "I'll have you trained yet, Rhodes."

He chuckled. "We'll see about that, Carlisle."

* * *

"Where've you been?" Charlie's mum demanded as he attempted to nonchalantly wander back into Gemma and Everett's house.

"Out," he answered evasively, prompting her to cock an eyebrow at him from her spot on the two-seater couch in the main living area.

"Where?"

How was it that he was in his mid-forties and his mother was still tracking his movements as though he was an errant teenager? Not that he'd ever been even remotely delinquent, even back then.

With a long-suffering sigh, he strode over beside her and plopped down on the other end of the couch. "I was running a few errands and exploring a bit more, if you must know." It was a vague response, but with a stretch of the imagination, it wasn't entirely a lie.

His mother's eyes narrowed. She was clearly sceptical. "On your own?"

"How many mates do you reckon I have here, Mum?"

Her lips pursed and she frowned at him. "Why would you want to be alone on your last day here?"

It struck him, then, that she might be feeling a little lost with Everett having just left and the reality that she was not returning to the UK with her other son finally sinking in. Charlie softened his tone, "I just wanted to clear my head a bit."

Now he felt marginally guilty that he'd selfishly spent the day indulging his more primal urges with Sara, when his mum had probably wanted Charlie to spend what little time he had left in the country with her. And he had promised his new girlfriend that their relationship was just between them for the time being, so he couldn't even offer Beatrice an explanation that would appease her.

"Well, I can understand that," she responded, taking him by surprise. "You've been working through some heavy stuff."

Feeling even guiltier, he took her ready-made excuse and ran with it. "Yeah," he nodded, "but I'm honestly good now," he assured her, "I promise."

His mum looked him over again with obvious scrutiny before she relaxed her shoulders and smiled. "You do seem more yourself. Less troubled."

He bobbed his head again. "Still, it would have been nicer to spend the day together, yeah?"

Giving a minute shake of her head, she waved him off. "Pish. You'll be back in a few months for Christmas."

Indeed he would. And he had a whole slew of new reasons to look forward to that visit.

His mum was still talking. "Perhaps one year we might convince Everett and Gemma to bring Zoe to London instead. We could even travel up to Aberdeen and hopefully give the girls their first white Christmas."

Sara would love that. Unbidden, an image of her materialised in his head. He saw her wrapped up in a thick winter coat with faux fur cuffs and a collar, with her nose red and eyes bright, and flecks of freshly fallen snow dotting her dark hair. A soft smile curled his lips.

Christ, he had it bad.

* * *

Charlie found that keeping his new relationship secret was easy once he was back in London. None of his mates or colleagues were in touch with his family, which put less pressure on him. If he slipped up and mentioned Sara, they wouldn't bat an eyelid.

Of course, when he did finally acknowledge that he'd met someone, they gave him shit about it as his mates were wont to do.

"You're sayin'," Jim laughed, waving a half pint of beer at him, the amber liquid sloshing about inside the glass, "Mister 'I don't do relationships' is dating some bird halfway across the world?"

Charlie sank further into his booth seat, shaking his head. "She's not 'some bird'," he chastised, snorting, "who talks like that?"

"You're evading the question." Their mate, Mick, chimed in on Jim's other side, across from Charlie. Mick tapped on the tabletop between them with his index finger. "Not only are you dating, you've dived right on in to long-distance. Just how many knocks to the head have you taken?"

"I know I'm going to regret asking this," Charlie responded with exasperation, "but why?"

"You're doing all the hard shit with none of the pay off," Mick extrapolated, counting off on his fingers, "You gotta talk, email, send messages, be emotionally available or whatever, but you're still not getting laid."

Jim chortled while Charlie glowered across the table. "You're an idiot," he informed the man directly across from him, before he jabbed his index finger in Jim's direction without even bothering to look at him, "and you're encouraging him."

"The man makes a decent point," Jim shrugged before taking another draw from his glass. He hissed his pleasure after he swallowed and jutted his chin upwards towards Charlie. "You're doin' it all arse backwards."

Charlie wasn't about to divulge the bathroom romp that had set this whole thing into motion, nor the exploratory 'getting to know you' sex which had taken place the next day. He also wasn't going to tell his mates that, in the three weeks he'd been back in the UK, he had received a number of photos of his stunning new girlfriend in various states of undress, and in indecent enough poses that some had been enough to make him blush. Many of the accompanying text messages that he and Sara exchanged had him more than warm under the collar, and they had already experimented with some mutual pleasure via Facetime.

Despite the oceans between them, sex was most certainly not lacking in their relationship.

In fact, nothing really seemed to be lacking. Through the time differences, he and Sara maintained fairly effortless conversations, still managing to bicker and tease one another while they introduced each other into the mundane elements of their lives. Her shift work actually worked in their favour, too, with the pair of them able to speak to one another more frequently than if they needed to truly factor in their differing time zones.

Honestly, Charlie was a little concerned that it seemed *too* easy. Sure, it had only been three weeks, but the same length of time physically apart had almost destroyed Rhett's relationship.

"You're not your damn brother," Mick informed him; Charlie was startled to realise that he'd voiced those last thoughts out loud.

Finishing off the last of his beer, Charlie set his empty pint down and wiped his mouth on the back of his hand. "Yeah, and by all accounts, I'm the antisocial one of the two of us."

"Yeah, you're pretty antisocial," Jim scoffed with a liberal dose of sarcasm, gesturing at their surrounds, and absently nodding and smiling at someone he recognised. He turned his attention back to Charlie. "Is that why you're out at a pub with your mates, then?"

"Shove off, you know what I meant," Charlie huffed with yet another roll of his eyes. "I'm not the type to find this sort of thing –the talking and stuff– so easy."

The other two men nodded in unison. "Exactly the point I was trying to make," Mick sounded far too smug.

Jim agreed, extrapolating, "And it's why I was surprised that you're not only dating, you're doin' it long-distance."

Taking a deep breath, Charlie was forced to acknowledge that they had, in their own stupid way, expressed the same surprise he was feeling. "Fine," he replied, catching the bartender's eye and gesturing for another round with his index and middle fingers held up together, "then, yeah, I guess it's a bit unexpected."

His mates grinned back at him.

"But you're clearly head over heels for this one," Mick had turned thoughtful, "if you're finding it easy to keep things going, especially without a bit of rumpy pumpy."

Charlie snorted. "You're a right git, you know that?" he said, then thanked the waitress who had arrived at their booth with three more pints. She left with an amused smirk on her face, and he wondered just how much of the discussion she'd just overheard.

"She hot?" Jim redirected the conversation, adding, "Your Australian chick?" As if Charlie wasn't already aware of to whom he was referring.

"Yes." In fact, Charlie thought Sara was insanely hot. The photos she'd sent him of herself in lacy scraps of lingerie reminded him immediately of their short time together, her long model's legs wrapped around his waist while her dark brown eyes burned holes into his green pair.

Jim's eyes lit up. "Got a photo?" He leaned across the table eagerly. At his side, Mick did the same.

Knowing they wouldn't let up until he gave in, Charlie sighed and nodded, fishing his phone from his pocket. Secretly, he wanted to show her off. She was a stunner in every sense, and he was the lucky bastard she wanted to be with. He knew that it made him a bit of a wanker to feel this way, but he couldn't help it. Sara was gorgeous –inside and out– and damn right he was going to share that whenever he got the chance!

He pulled up her Facebook and found a photo of her, Gemma and Zoe together. In it, she wore skinny jeans with a black singlet top, and a wide-brimmed, floppy hat. She carried her sunglasses in her hand as she laughed at something in the photographer's direction. Her other hand was held in his niece's tight grip. She was a vision –as she always was– and his heart gave a little lurch because he missed her laugh and the way her eyes brightened when she was happy.

"Sara's the brunette," he said, turning the phone to face his friends. "The blonde is Gemma, Rhett's girlfriend. And the kid is Zoe, my niece."

Jim gave a low whistle, "Nice," he appraised, and Charlie was willing to give him the benefit of the doubt that he wasn't being creepy. "Makes sense you'd bag a model."

"She's a nurse."

"Model type, then. I mean, do girls like that go for ordinary lookers like me? No. But big, muscled, handsome blokes like you? Not a problem."

Charlie frowned. "I'm not with her for her looks, and she's not with me for mine, either." Yes, they shared a mutual appreciation of each other's aesthetics, but they were both deeper than that, and it annoyed him that his friend might think otherwise. The part of him that had been raised by a strong, independent woman reared up. He shook his head with obvious disappointment. "And if you're only chasing after women for their looks, mate, that's where you're going wrong."

Meanwhile, Mick looked at the photo, then back up at him. "And she's, what, fifteen years younger than you?"

"Eleven," Charlie corrected, his already present frown deepening. "Not that it makes any difference."

He locked his screen and slipped the phone back into his pocket. He didn't think it was a particularly shocking age gap at all, and it wasn't anyone's right to judge even if there had been more years between them. Hell, he and Sara hadn't even bothered discussing it, so clearly it didn't bother her either.

Mick held his hands up in the universal gesture of surrender. "Easy, mate. I'm just thinking ahead."

"Ahead?"

"Just look at that picture, Charlie," Mick answered, taking a swig of his pint. He brushed his own brown hair back and gestured vaguely. "She's my age, right? And I know women my age. Most of 'em want to settle down. Get married. Have kids. Not all, but most. So, you know, you should probably prepare for her telling you that."

"She's already told me she does," Charlie grumbled, then automatically regretted it as both his friends' eyes widened comically. They knew he had never wanted to settle down, and that he certainly had never before entertained the concept of having children of his own.

"And you didn't end it on the spot?" Jim sounded part horrified, part awed. "Who is this woman?"

Charlie chose to ignore that. "Ours is a...unique situation," he admitted, and Mick choked on his current mouthful of beer.

"Please don't tell me you've already knocked her up?"

"Nah, that's Rhett's trick, not mine," Charlie joked, watching matching expressions of relief pass over the other men's faces. "But we've known each other for a few years. So we both already kind of knew where the other stood."

"And yet you're still taking a shot with her?" Mick sounded sceptical.

Charlie nodded. "It sort of just..." he gestured vaguely with his hands, "happened. So we wanted to see whether it was a one-off, or if we actually could make things work."

He was beginning to regret mentioning Sara at all. And these were his mates! He could only imagine what telling his mum and brother would be like. Sara had definitely been right to want to keep things between them as they worked stuff out.

"And?" Jim asked. "What happens if they do work? You still don't want to settle down, and she does."

Not wanting to admit that he was already on the cusp of changing his mind about not settling down, Charlie shrugged. They wouldn't believe it if he told them that those thoughts had begun festering before he'd even considered that he might have a chance with Sara. Hell, putting it into this context, he almost didn't believe it and he'd lived it.

"Look," he ran his index finger up the side of his glass and through the condensation as he attempted to close the conversation, "it's still early days. I'll cross that bridge when I get to it." He shook his head. "*If* I get to it."

117

Thankfully, they backed off, and Jim gleefully switched the subject to football. "Alright, so Chelsea's looking strong this season…"

Mick scoffed, "You're off your rocker. They're going to get creamed when they go up against Arsenal."

Charlie smirked into his beer as his friends continued to squabble, relieved that things were heading back to normal.

* * *

"I miss you," Sara greeted from the screen of Charlie's phone, setting her own up on her bedside table. She lay on her side on her pillow, and he wished he could reach out and smooth away an errant lock of hair for her.

"I miss you, too." It was midday for him, and ten o'clock at night for her. He felt a little strange to be settling in to eat lunch while she readied herself for sleep. "How was work?"

"Slow today, which was a nice change." She yawned widely. "But somehow more tiring than if it had been busy."

"I should let you get to sleep, then." He didn't love the idea of not spending their usual time together, but he also knew it wouldn't be fair to keep her up when she was so obviously exhausted.

Sara shook her head. "No. Tell me about you. Did you end up getting the…that…roof *thing* finished in time for your project?"

He chuckled and nodded. "We did. The trusses were corrected and fitted in time to officially begin prepping the house for lock up. Roof's going on next week."

There had been a delay with the manufacturer sending trusses which had been made to the wrong specifications. He and his team had experienced a stressful few days trying to work around the problem. Charlie appreciated that she'd listened enough to ask about it, even if she hadn't quite remembered what the issue was. He didn't blame her for that, though. The way she rattled off medical terminology sometimes felt as though she was speaking a whole different language. He was certain she felt the same way about his job.

118

"Mmm," her eyelids were getting heavy. Charlie could tell even through the small screen of his phone. "You've still gotta send me a photo of you on the job. Shirtless and sweaty. Tradie porn style."

He laughed. "You know I spend more time in the office than on site these days."

The response only elicited a pout. "Please?"

He could already hear the guys ribbing him if he were to get caught. Still, he couldn't say 'no', not when she was still sending him new and exciting photos of herself every other day. "Alright," he agreed, "just one."

"Yay!" she clapped her hands together, up beside her face on the pillow. "Make sure you're wearing your tool belt."

"I will," he humoured her fondly.

"You'd better not chicken out."

Arching an eyebrow, he asked, "Or what?"

She went quiet and contemplative, visibly considering her options. "Or I'll stop sending my own photos through." The sleepiness in her expression gave way to something a little more playful and teasing. "You don't wanna miss out on the other tricks I have up my sleeve, do you?"

No, he did not, but he was not going to admit that without toying with her.

He tilted his head from side to side. "Meh," Charlie answered, trying to keep the amusement out of his voice, "you've sent me quite a lot already. More than enough to get me through the next couple of months."

"Is that so?" There was a hint of danger in Sara's tone, but she remained smiling. He enjoyed moments like these, where they were both silly and teased each other in jest.

"Yeah," he was still feigning nonchalance, "it's only been a month, Sarz. Have to leave something to the imagination, don't we?"

"Well, when you put it that way, it makes sense," she nodded and offered him a saccharinely sweet smile that he knew spelled trouble. "You'll just have to wait a while longer to meet Bob, then."

"What? No!" he sat up straighter, thwarted once again at his own game. "No, I think you should show me how Bob treats you."

Unable to contain her laughter, she shook her head and waggled an index finger at him. "Nuh uh. You said it yourself: I've sent too much already."

"I never said it was *too* much." Charlie knew he'd been bested, but hearing her laugh, even transmitted through his phone's tinny speaker, lifted his spirits. "I think I'd benefit from seeing Bob in action. I might learn something new."

"Hmmm," she considered, "maybe if you're a good boy and you send me the photo I've asked for."

"I will," he vowed, deciding that the reward would be well and truly worth the potential embarrassment, "and I'll even throw in one of me playing football."

"Rugby or soccer?"

"Soccer." His team wore forest green jerseys over white shorts. He knew the colour suited him.

"Okay. Deal," Sara declared, grinning smugly. "You send those through, and I'll finally introduce you to Bob." She lowered her voice, "You'll wanna be alone for that."

How was it she could go from cute and sleepy to a sexual siren in the blink of an eye? He swallowed roughly. "Can I ask why? Maybe get a little preview?"

She laughed again and shook her head, ending with another wide yawn. "Not tonight, buster. I'm completely wiped."

"Go to sleep," he responded gently, all playfulness gone, "and we'll talk in a couple of days."

"Alright," Sara nodded. "Miss you."

"Miss you, too, love."

She blew him a kiss before she reached forward and terminated the call.

* * *

A week later, Charlie managed to take a photo of himself working at the job site. He'd been lugging bricks from one end of the site to the other and, when the other guys went off on their lunch break, he'd opted to stay back on his own. Realising that this was his chance, he took it. Sweaty –and oddly excited– he whipped off his shirt, propped his phone up on a pile of bricks with its timer set, and smirked as it snapped a photo of him.

He sent it to Sara with a kiss blowing emoji, not expecting a reply for a while because he knew she was working, and yet his phone buzzed in his pocket five minutes later.

'*Holy shit,*' Sara's response read, '*Bob's definitely getting a workout tonight.*' He didn't think the winking emoji that followed was necessary, considering that the image she'd put in his head immediately distracted him from everything else.

Naturally, a lot of him wished he was there with her, so that she'd have no need for her battery-operated companion, but the other part –the one that had gotten excited taking the photo for her– had never experienced anything quite like this in a relationship before. The anticipation was out of this world. He wasn't certain he would be able to finish his workday without a raging erection while knowing what her evening plans were to be.

Subtly adjusting himself, he wrote back a cheeky '*Glad you enjoyed it, love*' before he attempted to get back on task. But his mind kept drifting. He found himself checking the clock, calculating what time her shift would end and how long it would take her to get home. Then, of course, he imagined her in the shower –because she hated bringing the smell of the hospital home on her– and that on its own just about short-circuited his brain.

Would she take Bob into the shower with her? She had confessed that her favourite toy was waterproof –and the ideas *that* had given him had been far too delicious not to share with her during one of their calls– so it wasn't out of the realm of possibilities. But she'd promised to *show* him, and her phone was not waterproof.

"Oi, Rhodes!" Luke, one of the other builders, snapped his fingers in Charlie's face, asking, "Where'd you just go?"

"Australia," Jim supplied cheekily as he sauntered past. Charlie flipped him off.

"Sorry," he turned back to Luke, feeling a bit sheepish, "what's up?"

"The truck's arrived with some of the rough-in stuff," Luke informed him, pointing to the other end of the site where a truck was parked up on the curb. "Give us a hand unloading?"

"Sure."

Charlie was grateful for the distraction, still embarrassed that he had been caught daydreaming about his girlfriend while on the job. He worked quickly with Luke and Jim to get the supplies unloaded and stored away securely and, when they were done, he used the hem of his shirt to mop at his forehead.

"Oh, put it away," Jim scoffed. "None of us want to see that."

For the second time that afternoon, Charlie flipped him the bird.

"Right, well, I'd say that's enough for the day," Luke proclaimed, checking his watch as he interrupted the playful argument before it could escalate. "Comin' down the pub for a pint or three?"

"Nah," Charlie shook his head, "I'll give it a pass for today."

"Got a phone date?" Jim teased, causing Charlie to punch at his bicep.

"Something like that."

Wanting to make it home in one piece, he left his phone untouched in his pocket and drove back to his flat. He had worried that he'd be lonely with his mum across the world, but between this new relationship with Sara and an increased workload, he'd barely spent any time actually on his own. He came back to his flat to sleep and shower and to have his 'dates' with Sara but, aside from that, he'd not had as much of a chance to mope about as he had originally anticipated he might.

After he let himself in the front door, he finally gave himself permission to check his messages.

There were four from Sara.

'Meet Bob' the first one simply read.

The second was a picture of a bright pink plastic and silicone monstrosity. Charlie's lips curled upwards into a grin because he should have guessed that her vibrator wouldn't be anything other than outlandish.

The third message was another text. *'Now, let me show you what he can do.'*

But the fourth message…Charlie swallowed convulsively. It was a video. She'd filmed herself.

Using Bob.

She'd filmed herself using Bob.

Because *of course* she had. Sara didn't do things in half measures. She was brazen, confident, and determined, and the combination of all three was hot as hell.

They had been dating –long-distance at that– for just over a month, but Charlie didn't think he'd ever felt this way about a woman before. Then again, he'd never been with anyone like Sara before.

He sat down heavily on his sofa and, after a ridiculous check over both his shoulders, pressed play on the video she'd sent.

At once, he recognised her bed. Even a month later, he was convinced he could close his eyes and remember the feel of her mattress and the scent of her freshly laundered sheets. If he tried hard enough, he could pretend he was right there beside her, instead of watching through his tiny phone screen while she teased herself with the pink eyesore.

He longed to reach out and touch her, to bring her to the same peaks of pleasure that she was taking herself to. In the video, she was making the same breathy sounds of enjoyment she had made for him the day before he'd left the country, and he couldn't tear his eyes away as she pushed herself over the edge into the blissful abyss of her orgasm. He was hard, but he hadn't touched himself, wanting to focus purely on watching her.

The trust she so obviously had in him was astounding. As confident and bold as she was, Charlie didn't think she would send a video like this to just any lover. Somehow, he knew that this was just for him. That it was a side of herself she'd shared *only* with him. He didn't know how he knew it, and he wouldn't ever ask her, but it felt special.

And it was fucking hot.

'*You are a wonder.*' He sent the message to her before he contemplated watching the video again. '*Absolutely gorgeous.*' His fingers hovered over the keypad for a moment before he added, '*I miss you.*'

It startled him a little to realise that he'd almost typed three other words instead.

Chapter Nine

Keeping her relationship with Charlie secret was damn near impossible for Sara. All the people she was close with had some sort of connection to Gemma, either because they worked together and were friends with her as well, or, in Jeff's case, because he was essentially family, too.

It sucked.

Sara knew that she had been the one to set the rule, so she had nobody to blame but herself. And her reasoning for it still stood. The last thing she needed was their respective families sticking their noses in before they even knew how –or even if– things between them would work out. That would spell complete disaster and she knew it.

But she was so happy. Her connection with Charlie surpassed even her wildest imaginings. They had genuine chemistry and, though she was a little afraid of jinxing things so early on in their relationship, she was certain that she felt *the spark* between them.

Honestly, she'd been starting to suspect that it was a myth. People didn't actually feel that way about each other in reality. Gemma was talking shit.

But then there was Charlie.

When she was with him –even via Facetime– she felt it. The spark. A tumultuous feeling of excitement, warmth, and endless possibilities. A craving to connect with him in every imaginable way. She practically floated on air whenever he messaged her, or, better still, whenever they spoke. It sounded silly, but he made her feel special in a way none of her previous boyfriends ever had, and she couldn't put her finger on why.

Yes, he was tall and built like a Greek god, and he had an accent to swoon over, but she'd dated attractive men before and had never felt like a giddy teenager around them.

Charlie was different. They were different *together*.

If she was being completely honest with herself, it had been that way since they'd met. There had been sparks between them as they'd argued and gotten under one another's skin. She could already hear Marcus' voice in her head, chuckling and telling her that children often behaved that way when they wanted each other's attention but were unable to verbalise it.

Had she always wanted Charlie's attention? It was beginning to feel as though she might have.

And she was almost certain those feelings were mutual.

Sara smiled to herself and re-read the last message that she had received from him. The one he had sent after he'd gotten her video.

God, she'd sent him home-made porn!

Her cheeks burned in mortification. What had she been thinking? The risqué photos had been one thing, but the video? There was nothing to hide behind in that. She was literally baring everything for him, trusting him to keep it to himself and to not ridicule her.

Sara had panicked after she had sent it and had half considered deleting the message before Charlie could see it…but she hadn't. She'd left it for him, wanting his reaction. She had wished she could have seen his expression in person, but the words of praise that had finally come through while she'd been sleeping had settled any fears or nerves she'd had.

'I'm glad you enjoyed it,' she typed back now that she was properly awake, sending the emoji blowing a kiss. 'I'll get to re-enact it in person soon enough.'

It was easier to be flirtatious than to acknowledge that her feelings were becoming more intense with each passing day.

It had only been a month. And they'd only been together physically for one day of that month, right at the beginning. Was it possible to fall for someone over phone calls and messages? Once upon a time, she would have scoffed at such a suggestion –people found it much easier to lie and put on a façade that way– but now she felt differently.

Charlie wasn't any different via Facetime or Messenger than he was in person. There was no act with him. And she was being her genuine self in return, if perhaps a little more adventurous.

At the back of her mind, she could once again hear her mother's voice warning her that independence was easier than loving and losing, but Sara refused to believe that. She liked the way that Charlie made her feel. How could loneliness be better than this?

Her phone lit up with an incoming message, cutting into her train of thought.

'Love, no offense to Bob, but I doubt you'll be needing his services when I'm there.'

She cackled to herself. *'Cocky bastard, aren't you?'*

'Don't act like you don't love it.'

Sara snorted. She did enjoy their banter and he knew it. Glancing at the clock in the top left corner of her screen, she frowned. *'Isn't it almost 2 a.m. there? Why aren't you asleep?'*

'Today'll be Saturday,' he replied, and she could almost hear his voice as she read the words, his accent curling around the words charmingly. *'I wanted to catch you first.'*

"Awww," she murmured, feeling her heart flutter. He'd kept this sweet side of him well hidden over the years, not that she had given him any reason to show it to her before. *'Well, you've caught me,'* she typed back, sending a gif of a cartoon bunny coyly batting her lashes. *'What are you going to do with me?'*

Once again, she knew she was deflecting. But there was no way she was going to delve into her hidden emotions with him via her Messenger app. These were the sorts of feelings which required hours of contemplation and introspection, accompanied by wine and a deep and meaningful chat with her friends.

But that took her right back to her initial conundrum.

She couldn't talk about any of this with her friends.

Actually, she thought, finally pulling herself out of bed and traipsing across the short distance to her walk-in wardrobe, *I could. All I need to do is pretend that I'm dating someone local.* She plucked a fresh set of scrubs off a nearby coat hanger. *That'll throw them off the scent.*

Gemma, in particular, had already observed that she was behaving oddly. Like Eve, she had commented on the way Sara smiled at her phone, but she'd also noticed the evenings that Sara had been 'busy', asking her outright if she had a hot date. Sara had said "Something like that" and changed the subject. But now that it had been a month –with no sign of things going south– maybe she could tell her bestie that she was seeing someone without giving away too many details?

Dressing in her work clothes, Sara decided her most recent idea seemed to be the safest course of action. She was desperate to talk over her feelings with her best friends, needing their affirmation that she wasn't going crazy, and that it was perfectly natural to fall head over heels so quickly. She already knew Gemma would be on board – she'd fallen head over heels with Everett within a week.

But this wasn't Sara's usual modus operandi and she felt very much like a fish out of water. Especially with her mum's words continuing to haunt her.

Her phone rang –an audio call through Messenger– and she startled, racing across the room and fumbling through her blanket to find the device.

"There are many things I'd like to do with you, love," Charlie's voice was deep and heavy with sleep as well as innuendo, "but mostly I just want to kiss you again."

"Aww, Charlie," she sighed at the sweet answer. Sometimes he made it very difficult to keep things light and playful. Who'd have thought the gruff builder would have had it in him? "I want that, too." She sat on the edge of her bed and offered, "Christmas is only a couple of months away now."

That would be yet another test for them: seeing if they could date in person as well as they could long-distance. It sounded easier on the surface, but what if this spark was so strong purely because of the anticipation that was building? After all, there was a certain excitement in wanting what you couldn't have. What if, after they were reunited, things became stale and boring?

"I can't remember the last time I was so anxious for Christmas," he confessed over the line before yawning, "I think I would've been about five."

"Well, Santa's gonna bring you something much more exciting than a toy truck this year."

She relished in his deep chuckle. "A G.I. Joe?"

Sara snorted inelegantly. "Keep guessing."

"A remote-control car?"

"Well, maybe I might get myself a new toy with a remote," she teased back, giggling as he groaned. "You can help me play with it, though. I'm good at sharing."

"You'll be the death of me, Sara, you know that?"

She grinned. "I have always enjoyed torturing you."

"And don't I know it," he yawned down the line again. Her smile softened. "Get some sleep, babe."

"I will. I just wanted to hear your voice."

And there he went again, chipping away at her defences and making her feel things she didn't think she was prepared to feel. "Mmm," she agreed, "I'll admit, hearing your sexy accent is a great way to start my day."

"Is that all I am to you?" he teased, and she heard him smother yet another yawn. "Accent porn?"

"Oh, you're *many* different types of porn to me. Now, go to bed."

"Alright, alright. I'm going." She could hear the smirk in his voice as he added, "I do like it when you get all authoritative."

"Don't give me ideas, Rhodes," she sassed back with a smile.

"I wouldn't dream of it."

* * *

"Another message from lover boy?" Jeff teased, nodding at the phone in Sara's hand.

Hastily stuffing it back into her pocket, she nodded. It had been a week since she'd decided that she would tell a few white lies to her friends, though she hadn't yet done so. Some part of her felt a little uneasy at the thought of misleading them, and she wasn't quite sure how to bring it up when they all seemed to be respecting her initial wishes to stay out of it.

"Yeah," she answered. Her cheeks flushed at some of the things Charlie had written. Aware that she was catching up with her family, his intention had been to ruffle her feathers...and it had worked. She was already plotting her revenge.

Jeff leaned across the kitchen counter, where he'd been prepping a charcuterie board, and pinned her with a knowing stare. "How long have you been seeing this one?"

"Something like five or six weeks." Aiming for nonchalance, she shrugged a shoulder. "It's nothing serious."

Liar! The voice in her head screamed at her. *Lying liar!* She knew her feelings for Charlie were becoming quite serious, and this scared her.

"Maybe not yet," Jeff responded, his cheeses forgotten, "but I can tell there's something different with this one. *You're* different."

She rolled her eyes and plucked a stuffed olive from the spread in front of her friend. "As if."

Sara wasn't sure why she was fighting this when she knew that she agreed with him. This was her prime chance to unload and finally get some affirmation that her feelings were normal, that she wasn't being an idiot by jumping into something so deep so soon. But the words wouldn't come. Admitting them out loud was harder than she thought it would be.

"Sarz," Jeff shook his head, his black hair falling into his eyes. "You're attached to your phone. You light up when you get a message. You're quieter...maybe more contemplative? I don't know. All I know is you actually seem serious with this one. Even when you were with Roger—"

"Ugh. Don't speak his name. Let's call him...*Moldywarts* or something." She knew Gemma would have appreciated the throwaway line more than Jeff, but he still snorted.

Jeff pointed his cheese knife at her emphatically as he continued, "You were with him on and off for years. *Years*, Sara. But...and don't take this the wrong way–"

"You know I'm going to, now."

He ignored her interruption. "Even then, you didn't seem invested, you know? I think we all knew you were just having fun with him – and there's absolutely nothing wrong with that."

"Listen, Judgey McJudgerson," she poked a finger in Jeff's direction, "just because you've been with the love of your life for forever–"

"Ten years."

"*Forever*," she insisted, sniffing primly, "and you're still all loved-up and are getting married in less than a year." Jeff cheered. She narrowed her gaze. "Just because you're on that trajectory doesn't mean everyone else is. Or are thinking about it. Or…whatever."

"No, that's true," Jeff pushed the wooden board of savoury treats closer to her as she continued to eye them, and then she snagged a piece of prosciutto. "But I think you *are* thinking about it with this one, and it scares you." He tilted his head and smirked. "Am I on the right track?"

"Oh, fuck off," she complained, trying to hide her smile, "you're not *always* right, you know."

He cut himself a triangle of brie and slid it onto an artisanal cracker, then waved the stacked cracker between them as he responded, "But I am this time, aren't I?"

"Eat your damn cheese."

"Cheese?" Gemma seemingly appeared from out of thin air. She came to stand beside Sara in front of the kitchen bench. "You guys have cheese and aren't sharing? I think I hate you both."

Jeff chewed and swallowed his treat, then gestured at Sara. "This one distracted me. I was making up a board to bring outside."

"She just wants all the cheese to herself," Gemma laughed, reaching for the brie and the knife, "I'm onto her."

"Actually, she was finally opening up about her secret fling," Jeff grinned, and Gemma squealed before she turned and smacked at her best friend's upper arm.

"You told him before me?"

"To be fair," Sara sighed fondly, "I didn't tell him anything. He's been doing most of the talking," she arched an eyebrow at Jeff, daring him to refute her, "as usual."

"I was interrogating her," Jeff informed his soon-to-be actual sister-in-law, and it amused Sara that the declaration was made with absolutely zero shame. "And you interrupted right when she was about to cave in and admit I'm right."

Gemma eyed Sara intently while she asked Jeff, "Right about what?"

"That she thinks this one is *The One*." They could all hear the capitalisation of the last two words.

Gasping, Gemma grabbed at her best friend's hand. "Really? Oh, I need all the details!"

"Ha!" Sara countered, "This coming from the woman who *still* won't talk about her magical sex life with her hot actor boyfriend."

She mostly teased her bestie about this on principle now, as it had been four years since her friend's fateful Gold Coast encounter and Gemma had remained tight-lipped. Having now experienced what the older Rhodes man had to offer, though, Sara couldn't say her curiosity wasn't a little piqued again.

"And I never will," Gemma informed her, before prodding, "but you're not deflecting this time. Is this guy really *The One*?"

Sara held her hands up in surrender. "I've only been seeing him–" and even then, there hadn't been a lot of in-person sight involved "–for, like, six weeks."

"But she's definitely throwing off 'this is serious' vibes," Jeff added, sotto voce, pushing more cheese along the counter in Gemma's direction.

Gemma cut some more brie and placed it onto a cracker while she eyed Sara speculatively. "He's right. You've been cagier about this one. Usually, you're dying to give me all the details, including the ones I have *zero* interest in." She bit into her snack and, around her mouthful of food, continued, "But you've been a vault this time."

Sara had to admit it: that was definitely out of character for her. She had no way to justify it, either. Well, other than to confess that Jeff had hit the

131

nail on the head. This time *was* different.

"Maybe I've matured?" She offered, her lips pulling into a pout as her friends shared a glance and then burst into laughter. "Screw you both."

Gemma attempted to appear apologetic and smoothed her hand down Sara's arm in a consoling gesture. "I'm sorry," she said, "we're just playing. We won't push you if you're not ready to talk about it." She pinned Jeff with a hard glare. "Right?"

He held his hands up in surrender, but muttered, "Spoil sport."

Unable to contain her sigh, Sara shook her head. "The thing is, I *want* to talk about it. I do. But…it's complicated." She knew those words would only feed their curiosity. "And before you ask – no, he's not married, and I'm not pregnant."

And yet, somehow, she felt as though her situation might have been easier if either of those issues were the cause of her discomfort.

"Then what's the problem?" Jeff asked, direct as ever.

Why was it so hard to confess that she was afraid of humiliating herself?

While Sara pondered on that, Gemma groaned. "Please don't tell me you've taken Roger back again."

"Ugh, no." Sara's response was immediate and resounding. She stared back at her BFF in horror. "Gross."

For her part, Gemma just shrugged. "Well, what else am I supposed to think?"

"It's nothing like that, I swear." Well, aside from the fact that she was dating a man she'd once sworn black and blue that she'd detested. Not wanting her friends to keep guessing –especially on the off chance one of them actually got it right– she blurted, "I just feel like I'm falling too hard, too fast. That's not a me thing. I don't do that, you know?" Except apparently now she did.

"So I was right!" Jeff pumped the air with one of his fists. "Nailed it."

Gemma rolled her eyes at his antics before landing an empathetic stare back in Sara's direction. "That just proves this one is different, right? That your feelings are real."

"Or that my biological clock is now ticking rapidly towards implosion, causing me to become less picky in my old age."

Gemma scoffed and popped an olive in her mouth. "Oh, please," she argued, chewing and swallowing. She planted her hands on her hips. "If that were the case, you would have settled for someone else long before now."

"Well, alright, maybe…"

Gemma pulled her in for a sideways hug. "C'mon, tell me about this guy."

Sara nodded. "He's…" Oh, God, how was she supposed to describe Charlie without giving it all away? "Mid-forties, tall, handsome, fit." And an accent that made her a little weak at the knees.

"So, your usual type, then?" Jeff offered with an ample amount of snark. He piled a bit of salami and brie together on another cracker. "What's different about him to all the others?"

Lips curling up into a smile, Sara thought about Charlie's best qualities. "He's funny. He makes me laugh, like, constantly. And he acts like this tough guy, y'know? But he's secretly super sweet…I mean, he just does things for me, or whatever, because he 'thought of me', and they take me completely by surprise."

Gemma was giving Sara one of her soft, warm looks of gentle awe. Sara had to look away, mildly uncomfortable under her best friend's appraising stare.

"We can talk for hours without repeating ourselves, or without conversation getting boring," she continued, "and when I'm with him–" or just talking to him via Facetime "–he makes me feel all giddy and ridiculous in a way I'm pretty sure I've never felt before. Like," she paused, considering her analogy, "like I'm a kid with a crush."

"Well, you know I can relate to that," Gemma nudged their shoulders together, "and it really does sound like maybe you've finally found someone you're properly compatible with." She grinned – a sure sign that her next words would be trouble. "I'd even say it sounds like you've found *exactly* what you wanted."

"Yeah, well, I thought what I wanted was a myth."

Jeff arched his eyebrows at her. "So, what? You think this guy's too good to be true?"

"No, he's genuine," Sara knew that much. She shrugged. "I just have no idea what I'm doing."

"None of us actually do," Gemma was quick to assure her. "Look at me and Everett: ours was a hot mess of a situation, but we made it work. God only knows how…"

Sara shook her head. "Because you *work*. You just *click*, and you both care enough to get through all the shit together."

Her best friends were smirking at her, and she realised that she had pretty much addressed her own concerns while defending Gemma's relationship. Because Charlie *was* genuine, and, like his brother, he seemed invested enough to make things work, too. And *boy* did they 'click'. She'd never experienced a connection that felt so effortless before.

"Well, fuck you both," she huffed, unable to contain her smile.

"Hey, little ears can hear you!" Brennan's voice interrupted, and Sara and Gemma turned to find him standing behind them with his hands clapped over Zoe's ears. He pulled his hands away once he seemed certain the swearing had stopped, much to Sara's amusement. "What's taking you so long with the snacks?"

"Sarz was finally telling us about her *boyfriend*," Gemma taunted in a sing-song voice, giggling and ducking out of the way as Sara swatted at her.

"Well, bring the food outside and be prepared to give me a recap," Brennan demanded. "I'll get the wine."

"And the juice," Zoe added, nodding imperiously.

"And the juice," Brennan agreed.

And so, settled around the outdoor table, surrounded by the friends she considered her family, Sara did just that, though she was careful not to drop any hints which might give Charlie's identity away.

By the end of their catch-up, she felt renewed confidence in her relationship, and in her feelings. Perhaps she was falling a bit quickly, but –after telling her friends about some of the things her mystery man had said and done– she didn't think that she was the only one. This, more than anything, calmed her nerves.

However, she still wasn't going to tell Charlie how she felt about him. That was a conversation best had in person.

Chapter Nine

* * *

"Christmas is just around the corner," Charlie told Sara gleefully.

It was early December, and things had been progressing well. With her worries assuaged by her increasingly curious friends ('When are we gonna meet this guy?' was a frequent question for her continued deflection), Sara had comfortably slipped back into her routine with Charlie.

They still sent each other raunchy messages and photos, though she hadn't repeated her foray into amateur porn. They spoke via Facetime where possible, and if she had thought she'd fallen hard for him before, it was nothing compared to the way she felt now. As the weeks had passed, she'd shared memories of her childhood with him that she'd never really spoken about with anyone, and he'd done the same.

Despite not having seen him face-to-face since the day they'd decided to give a relationship a shot, Sara had never felt closer to a man before. The only other person she'd shared any sort of similar connection with had been Gemma, and that was a purely platonic, sisterly vibe. She still wanted to fuck Charlie.

"Thank God," she replied, falling back onto her mountain of pillows with a sigh. "Not being able to kiss you is driving me crazy."

His chuckle sent a warm thrill through her. "I'm right there with you, love, but not too long now and we'll get to make up for it in spades."

She bit her lip, and he frowned at her from her phone screen.

"What's wrong?"

"Nothing's wrong." Sara knew he wasn't going to be a fan of her next words. "But I've been thinking..."

She watched as his expression shuttered and quickly realised that he might just be bracing himself for the worst.

"I'm not breaking up with you, idiot," she shook her head, the edges of her lips curling upwards. "Stop imagining the worst."

Charlie rolled his eyes, but colour had returned to his cheeks. He resettled himself against the back of his couch. "What was I supposed to think?"

"I was just telling you how badly I miss kissing you," propping herself up on her elbow, she scoffed, "why would I follow that up with a breakup? Via fucking Facetime, no less."

He shrugged back at her. "I'm not used to things going so well for me, I suppose."

The confession made her heart sink and hopes swell. It was an odd combination, and it made her feel even guiltier for the idea she wanted to run by him. But it didn't change her feelings about the situation, so she took a breath and threw it out there.

"I just...well, I think we should still keep this," she pointed at herself, then in his general direction, waving her hand towards her phone where it was propped up on her bedside table, "quiet over Christmas."

With both his sandy blonde eyebrows winging upwards, he asked, "Why? Haven't we proven that we work?"

"In theory, yeah..."

"In theory?!" Charlie was sitting up straighter now as he glowered through the screen at her. "How the hell is this just theory?"

Sara licked her lips, considering how best to explain what she meant. "I just mean, y'know, we've proven that communication and long-distance isn't going to be an issue for us..."

"But somehow that's not enough?" His frown deepened. "Are you embarrassed to be seeing me? Is that it?"

"What? No! Why would...you know what? No. Just no." She pinched the bridge of her nose and rushed to finish her explanation. "We're usually good at the talking thing. But we've only spent one physical day together. What if..." swallowing, she moved her hand and stared balefully into her phone screen, "what if all of that chemistry was only there because we were on borrowed time, and it was new and exciting?"

He blinked at her, stunned. "What?"

"I know it sounds dumb, but...but what if we get to spend more time together and it just...I don't know...fizzles out?"

"Fizzles out?" he repeated, still seemingly dumbstruck by the suggestion alone. His shoulders slumped with defeat. "Is that what you think will happen?"

"No! Of course not! But don't you want to make absolutely sure that what we had back in September wasn't a fluke?"

She'd thought a lot about this over the past few months. And as strongly as she felt for him, Sara still needed actual tangible proof that it was all going to keep working out once they were reunited.

Of course, she knew it sounded ridiculous. Surely, the hardest part was the physical distance between them, right? Wasn't that what had almost destroyed Gemma's relationship?

Your relationship is nothing like Gemma's, some voice inside her said. Seeing as it was her own voice, she had to concede it was right. That *she* was right. Despite all of their similarities, she and Gemma were completely different. And even though Everett and Charlie were brothers, with many of the same fundamental ideals, they were also nothing alike. And, all being said and done, the two separate relationships were built on entirely different foundations. Her internal voice of reason stepped up again. *Stop comparing yours to hers.*

But that only brought her back to wondering if —because of those very differences— being together for an extended amount of time might actually be her and Charlie's undoing.

"A fluke?" Charlie echoed.

Sara nodded, brushing her long dark hair back with her free hand. "I'm not saying it was," she placated, "but we were both in weird places, emotionally and mentally, at the time, right?" Over the past couple of months, they had also spoken about that a bit.

It had surprised her when he had admitted that he'd been struggling with the idea of being alone for the rest of his life, that casual flings weren't doing it for him anymore. He still didn't know if he wanted the whole picket-fence life with kids and a dog, but Sara had assured him that they had time to work all of that out together.

In turn, she had then informed him that she'd imagined that fairy-tale sort of life for so long but could also see the pros in remaining child free. Honestly, Sara had mused aloud, she'd wanted a kid because it was someone to love, and to love her in return, and watching Gemma and Zoe together had set off a maternal ache deep inside her. But she had Zoe as an honorary niece, and, in the right relationship, she believed she could still live a happy life, with or without kids of her own.

The crux of the matter was, she had been desperately searching for a connection first and foremost. It seemed almost too good to be true that he had as well.

"We were," Charlie nodded slowly behind the mild pixelation temporarily distorting her screen. She lamented her crappy internet speeds. "But I don't think that made our chemistry any less real."

"What if it intensified it or something? And this," once again she gestured between them, "this forced anticipation thing is just pushing that same feeling along? What if we get to spend more than a couple of days together and it's not as great in person as it is online?"

She watched him scrub his hand over his face – a sure sign he felt a little irritated or out of his depth. "Sara, love, I think you're worrying yourself over nothing. But," he exhaled loudly, the sound accompanied by a short, sharp shake of his head, "if you're that concerned about it, we'll keep it secret a bit longer."

He didn't appear at all happy to be making this compromise, and she knew he hated keeping things from his family, but all Sara could feel was relief at his agreement.

Between wanting to avoid Brennan and Jeff playing out the overprotective brother act and knowing that Beatrice would probably attempt to smother her with maternal love, Sara didn't want to risk making such a big, dynamic-altering announcement over Christmas. Outside of not wanting to face the meddling from their families, the humiliation and awkwardness should their relationship fall apart soon after disclosing its existence was not something she wanted to experience.

"Thank you," she responded quietly, reaching out with her free hand to stroke at Charlie's face on her screen. "I just want to be sure."

"I understand," he nodded, mustering a small smile for her even though she knew he wasn't fully on board with her plan, or her justification.

"I…" she cut herself off, too close to making a declaration she was still not ready for. "I miss you."

The expression on his face gentled and his smile became more genuine, "I miss you, too."

* * *

Just as they always did, the Christmas holidays finally arrived in a fanfare of humidity and rain. Sara couldn't recall the last Christmas Day that wasn't stinking hot and simultaneously rainy as hell. The mugginess in the air clung to her skin and made her hair lank and gross. Every year she made it her aim to spend all of her time inside the blissful air-conditioning of either her house or one of her family's.

This Christmas, however, had the additional bonus of her lover sharing Gemma's house.

It had taken all her willpower to not squeal and throw herself at Charlie when he'd sauntered into Gemma and Everett's lounge room, rolling his suitcase behind him. Zoe, on the other hand, had shown no such restraint. This time around, Everett and Beatrice had met him at the airport without the three-year-old. While they waited for the entourage to return to the house, Zoe had regaled Gemma and Sara with how desperately she missed her Uncle Charlie. Sara had found it difficult not to agree.

While he stooped to catch his flying niece in his arms, Sara took the opportunity to drink him in. He was just as handsome as she remembered, though she noticed that his biceps seemed larger in the tight, black polo he was wearing, and his chin and cheeks bore the obvious stubble of at least a day of forgone shaving. He had dark circles beneath his green eyes, and his hair was mussed and oily. Given that he'd just spent the better part of twenty-four hours on an aircraft, Sara knew he was probably exhausted and desperate for a shower.

She wanted to hop into both his shower and his bed with him.

When their eyes met over Zoe's little shoulder, she knew he was having very similar thoughts.

Why had she thought it was such a good idea to keep their relationship on the down-low again?

This question was answered by his mother's excited chatter as she pestered him for all the updates in his life –as though he didn't call her at least once a week– and then Everett's exasperated interruption to leave the poor man to get his bearings.

"He'll be here for a month," Everett told Beatrice, but though the words were firm, his tone was warm. "Let him get at least one night's sleep before you interrogate him."

Sara really liked Charlie's family. Beatrice was lovely. They had gotten to know each other fairly well, as Gemma had been sure to include the Rhodes matriarch in all their family get-togethers, even with Everett overseas. Moreover, Sara and Everett had gotten along since she'd first officially met him, though she still liked to exaggeratedly flirt with him because it amused Gemma to watch her beau squirm.

Once Sara's relationship with Charlie was out in the open, all of their dynamics would change permanently.

She wasn't ready for that. Not yet.

Which meant that they would have to be subtle.

Unfortunately, 'subtle' wasn't a word generally used to describe her or Charlie.

But they had to try.

It wasn't until long after dinner on that first evening when Sara and Charlie finally had a moment alone. Having excused herself to the bathroom, she sneaked down the hallway and let herself into the guest room Charlie usually stayed in. He had begged off for an early night's sleep, claiming jet lag. She hoped she would catch him awake.

She was not disappointed.

"Took you bloody long enough," he complained good-naturedly, already swinging his legs over the side of the bed and pushing himself to his feet.

She was about to inform him that she hadn't wanted to appear at all suspicious with her timing, but before she had the chance, he crossed the space between them quickly and pulled her against him, moving his lips to hers and groaning into her mouth at first contact.

Her hands flew to his bare pecs –and it was only then that she noticed he was only wearing a pair of dark green satin boxer shorts and nothing else– and she melted into the kiss as he deepened it. It sounded corny, but she lost track of time and space as they reconnected. Not until he pulled back and rested his forehead against hers, murmuring sweet words about how terribly he'd missed her, did her brain unscramble.

"I've missed you, too," she responded emphatically.

His hands, currently on her hips, tightened their hold as he began to speak, but a knock at the door had them both freezing in place.

"Charlie?" Everett's voice followed the sound. "You awake?"

If she had thought it would be as simple as remaining silent and waiting for her BFF's boyfriend to wander away, Sara was proven wrong as the door handle behind her back turned.

"Shit," she breathed and dove behind the opening door, hoping Everett wouldn't attempt to open it the entire way.

"What?" she heard Charlie demand, clearly irritated.

"Are you alright?" Everett asked. There was a curious lilt to his voice. "It's unlike you to turn in so soon, even after a long flight. I just wanted to check in on you."

She heard the older man sigh. "I'm fine. Just tired."

There was a brief pause before Everett pushed the issue. "Are you sure? You're not still having a mid-life crisis?"

Sara frowned at the painted timber separating her from Gemma's beau, even while her heart continued to jackhammer at how close they'd already come to getting caught. *What mid-life crisis?*

"For fuck's sake," Charlie complained in response, "I said I'm fine. Just jet-lagged and completely buggered. *That* could be due to my old age, you muppet."

"Hey," came the reply from the younger of the brothers, "I didn't say you were old. I was just–"

"I know," Charlie cut him off, still sounding annoyed. Sara was aware that he was trying to hurry his brother back out of the room. "I know *you were just*," he mocked, "but I'm good. I promise. Just tired."

She watched through the crack of the door-jam as Everett backed up into the hallway. "Alright, alright," he acknowledged, "I'm sorry for disturbing you, then."

"Goodnight, Rhett." Charlie's response was firm.

Everett sighed. "Goodnight."

Charlie shut the door in his face.

Sara listened as Everett's footsteps retreated down the hall before she let out the breath she'd been holding. "Well, that was close," she murmured, taking two steps forward and smoothing her hands over Charlie's bare chest. "Mid-life crisis?"

He rolled his eyes towards the ceiling. "That's a long story."

"I want to hear it."

"We don't have the time at the minute," he countered. "Unless…"

Guessing what he was going to say, she shook her head. "No."

Ignoring her, Charlie pressed his lips to her neck, smirking against her skin as she squirmed, ticklish. "We could just tell them."

"Charlie…"

"I know, I know. You're not ready." She could hear the disappointment in his tone and once again felt guilty that she was forcing him to hide from his family.

Nudging his cheek with her head, she shifted so she could place a quick, chaste kiss to his lips. "Thank you for understanding."

"Hmm," he replied, stepping back and nodding. "You'd best get back out there, then. They'll send a search party if you're gone much longer."

As she slipped back out of the door and down the hallway, Sara knew the topic was going to remain a bone of contention between them.

However, in the lead up to Christmas, she discovered that the sneaking around was actually kind of hot. There was an additional thrill to their interactions – her adrenaline spiking with the notion that with every brush of their hands, or each lingering glance, they increased their chances of getting caught.

Charlie hadn't yet managed to steal away to her house, though, which only made the anticipation of such more unbearable. This pushed her to be bolder with her teasing, taking every opportunity available to bend over in front of him, or *accidentally* press her body against his when she just happened to be passing him in the hallway.

"This is killing me," he informed her, catching her by the wrist as she sauntered back from the linen cupboard. She had Gemma's requested tablecloths, napkins, and placemats under her other arm, but giggled and dropped them as Charlie pressed her up against one of the walls in the hallway. "You're a bloody tease, Carlisle."

"Oooh, surnames," she sassed back, dragging her fingers across the smooth skin just under the hem of his shirt, "I'm really in trouble, huh?"

The pupils of his green eyes dilated. "You're a menace," he practically growled, "and you know it."

Jutting her chin upwards, she grinned in challenge. "So what are you going to do about it?"

She could hear footsteps coming their way. Her heart rate sped up as he leaned in closer, his lips ghosting over hers. "I'm going to return the favour," he replied in a low voice which promised all sorts of delicious, devious delights, before he dropped to his knees to 'help' her pick up her discarded linens, just in time for Everett to stumble upon them.

"Everything alright?" he asked, glancing between them.

Sara hoped that he would attribute her flushed cheeks to her embarrassment over her supposed clumsiness. "Yeah," she nodded, hastily grabbing the messy pile from Charlie's hands. She cringed a little, knowing that Gemma wasn't going to be happy that her ironing had been for naught. "Just a klutz."

"Best watch what you're doing next time, love," Charlie suggested. She could hear the promise in his words which –thankfully– seemed to have gone right over the younger man's head.

Everett frowned at his older brother. "Charlie," he said in warning while Sara bit her tongue to prevent herself from laughing, "behave."

Green eyes locked with hers. When her lover spoke, his response was full of cheek. "Now, where's the fun in that?"

* * *

Late on Christmas Eve, hours after their family dinner had ended, Charlie finally managed to sneak out of Gemma and Everett's house. He'd texted Sara to let her know that he'd been able to get an Uber. The anticipation of finally getting him all alone was almost too much to bear as she waited in her lounge room. She sat on the couch, bouncing her leg with nervous energy. Just the thought of having him back in her bed –or on the couch, or even on the dining room table– had her taut like a bow. His earlier threat to return the same sexual torture she'd put him through rang in her ears. Squeezing her thighs together, Sara wondered how on earth just the thought of being with him could have her so turned on.

When her doorbell chimed, she practically sprang from the couch and raced the short distance to the front door, swinging it open without any semblance of grace.

"About bloody time," she parroted words he'd similarly spoken to her days earlier; he smirked at her from the doorstep.

"On edge, are we?"

Rolling her eyes, she took a fistful of fabric from his t-shirt and yanked him across the threshold, practically slamming the door shut behind him. She paid little attention to anything else as she wrapped her arms around his neck and landed a demanding kiss to his lips.

His hands slid down her sides, under her backside and, through the lust-induced fog in her mind, she realised his intention.

Wrapping her legs around his waist, she silently marvelled at how effortlessly he lifted and carried her down the hallway, to her bedroom, and deposited her gently in the middle of her bed.

"I like the getup," he grinned, gesturing at the sheer Christmas themed negligee she was wearing. (She had put it on as soon as he'd texted to say he was coming over.) He climbed onto the bed and greedily moved his fingers to the spaghetti straps on her shoulders. "But I think it'll look much nicer on the floor."

She threw her head back and laughed. "Corny, Rhodes. So corny."

"And yet," his hands were under the sheer material, skimming over her stomach and back, guiding the offending garment up and eventually over her head, "the complete truth."

Sara found she was unable to argue with that.

✳ ✳ ✳

After enjoying Charlie's extended stay over Christmas and New Year, Sara was sad to see him leave. Going back to Facetime chats and raunchy messages was fun, but she missed having him nearby. Still, they were going well. Sara knew that they were. But that didn't prevent a niggling sense of doubt from forming in the back of her mind. After all, how good could things be if she was forcing herself to lie to not only her family, but his as well? And yet, the thought of them finding out terrified her.

Was that an omen? A sign that maybe she should rethink dating Charlie altogether?

She didn't want to consider that, but it was there, lurking in the shadows of her brain: a depressing, constant sense of doubt.

It'll change when we tell everyone, she reminded herself, trying to shake it off. *We just need to prove we're not going to fail at this.*

It was a vicious cycle of thoughts. She didn't want their families knowing they were dating until they could demonstrate that it wasn't just a passing fancy…but until they knew about it, it didn't feel like their relationship could work out.

The thing was, she couldn't bear to deal with the fallout if they told everyone too soon. It would be painful, humiliating, and awkward for the rest of their lives.

What potential was there for them if she couldn't bring herself to just tell her family the truth, though? And why couldn't she tell them? Did she harbour some sort of embarrassment somewhere deep down in her subconscious? Surely not. So, was she afraid that there wasn't actually a future with Charlie after all? How long would it be before he lost his patience with her and demanded that she tell them before she was ready?

And so the cycle continued.

You're being stupid, she told herself, *snap out of it.*

And so she did. Or she tried. She pasted on a smile and brought herself back to the present, back into the conversation with Eve (who had, over coffee in their usual meeting spot, begged to meet the man who had her behaving so uncharacteristically) and sidestepped a few more questions about her mystery man.

The fact that Sara couldn't even tell Eve –because she was afraid Eve might slip up and tell Gemma or Jeff– set off the cycle of uncertainty all over again.

Sipping at her latte, Sara tried to ignore the doubts.

It was *fine*.

Her relationship with Charlie would be fine.

She was fine.

Everything was fine.

Perfectly fine.

* * *

"Son of a bitch," Sara cursed as she logged in to her work's online dashboard and opened up the next month's roster. There, in irritatingly bright, chirpy colours, was her undoing. She and Gemma had landed the worst shifts over Easter, working late afternoon to late at night every day, up to and including Easter Sunday.

What was she going to say to Charlie?

She'd had months to organise time off if she'd wanted to, but she'd left it to fate, not wanting to have to explain to her best friend why she suddenly wanted that week off work. She could have said something about needing to spend time with her mystery boyfriend, but then would have had to justify why they still couldn't meet him…not to mention why she was spending so much time with them if she'd taken it off to be with him. It wouldn't add up and she had known it.

Everett was in the country for an extended stay this time, in between filming schedules, so Gemma hadn't bothered applying for leave, either. Sara didn't know whether having her friend with her on shift was a good thing or not. As bitterness and helplessness seeped into her bones, she figured it wasn't great. Gems would take one look at her and know something was wrong.

Over the course of the last few months, Sara had managed to talk herself into believing that as long as she and Charlie got to spend a bit more time together over Easter everything would be fine. They'd be able to prove that their relationship was working out, and they could then come clean to their families.

But now...

Now that plan was dead on arrival, really.

So what did that mean for them now? She couldn't exactly spend Easter away from him –and be stuck feeling bitter and alone and exhausted– and then turn around and tell their families that they were dating and everything was working out perfectly, could she?

It was starting to feel hopeless. Oncoming tears stung in her sinuses.

She felt so stupid.

Stupid for ever thinking that they could work out. Stupid for thinking that their plan –*her* plan– would be successful. Now she could see that she'd just gotten lucky over Christmas. Here was reality, ready to show her that she wasn't allowed nice things from the universe. She never had been.

Well, that was how it felt, anyway.

Suddenly, in a pique of melancholy and stress-induced despair, she felt just like her eighteen-year-old self again, awash in grief as she said goodbye to her life plans.

On some level, she knew that this situation didn't come close to what she'd gone through when she'd lost her mum at such a young age, but she was working herself up into a state. Her mother's own words about avoiding heartache were rattling around in her brain again, making her feel even worse. Rationality flew out the window the second Sara had realised that things weren't turning out the way she had planned, and she couldn't calm herself enough to settle her thoughts.

She didn't know how to fix this.

If she asked for the time off or to switch shifts with someone else, Gemma and Jeff would want to know why.

If she told Charlie that she hadn't asked for the time off because she hadn't wanted Gemma to know, he would be disappointed and frustrated.

She was damned if she did, doomed if she didn't.

Trying to be strong, or perhaps trying to avoid the issue altogether, Sara spent the next couple of weeks repeating the mantra *'Everything will be fine'* in her head.

It didn't help.

However, when she spoke to Charlie the night before he was due to leave for Australia and she still hadn't told him, something inside her snapped, and an odd sense of calm overtook her.

She knew what she had to do.

The mantra was back.

Everything would be just fine.

Chapter Ten

Before Charlie knew, it was Easter. While their relationship was going strong, he wasn't oblivious to the way Sara kept skirting the issue of telling their families. Although he had attempted to understand in those early months, the fact that they had been dating for six months and she was still uneasy about confessing was beginning to rattle him.

How could he not take it personally when her justifications seemed flimsy at best?

"We'll do it in person," she told him during their last Facetime call before he was to get on a flight back to Australia. "After the excitement of Easter's over," she explained.

He tried to tell himself that he was being paranoid about the tension he could hear in her voice. But, to mollify, he went with it.

He should have known, though, that it wouldn't be as simple as Sara had made it sound.

"On your own this time?" he greeted his brother at the Arrivals gate, scanning the crowd for his mother. His flight had landed fairly late in the evening, so it made sense that Zoe would be in bed and Gemma would be home looking after her.

Everett frowned. "Unfortunately, Gemma and Sara drew the short straw for the Easter roster," he explained as they walked through the throng of people, "so Mum's at home with Zoe."

Charlie's mood –already low to begin with– soured further. Sara hadn't mentioned working through Easter to him, and she certainly hadn't informed him that she'd be on night shift. He knew she had no real control over her hours, but he thought it was the sort of thing one told their long-distance lover, particularly when said lover was returning to the country for a week.

It niggled at him for the rest of the night.

Why hadn't she told him?

He even went so far as to send her a message sarcastically thanking her for the heads-up. It went unread until long after he fell asleep. When he woke up and checked his messages, he found a single word reply. *'Sorry.'*

Charlie fought the urge to hurl his phone across the room.

Over the course of the day, he did his best to seem happy and unaffected, but when Gemma joined them after midday, bleary eyed and dressed in her scrubs for yet another evening shift, Charlie felt the irritation seeping into his bones again. Sara hadn't sent him anymore messages. He wondered why he had suddenly gotten the cold shoulder. The last time they'd spoken, things had seemed okay, though he knew he had pressed her about finally coming clean to everyone about their relationship.

Surely that wasn't the reason for the sudden and completely unexpected breakdown in communication. *It couldn't be.* Charlie and Sara had worked hard over the last six months to avoid the same pitfalls of long-distance relationships that had plagued Gemma and Rhett early on in their relationship. Charlie had even felt vainglorious at the realisation that he'd found it easy to remain open and honest with Sara whenever he was missing her – something his arguably more charismatic brother had struggled to do with Gemma. But perhaps he had been too smug, too soon.

"Hello," from across the table, his mother waved a hand in his face, "earth to Charlie."

Blinking and shaking his head, he attempted to focus on the discussion taking place around him. "Sorry," he offered lamely. "I'm still a bit jet-lagged, I think."

She didn't seem convinced, but she thankfully let it drop in lieu of catching him up with the rest of the conversation. "Well, Zoe was just telling us about the Easter Bunny." Here Beatrice smiled warmly at her granddaughter, reminding Charlie of exactly why she'd moved across the ocean. "Isn't that right, darling?"

Zoe bobbed her head with the excitement that only a three-year-old could possess. Her wild mane of dark hair swished about her pixie-like features and eyes the same shade of blue as Everett's glittered across the table at him. "Yup," she popped the 'p' sound, "he's gonna bring chocolate 'n hide it when I'm sleeping."

In the few months since Christmas, she'd started pronouncing her letter 'L's properly. With Zoe practically half-way to four now, Charlie realised that she had truly lost the last of her baby-like tendencies. Even her sentences were better developed. He sighed, feeling that same familiar pang of missing out as he had during his fateful visit for her birthday.

He swallowed and mustered as much enthusiasm as he could. "Is that so?"

"Uh huh."

"And is this chocolate fair game?" He leaned forward and grinned at her. "If I find it first, do I get to eat it?"

She erupted into a peal of giggles that genuinely lifted his mood. "No, Uncle Charlie," she slapped at the surface of the table, "it's *my* chocolate."

"I'm hearing a challenge," he teased, laughing as she hollered "Noooo!"

Everett snorted and nudged him with his elbow. "Stop teasing her," he requested with a laugh of his own, before addressing his daughter. "He's stirring you up, darling. Uncle Charlie won't eat your chocolate."

She blew a raspberry in Charlie's direction. He laughed again, leaning sideways to offer his brother his assessment. "She might look just like you, Rhett, but she's Gemma's kid through and through."

"You say that like it's a bad thing." Sara's voice startled Charlie. He just about gave himself whiplash as he turned his head to watch her saunter into the room and then drop into the vacant seat on Zoe's other side. She stroked Zoe's hair lovingly. "There's nothing wrong with being a strong woman with a backbone, ZoZo. You remember that."

Charlie wanted nothing more than to demand answers on the spot. But, knowing that it would likely only make matters worse to out their relationship now, he settled for meeting his lover's gaze and silently asking with his eyes if everything was alright. If *they* were alright. Her minute nod did little to settle the uncomfortable swirling in his gut which was saying otherwise.

What had gone wrong?

"I never said there was," he argued, if only to continue the conversation with her. He nudged his brother for back up. "Did I?"

Everett —the traitor— played Switzerland. He held his hands up in surrender. "I'm not getting in between another of your arguments."

"Well, you're no use to me, then," Charlie dismissed him. He turned his head and smiled at his niece. "I like feisty women," he informed her in a poorly shrouded message for Sara, simultaneously ducking the hand that swung out to hit him upside the head for being inappropriate. "So you go right ahead and be as fiery as you like, little love."

Sara smirked at him, before leaning back and craning her neck to call out for Gemma. "We're gonna have to make a move if you don't want to be late."

His heart sank.

There was still no chance to talk.

His mum spoke up then, *tsking* at her. "Oh, darling, between this gent you've been seeing and work, we hardly get to see you anymore."

Charlie's eyebrow raised. She'd told them she'd been seeing someone? He wasn't aware of that. He shot her a cheeky grin, hoping she would find his playful teasing charming. "Seeing someone new, are you?"

The look she gave him in return was one of warning. "What's it to you?"

Before he could come up with a light-hearted retort, his mum was leaning forward conspiratorially. "She's been very hush hush about him," she said, reaching across Zoe to pat Sara's hand atop the dining table. "Says he's some local man she met online. They've been spending a lot of time together."

Unsure of what to make of this new development, he tried to catch his girlfriend's gaze again, but she looked away. Becoming uneasy now, he couldn't help but ask no one in particular, "You've not met this bloke?"

"No," Gemma answered this time, sashaying back into the room with her work bag at the ready, "but I'm pretty sure I saw him the other day."

The amusement he'd been feeling gave way to a whole new feeling: surprise. It matched the shock on Sara's face. Charlie swallowed as he watched Sara narrow her gaze at Gemma and demand, "What? When?"

"That tall, dark, and handsome guy you were with in the food court on your break?"

"Jesus, Gems, that was Max."

The fleeting moment of panic that Charlie had felt receded. She'd told him about Max –a friend she'd made from a failed Tinder date– and the fact that they often met for a quick coffee or sometimes lunch. He felt incredibly guilty for momentarily believing she might have cheated. That was not fair to her at all, even if he was in a bit of a mood with her.

"Oh," Gemma's face fell. "Damn. He was hot."

"I'm still in the room," Rhett reminded his girlfriend drily. She rolled her eyes at him.

"I'm taken, not dead. My eyes work just fine."

And with that, the conversation about Sara's love life passed them by, but it left a bitter taste in Charlie's mouth all the same.

Why hadn't she told him that she'd fed their families some half-truths? And why was she still so reticent to set the story straight?

* * *

'*So, are you going to tell me why I'm in the doghouse, or do I have to guess?*' Charlie pressed send on the message before he could overthink it. He'd begged off to bed early after eating dinner with his mum, brother, and niece, citing a headache. They'd already picked up on his declining mood. There was no sense giving them more ammunition.

He was halfway through his week-long stay, and he'd not had a moment alone with his girlfriend. He had seen her twice more when she'd come to collect Gemma for work, but each time was fleeting and, in some capacity or other, was spent in the company of their families. The next day was officially

Easter Sunday –and would also apparently be the girls' last night of working the night shift– so he was hoping he might get to spend at least a couple of days with Sara after that, as long as she was speaking to him.

When her reply finally came through it was defensive. He could hear her voice –dripping with disdain– as he read it: *'I'm terribly sorry that my having to work is hurting your feelings, precious.'*

His feelings truly were hurt.

He couldn't understand the sudden shift in their relationship, and not understanding made him feel foolish.

Charlie didn't like feeling that way. However, he knew that lashing out in return was not going to be the answer, even if his instinct was to do just that.

'Sara,' he typed back after taking a deep breath, *'please. I'm only here a few more days.'*

He hoped she would understand what he hadn't said: that he desperately wanted to fix whatever was wrong and go back to the way things had been before he'd boarded the plane to Australia.

'I can't change my roster,' she wrote back. He frowned at his phone. He couldn't give a rat's arse about her damn roster. Had she missed the point, or was she being deliberately obtuse?

Glancing at the clock on his screen, he was startled to find that it was after 11 o'clock. Her shift was ending soon. If he could leave the house without his brother noticing, he had a better chance of hashing this out with her face-to-face.

Without overthinking the matter, he hurriedly dressed in the clothes he'd previously discarded and crept down the hallway. The lights were all out in the house: a sign that Rhett had also retired for the night. Idly, Charlie wondered whether the Easter Bunny had already been, or whether his brother would set out the chocolates in the wee hours of the morning instead. They were all looking forward to Zoe's first real Easter egg hunt, as it was the first year that she'd understood what was going on.

Shaking the random thoughts away, Charlie let himself out the front door and walked down the driveway, praying the gate wouldn't squeak when he opened it to let himself out onto the street. He ordered an Uber once he was a few houses down the road.

It was a clear night. Stars dotted the black sky. A crescent moon peeked out from behind a foggy-looking cloud. In the suburbs, everything was quiet and still. There was a slight breeze in the air, but it still felt warm to him, even though he'd seen a lot of the locals already wearing winter clothing – jumpers and sweaters and the like. As far as he was concerned, the people here had no idea what cold really was.

But, despite the warmth of the sub-tropical climate, he felt goosebumps break over his skin as he waited for his ride. Nervous anticipation built up inside him. Unlike his visits to Sara over Christmas, this felt ominous. Everything about this trip had felt off, and he resented that.

The Uber ride took no time at all. To pass the time, he sat on Sara's doorstep and waited for her to return home, mindlessly scrolling through his Facebook feed. When the light from her headlights finally illuminated the driveway, it was close to one in the morning. Pushing himself to his feet, Charlie couldn't see her face –too blinded by the headlights– but he knew that she had seen him. He followed her car into the garage and hung back as she dragged herself out from the driver's seat.

She looked tired. Her hair was pulled into a messy bun atop her head, and she must have taken off her scrubs at the hospital, because she was wearing a loose pair of tracksuit pants and a t-shirt. There were dark circles under her eyes, and her shoulders were slumped. For a moment, he wondered if perhaps he shouldn't have come.

The reminder that he was flying back to the UK in another three days was the only reason he pushed on with his plan to try and resolve things sooner rather than later.

"Hey," he smiled softly at her, but maintained his distance. It was one thing to spring a surprise visit on her, another to crowd her when she was clearly dead on her feet.

She pressed the button on the wall to close the garage door and sighed. "Hey." It wasn't the most enthusiastic of greetings, but she hadn't demanded he leave, either.

"I'm sorry to just turn up without warning," he offered as an olive branch, following her through the door leading from the garage to her hallway, "but I've missed you."

She had to know by now that those words had a subtext all of their own.

"I know." As Charlie's heart fell at the lacklustre response, he followed Sara into the kitchen where she dropped her bag and keys on the counter with a clatter. She turned to finally look him in the eye. "I'm sorry. It's been a shitty couple of weeks. I'm not the best company right now."

It was the most she'd spoken to him –via message or otherwise– and he grabbed at the chance to communicate again like a lifeline. "I'll take any version of you over none." The words felt silly and theatrical, but they were genuine nonetheless.

"Damn it, Charlie," she huffed, placing a hand on her hip, "can't you just be a dick for once?"

Now he was confused again. "Why?"

"Because you being a nice guy makes this all harder."

He wasn't an idiot. He knew what those words heralded. "It's easier to break up with someone when they give you an actual reason, eh?" He didn't want to do this. He didn't want to give her the out that she was looking for. But his heart was hammering in his chest and his feelings were hurt. *He* was hurt. As far as he could tell, this was coming out of nowhere. He couldn't help being bitter. "What the fuck, Sara?"

She shrugged at him, but he held firm.

"No." Shaking his head, Charlie needed to know what had changed. "When we last spoke –really spoke– we were good. Then I hopped on a plane and, the next thing I know, it's all gone to shit."

As he ranted, she stood in front of him, trailing her teeth with her tongue. He knew her well enough by now to know that it was a sign of her irritation, but he couldn't care less. He deserved answers.

"We're not going anywhere!" She eventually snapped at him, raising her hands into the air. "How long did you honestly think we were going to work out for?"

What?

No, seriously, *what?*

He scowled and folded his arms. "Where is this coming from?"

"I don't know, I just...I got my roster for Easter and it all just sort of hit me, you know?" Sara's dark brown eyes pooled with tears, and her voice got tight, but she was finally letting it all out into the open. She had never been the type to cower away from a discussion, even an unpleasant one. This was proving to be no exception. "The whole long-distance thing...it's been a bit of fun, but there's no happy ending for us, is there? Not really."

"Are you kidding me right now?" Working his jaw, Charlie glanced at the ceiling to try and rein in his temper. "One stumbling block and you're ready to call it quits?"

Her cheeks flushed, and she jabbed a finger into his chest. "Where do you see this all heading, then, hmm?"

He had no real answer for that. They'd only been dating for six months, and physically together for a few weeks at best. It was still new, as far as he was concerned, and he hadn't given much thought to the bigger picture.

"I..." A brief flash of what they could be invaded his mind. The stereotypical 'white picket fence' life that his brother had: A kid. A house. Happily ever after. But with him living in London and her in Brisbane...well, perhaps she'd made a fair point. He swallowed. "I don't know."

"Exactly!" It was a victory cry, but not a happy one. The index finger she'd jabbed him with was now directed upwards. "There's no real future for us."

In his mind, he bid a silent goodbye to the fantasy life he'd momentarily concocted. Now he felt bereft and bitter and stupid. "Well," he offered, his tone turning snide, "glad we didn't tell everyone after all."

Saying the words out loud only made him feel like more of a sappy twit. Had she known all along that they truly had no chance of succeeding? Was that why she'd demanded his silence the whole time? And why the hell had he convinced himself that there was a future for their long-distance relationship? He wasn't like his brother. He had no reason to build a life across the world.

Regret flitted across Sara's face. "Charlie..."

They'd really just been playing all along. The entire time, he had carried on his sex life with his hand, and she'd had her toys, and all they'd really given each other was the pretence that neither of them had to be lonely. But it clearly wasn't enough for her. If he were being honest, it probably wouldn't have been enough for him in the long run, either. But at least he'd been prepared to try.

"Was I just entertainment while you looked for someone better suited, then?"

She scowled up at him, her jaw hanging slack. "Excuse me?"

To tell the truth, his accusation had taken him as much by surprise as it did her. He genuinely had no idea where it had come from, but the more he thought about it, the more it made sense. "Well, Mum did say that you told them you'd found a local bloke…" God, he felt like such a naïve idiot.

"You're a fucking moron." Sara rolled her eyes. "I made up some guy to cover for the fact that I was sitting at home Facetiming you all the damn time."

That was what he had initially assumed, but he didn't know what to believe anymore, and he told her as much. In return, she slapped him.

He brought his hand to his stinging cheek, his eyes wide with surprise. He'd gone too far and he knew it. "Sara, I'm sorry, I–"

Sara shook her head. "Get out," she demanded, her oncoming tears making her voice tighter. Her hand trembled as she pointed towards the hallway. "Get out of my sight, Rhodes."

"Love, I–"

"*Now.*"

With one last baleful glance in her direction, Charlie nodded. "Fine," he agreed, but it wasn't the angry, post-breakup declaration that he'd hoped it would be. He sounded defeated and broken even to his own ears. "Goodnight, Sara."

* * *

If Charlie had thought that putting on a happy façade was difficult back in September, it hardly rated a mention in comparison to faking his way through the rest of his Easter stay. But he managed it, even when the entire family got together for a belated celebration on Easter Monday.

At the dinner table he sat himself well away from Sara, and instead enjoyed a distracting chat with Brennan about work which inspired him to focus on his career trajectory again. Between that and genuinely enjoying his time with Zoe, he was able to make it through to boarding the return plane to London.

The flight back was the longest he'd ever experienced. With no sassy three-year-old to divert his thoughts, he spent it in retrospection, alternating between anger, regret, and melancholy. Not even the ideas that Brennan had put in his head could keep his mind occupied for long.

After downing a few free whiskeys, he came to the conclusion that his mates had been right: he'd gone about it all arse backwards. A few more drinks once he was back in his apartment and he was done with trying to find love. If he couldn't make it work with someone as perfect for him as Sara had been, he'd have no hope with anyone else.

It was difficult falling into a routine without her messages, though. Charlie found himself continually reaching for his phone, half expecting her to send through a cute selfie or some hilarious thought of the day. But the days turned into weeks, and before he knew it, it had been a fortnight without her.

The time wasn't healing the pain of this loss.

She had been different. He had been different when he'd been with her. She knew things about his life that nobody else –not even his brother– knew. Though he'd never said the words, he'd fallen in love with Sara, and he was still kicking himself for not fighting harder to prevent what she seemed to feel was inevitable.

When Everett called him out of the blue, it took all of his willpower not to ask about her. Instead, he politely asked about their mum, and about Zoe and Gemma, which then led to his brother making a confession that rattled him.

"I'm going to propose."

Charlie had been tidying up his apartment and froze with the phone to his ear, a single sock –fished out from under the sofa– dangling in his left hand. "Propose?" he repeated, his previously forgotten feelings of envy for his brother's perfect relationship beginning to make their reappearance. "As in marriage?"

"No, as in put forward a business venture," Rhett's sarcasm rang down the line. "Yes 'as in marriage', you git."

Sitting down heavily on the sofa, Charlie blurted out, "Why?"

There was a moment of stunned silence. "What the hell do you mean, 'why'?" Everett asked in an indignant tone.

Clearly his brother had not expected any resistance towards his happy news. And why would he? Charlie loved Gemma like a sister, and Everett had already made the much larger commitment of having a child with the woman. Bugger it, he'd even bought a house with her and merged his entire life with hers. At this point, marriage only seemed like a formality.

"Sorry," Charlie sighed, leaning against the backrest as he directed his gaze to the ceiling, "you just surprised me."

Everett replied slowly with obvious scepticism, "I surprised you by telling you I'm going to propose to the mother of my child?"

"Well, when you put it that way…" Charlie attempted to joke, but it fell flat. He then tried to muster some enthusiasm. "In all seriousness, Rhett, that's wonderful news. When are you going to pop the question, then?"

Everett was back in Los Angeles again, this time for a three-month long filming stint. Knowing his younger brother as he did, Charlie didn't think the man would do anything impulsive. He was a romantic at heart –incredibly sentimental– and would likely attempt to plan his proposal down to the finest details.

"I'm not sure when yet," Rhett confessed, "however, I'd like to take Gemma back to the hotel where we met. Perhaps even book the same room that I…*we* stayed in."

See? Charlie thought to himself, a small smirk lifting his lips. *Sentimental sod.* "That's very *on brand* for you," he acknowledged, before gently adding, "and she'll love it."

"Hang on," the other man informed him, "I'm switching to video."

Clearly Charlie's attempt at enthusiasm hadn't been particularly convincing. Sitting up while his brother terminated the call, he shifted forward and propped his phone up on the coffee table, leaning it against the potted cactus he'd bought so he could comfortably have Facetime conversations with Sara.

Damn it, he thought at the same moment his phone began to alert him of his brother's incoming video call. *Why does everything have to go back to her?*

He pressed the accept button and his brother's concerned face filled the screen, the man's bushy, dark eyebrows practically meeting between his eyes as he frowned. There was no preamble before Everett demanded, "Tell me what's wrong."

"Nothing's wrong." Charlie was having flashbacks. Were they destined to have this same talk on repeat?

"Sure," his brother scoffed at him. From what Charlie could tell, Everett was in another trailer on set somewhere, which made sense. He never would have discussed such a private topic in public. "I give you life altering news, and you react the way you just did? I'm not buying it."

"To be fair, proposing to the woman you knocked up four years ago isn't exactly life altering. That horse has already bolted, mate."

"You're not half as amusing as you think you are," Rhett shot back at him before pinching the bridge of his nose and giving his head a short shake, bemusedly staring down through the camera. "And I'm not letting you goad me off track, either."

Charlie shrugged. It had been worth the attempt.

Everett continued to needle at him, expressing his worries that Charlie hadn't been himself since before Easter, until Charlie lost his temper altogether.

"For fuck's sake, I'm jealous, alright? Is that what you want to hear?" On the screen, his brother's eyes widened and he sat back, visibly stunned. But Charlie wasn't done. "Forty-six fucking years old, and I'm jealous of my kid brother and his perfect fucking relationship. Because *of course* you're talking marriage." He rolled his eyes, the self-deprecation dripping from his words. "Of bloody course you are. I get dumped, and you get married to her best friend. Sounds about right."

"Her best friend?" As Everett's jaw slackened, Charlie winced. So much for keeping the whole mess a secret from their families. "Sara?" his voice went up half an octave. "You…and *Sara*?"

"What of it?" The defensiveness was in direct response to his brother's incredulous tone. A knee-jerk reaction that he just couldn't control.

"She's practically half your age for one–"

"Fuck off. She's thirty-five," he defended, scowling, "and even if she were half my age, she'd still be an adult, so it's a fucking moot point."

"Still…"

"No. Not 'still'. It wasn't an issue for us."

Everett rolled his eyes. "Well, something was, wasn't it?"

Charlie ground his teeth and practically snarled his reply. "It didn't work out is all."

After another moment of silence, wherein Charlie assumed his brother was processing the information, Rhett asked, "Is this why you were so withdrawn over Easter?" Charlie offered another shrug, and his brother pressed on, "Was it just a fling that went badly? Because, honestly, I'm surprised you've managed to be civil, let alone…" he trailed off, performing a vague gesture with his hands which Charlie supposed alluded to sex.

"We've been seeing each other since the night you went back to LA after Zoe's birthday." Sara was going to kill him for spilling the beans.

The one thing she'd been afraid of was making everything awkward between their combined families. But there was no way Rhett wasn't going to immediately tell Gemma what he'd learned, and it felt cathartic to get it off his chest with his brother, in a way that hadn't quite worked with his mates. Everett knew Sara. He knew exactly what Charlie'd had and lost. And he also knew Charlie well enough to know that he didn't fall arse over tit for just anyone. This relationship had been special.

Everett counted out the timeline on his hand, gaping into the camera. "Six…six *months*? Six months, and not a word about it?"

Holding his hands in surrender, Charlie attempted to explain. "Not my fault. Sara wanted to keep it quiet until she was sure it'd work out."

Saying it out loud only made him feel more like an arse. Just how long would he have been willing to hide their relationship from his family, just so that she could avoid an awkward conversation or two on her own?

The expression on his brother's face matched those thoughts. "Six months, Charlie."

"I know," he exhaled, shoulders slumping in defeat. "She didn't want things between her and Mum to change. Or between her and Gemma, either." And she hadn't wanted to deal with Brennan and Jeff doing the same overprotective 'big brother' act that they'd performed when Everett had entered their lives. Charlie had done what he could to reassure her that the situations were quite different, but it hadn't made a difference. "Honestly, I think she just didn't want everyone to know that we'd tried and that it didn't work out."

Everett made a sympathetic sound at the back of his throat and nodded. "I can sort of understand where she's coming from there." He tilted his head to the side. "You're still going to have to interact, and with the rest of us knowing that you've been together..." he trailed off while Charlie huffed an unimpressed laugh.

"You're really helping me here," he replied sarcastically, picking at a loose thread on the couch cushion beside him. "Thanks so much."

His brother eyed him through the screen in silence, assessing him. He was likely reassessing Charlie's outburst over his proposal news, wondering why this would be affecting him so much. "She meant something to you," he eventually said, his eyes widening with the realisation. "Do you love her?"

Having never said the words to Sara, it felt absurd nodding and confessing it to his little brother. But he did so anyway. "Yeah," he responded, his tone still bitter. "Idiot that I am."

"You're not—"

"I am." He cut Everett off firmly. "It's pretty obvious she didn't feel the same way."

Rhett frowned. "Did she say—"

"She dropped me like a hot brick. She didn't have to say anything."

He watched as his brother shook his head and attempted a different approach. "Was it the long-distance?"

"No." Charlie was almost certain of that. They'd communicated so well, and things had been good. Or at least he'd thought they had. But then she *had* said they had no future living so far apart. "Maybe. I don't know."

That frustrated him the most. It had been so out of the blue and she hadn't given him much of a reason outside of their future being uncertain. But they could have –should have– been able to talk through it.

Everett raised his bushy eyebrows and soon enough Charlie found himself venting all of his frustrations and then some. His brother listened patiently as Charlie went over it a million different ways.

"We'd really worked hard on the communicating thing," he insisted, thumping his closed fist on his thigh. "It was good. Great even. And then somewhere between my getting on a plane and arriving in Brisbane for Easter, she'd decided it was hopeless and needed to end."

There was a small smirk tugging at the corners of Everett's mouth. "She loves you, you twit."

"How's that work, then?" Charlie demanded. "She tells me it's over and you see that as some grand, dramatic gesture of her undying affection? Don't tell me you've hit your head on set again."

Holding up his hand, Everett requested, "Hear me out."

Charlie sat back against the sofa and spread his arms wide. "The floor is yours."

"I think she panicked." Everett was leaning forward now, additional animation in him as he relayed his thoughts. "I think she fell head over heels for you and it scared the shit out of her. And I think she told you that you don't have a future together as a test." Now his face fell. "A test you failed, granted, but I don't think that all is lost at this point."

"A test?" Charlie snorted. "What was I supposed to do? Tell her that I saw rainbows and sunshine and marriage and children?"

"Quite frankly, yes." Everett said matter-of-factly. As he continued to speak, it became clear to Charlie that Everett had no plans to mince his words. "You're jealous of what I have with Gemma. You said so yourself. And I think that's a fairly strong indication of what you honestly want with Sara." He sat back, full of smug self-satisfaction, folding his arms across his chest as he leered into the camera. "Tell me I'm wrong."

Charlie knew he couldn't do that. "Sod off."

"I knew it!" Rhett pointed at him. "And that means that you are just as cowardly as she is."

"Steady on..."

"No, think about it. She wanted you to put yourself out there and you blew it. You let her drop your arse because you're equally afraid of what admitting your feelings and dreams for the future mean."

Charlie had liked it much better when the tables were turned and he was the one doling out sage advice over Everett's relationship woes. Being confronted with his own –and knowing that Everett was right– was not as fun.

"Alright, let's pretend you're right–"

"Which I am."

Charlie rolled his eyes. "Even if you are, I can't fix it now, can I?"

"Honestly," Everett scoffed and shook his head. "Think back on all the advice you've given me over the years. Most importantly, you're going to need to suck it up and talk to her."

"Yeah, well, I'm going to have to do that at any rate," Charlie sighed, "because your big mouth is going to tell Gemma all of this anyway, I'm guessing."

Everett didn't seem at all apologetic. He shrugged. "We don't keep secrets from one another. One of the many reasons our relationship remains a success."

With additional hope in him now, and the beginnings of a plan forming in his brain, Charlie grabbed the opportunity to shift the conversation away from his disastrous love life. "Then it's best you strike while the iron is hot and propose, isn't it?" He smirked. "Have you got a ring?"

Everett's cheeks turned pink and he nodded. "I found it at a local antique dealer," he confessed, "it's not a traditional ring, but it suits her perfectly."

Now that he was no longer feeling the sting of jealousy, Charlie revelled in the change in his little brother. The man was happy and besotted. Gemma had rightly and truly been good for him. "Go on, then," he teased, "I know you've likely got it there with you. Let's see it."

Everett grinned and leaned sideways for a moment, pulling the box from his pocket. Charlie complimented his choice and the conversation moved on. He found himself offering suggestions to streamline Rhett's proposal plan all the while, in the back of his mind, he was also thinking about ways to resolve the mess he and Sara had made of their relationship. She wasn't going to be happy to learn that he'd told Everett everything, but he felt ten times lighter for having done so.

And it gave him an excuse to make contact.

Chapter Eleven

Sara missed Charlie. In the couple of weeks since she'd had a momentary lapse in sanity and ended their relationship, he'd done as she had asked and had kept his metaphorical distance. She knew that she should have expected him to respect her wishes, but it hurt a lot more that he hadn't ignored them in favour of fighting for her. Which, okay, she knew was stupid, because him doing what she asked of him was a much better sign of his character than him not taking 'no' for an answer.

However, it wasn't that he hadn't tried to fix things –things that he hadn't even realised were broken– before she had shut him down. She knew that she had pushed him into losing his temper. It had been a deliberate ploy, thinking that if she was angry with him breaking up would hurt less, and that she was in control of the situation.

She was clearly an idiot.

The strategy had worked in the past with boyfriends she hadn't really been into. But Charlie was different. Their relationship had been different.

She loved him.

Now was a spectacularly shitty time to want to make that confession.

It sucked that she had no one to blame but herself.

And the worst part? The worst part was that she didn't know why she had sabotaged herself. Running on a depressing mix of premenstrual hormones, frustration and then hopelessness when she'd received her Easter roster, a switch inside her brain had just flipped. She had somehow managed to convince herself that being unable to spend much time with him over his last visit had meant that their relationship was completely doomed.

Even as she'd pushed him away, the voice of reason in her head (which sounded oddly like Gemma) had told her that she was being stupid, that she was making a mistake of epic proportions. But she'd shoved it aside, too far down the rabbit hole.

Hell, Charlie had tried so hard to talk her down as well, and what had she done? She'd needled, and pushed, and bitched him out until he had finally snapped and given her the reaction she had been looking for. Sara had wanted to be able to convince herself that it was proof they would never work out. That she'd done the right thing by ending it early.

But she hadn't.

She knew that she hadn't. And she knew that she had hurt him about as much as she had hurt herself.

However, despite all of that, she couldn't muster the courage to reach out to him. At the very least he deserved an apology but, in this matter, she was as cowardly as she was stubborn.

Maybe breaking up with him was for the best, Sara thought to herself bitterly. *He deserves better than this. Better than me.*

She wasn't used to feeling this way. Usually so confident and sure of herself, it wasn't pleasant to be faced with her own flaws. But how else should she feel when she'd thrown away the best relationship she'd ever had? All because she'd essentially had a temper tantrum over not getting to spend time with him.

And that was her own fault as well.

Sara had been so insistent on keeping what was going on with Charlie a secret that she hadn't wanted to reveal it by asking for the additional time off work. It had made more sense to risk it, to hope that she would wind up doing day shifts or something more manageable, rather than telling anyone that her boyfriend was flying in from the other side of the planet and would only be visiting for the week. That plan imploding –on the heels of getting her period (*ugh*) and working back-to-back twelve hour shifts for a week to cover some unexpected short staffing– had pushed her right over the edge.

She should have known better. Planned better. Been better.

So, yes, she felt as though Charlie could do better than her.

But she was still selfish. Still missed him. Still wished she could suck it up and call him, explain herself and beg forgiveness.

And yet every time Sara picked up her phone to try, she froze.

Even if he forgave her, what then? What if she did this to him again? She didn't trust herself not to. Not anymore.

And that took her right back to thinking he deserved better.

Perhaps her mother had been right all those years ago. It was easier to avoid the heartbreak of loss if you didn't pursue love to start with. It was all about control, which Sara had proven she did not have. Not in the least. Not over herself, nor over the mess she had made.

But, try as she might, Sara couldn't stop missing Charlie.

And so the cycle of her thoughts continued.

Her phone rang just before ten at night, startling her. The frantic beating of her heart only increased to see Charlie's name –still accompanied by the shirtless picture he'd taken for her in his tradie getup– on her screen.

Her hand shook as she pressed the green answer button and brought it to her ear. "Hello?"

"Sara," his voice rumbled down the line, and it soothed her to hear him sound as anxious as she felt. "Hi."

"Hi," she repeated redundantly. Wincing at how awkward this felt, she glanced up at the ceiling. "Why...um, what's up?"

She heard him exhale. "Love, I have to apologise, I–"

"No," she interrupted, sitting up straight against her headboard. Her heart was hammering in her rib cage. "No," she repeated, "*I'm* sorry. I was just having a really shitty week and then I was just pissed because of my roster and I–"

"I told Everett. About us." His quietly spoken confession cut her rambling short. "I didn't mean to. It...it was word vomit." She could picture him scrubbing his hand over his face, matching the contrition in his voice. "I'm sorry. I thought it best to warn you before Gemma…well, before Gemma."

Oh, God. Gems was never –*ever*– going to let this go. Sara let her head hit the padded headboard with a thud. "It's alright," she told him, feeling oddly calm about the situation. Still riding on a wave of self-flagellation, she shrugged though he couldn't see her and added, "I should never have made you keep it a secret to begin with."

There was a moment of silence, and she wished so badly to know what he was thinking. But if there was one thing she could always count on with Charlie, it was his honesty. Even now, when she was certain the last thing he wanted to do was talk to her, he had called to apologise to her for accidentally telling his brother about their failed relationship. He'd opted to give her fair warning before she had Gemma –and possibly his mother– giving her the third degree.

"I don't know what to say to that, to be honest," he finally replied. There was a hint of irritation in his tone. She couldn't blame him. "It's only all I was asking you to consider for months."

"I know. I'm sorry." Annoying tears sprung to her eyes and she blinked rapidly to clear them. "I'm an idiot."

"Damn it," he muttered under his breath, and she assumed he'd heard the wobble in her voice. He confirmed this seconds later by softly refuting, "You're not an idiot, love."

"I am!" Sara insisted, and the dam broke, all of her thoughts and emotions spilling over before she could rein them back in. "You were the best thing that's happened to me in a long time and I…I was so afraid of it not working… which is stupid because then it became one of those things, y'know?" She sniffled miserably. "A self-fulfilling prophecy or whatever."

It was ironic, she thought bitterly, that she could communicate better with him via long-distance than in the flesh. It was easier to be honest with him when she didn't have to face him. This realisation only made her feel more spineless and stupid.

"Oh, love," he sighed, but the empathy rolling down the phone line wasn't helping her. "That doesn't make you an idiot. It makes you human."

"Stop being so sweet and understanding," she demanded with a watery laugh at how ludicrous the request sounded to her own ears. "I ruined things, and broke up with you, and you're supposed to hate me for it."

Charlie snorted. "I take it back, you are an idiot," he teased lightly, before gently adding, "I can't hate you, Sara. I don't think I ever have. Not even back when you were a prissy pain in the arse."

"Let's face it, I'm still a prissy pain in the arse," she played along, finding it far too easy to fall back into the routine of bantering with him.

"Ah, but I know it's all for show."

How was she not supposed to love him?

"I miss you," she blurted, and her cheeks burned. She bit down on her tongue to prevent humiliating herself any further.

His reply, when it came, was quiet and contemplative. "I miss you, too."

Her hopes soared.

* * *

"Sara Carlisle!" Gemma had let herself into Sara's house with the spare key gifted to her for emergencies, and her voice echoed off the tiles as she stomped down the hallway. "I've got a bone to pick with you."

There were no other sounds. No pitter-patter of shorter legs trying to keep up with her. Sara's last hopes of being able to distract her best friend from the awkward conversation they were due to have died.

She smiled sheepishly as Gemma found her at the kitchen table, her hands wrapped around a warm mug of coffee. "Um, hi?"

"Don't you dare," Gemma huffed, dropping into the seat directly across from her. "I tell you everything –legitimately everything– about my life, and you kept a bomb of that magnitude from me?"

Though she was tempted to pick up the old personal joke that Gemma held her own sex life behind lock and key, Sara knew it wasn't the time. Gemma seemed genuinely hurt. Feeling a pang of guilt, Sara averted her gaze. "I'm sorry," she offered apologetically, "I wasn't thinking."

Because, honestly, her BFF would have kept her secret after doling out a fair amount of good-natured teasing, and Sara had come to realise that too late.

Stupid hindsight.

"This was the guy, wasn't it?" Gemma's tone had shifted drastically from the ire she'd stormed in with to something far more sympathetic. When Sara forced herself to look back up from her mug and across the table, there was understanding in her friend's hazel gaze. "The one you were falling for. It was Charlie."

Sara nodded slowly. "Yeah."

"That makes so much more sense," Gemma slapped the tabletop between them. "Why you were so cagey about it, why you never gave us a name or let us meet him, why you were so afraid of admitting that…" her voice dropped, as though she knew that the next words would be painful for Sara to hear, "that you loved him."

What more could Sara say? Another nod. Another "Yeah."

Gemma regarded her for a long moment. "What happened?"

"I'm sorry?"

Rolling her eyes, her friend extrapolated, "You were deliriously happy. You were in love. *Love*, Sarz. I've *never* seen you like that before. What changed? Was the long-distance too hard?"

A self-deprecating snort escaped her. "No. In fact, that was almost easier than the in-person stuff."

However, it was starting to dawn on her that the in-person stuff wouldn't have been as difficult if she hadn't been making him sneak around. She thought back on all the missed opportunities to just be together, all because she hadn't wanted their families sticking their noses in too soon.

"You're kidding," Gemma's tone was incredulous. "Even now –after, what, almost four years? – I *hate* the long-distance stuff with Everett. I know there's no changing it, but…" she stopped herself and shook out her shoulders. "Sorry. This isn't about me. This is about you. And Charlie." She frowned. "How the hell did we miss that?"

"We were pretty discreet," Sara shrugged, but couldn't help adding, "mostly."

"You know I'm going to get the whole story out of you, right?"

There was a playfulness to Gemma's tone now, and Sara knew it was just further proof that she'd fucked up by not telling her best friend sooner. How could she ever have thought that their relationship would change, just because she was dating Gemma's boyfriend's brother?

Wow, that's a mouthful.

Gemma seemed oblivious to the path Sara's thoughts had taken, because she went on, "I mean, I knew you were being civil, but if I'd had any inkling that you were into him, I'd have tried to set you both up ages ago."

That caught Sara's attention. Her self-deprecating musings halted, and she blinked at her bestie across the table like a deer in headlights. "Say what now?"

"I mean, you're kind of perfect for each other. If you hadn't been so angry with him at the start, I almost would've thought you enjoyed flirting with him."

Sara couldn't deny that these same thoughts had crossed her mind, but she wasn't telling Gemma that. Instead, she rolled her eyes. "Been writing your fanfics again? Not everything is a love story, Gems."

"You yourself said that you felt things with him you've never felt before," Gemma was pointing her finger at her to emphasise her point. "If I'd known it was Charlie? Well, it would have made a lot of sense. There's always been fireworks between you. *Of course* it was going to get intense fast."

Damn it, but Sara couldn't deny that either.

"Yeah," she conceded with only a little bit of resentment, "it did."

"So I'll ask again," Gemma was leaning across the table now, "what happened?"

"I blew it," Sara admitted, pushing her lukewarm coffee aside. "I got into a bad mental space about it, and I convinced myself that there was no future for us…and I ended it."

She was proud of herself for not sobbing as she made the confession. Speaking to Charlie the night before had soothed some of the self-inflicted emotional pain, and, while they weren't back together, the conversation had ignited a tiny spark of hope that maybe they could try again.

Gemma was frowning at her. "Can I be honest with you?" When Sara nodded, her best friend's expression morphed into empathy, "I think you're more like me than you think."

Sara blinked back at her in confusion. "What?"

"You put on this confident front. A mask. But you're as afraid of losing people as I am...maybe even more, because you actually had them to begin with."

Feeling her face fall, Sara shook her head and reached for her best friend. "Gems..."

But Gemma wasn't done. "I'm just saying that I think that, *maybe*, you pushed Charlie away because some part of you freaked out about how much you care about him."

Sara couldn't refute her best friend's hypothesis. Having lost both her parents so young, and with her mum's words about loving and losing having had such an impact on her, she'd promised herself not to indulge in her desire to cling too hard to anyone. Being a party girl, or a vapid trophy, with no emotional connection had been easier than allowing herself to genuinely fall in love.

With a deep sigh, Sara nodded. "Yeah," she agreed, "and then I sabotaged myself. I gave into my anxiety...and I pushed him away."

Gemma's voice was soft and full of understanding as she bobbed her head and asked, "But you love him?"

"I think you and I both know that my loving him isn't enough for everything to magically work out."

Even if Charlie loved her in return, they had a lot to talk about first. She still wanted a future with someone –with *him*– and if they couldn't figure out some sort of long-term plan? Well, there would be no point rekindling the relationship just because the sex was amazing.

"It's the best kind of start, though," Gemma insisted. "Trust me. If Everett and I could make it work, you've got a fighting chance." Her lips curled upwards wickedly. "And then we'll essentially be sisters-in-law...sister-in-laws...whichever of those is the right word!"

Sara couldn't help laughing. "We're already basically family, babe."

"But it would be official!"

"Only if your man grows a pair and puts a ring on it," Sara countered playfully, not bothering to say the same for Charlie and herself. It was far too early to be thinking of marriage with the man when they weren't even together anymore. "Dude knocked you up *years* ago. A ring's a formality at this point."

It was the same joke she'd been relying on for years now, and useful when she wanted to shift focus off herself. Gemma's response was as predictable as ever.

Her BFF rolled her eyes. "Stop it. I don't need a ring to know that we're in a strong, committed relationship. Or to know that you'd be my sister-in-law if you were dating his brother."

"Except that's what the whole 'in-law' part means…..'cos, 'y'know, it's binding it all by *law*."

"Shut up," Gemma chuckled, "you're ruining the moment."

They laughed together for a moment, and as Sara calmed her breathing, she reached across the table to take her best friend's hand. "Thank you," she said with genuine gratitude. "I'm sorry I didn't tell you about Charlie. I really am."

Gemma squeezed her hand. "I know, and I get it. You were going through some stuff. But I know now, and we're going to fix it."

"I've actually already started," Sara informed her, sitting back as she tucked her hair behind her ears.

Gemma's eyebrows went upwards; she stared back expectantly.

Unable to leave her in suspense for too long, Sara explained: "He called me last night to warn me that he'd told Everett. I took the opportunity to apologise. We talked a bit."

Her best friend was literally sitting on the edge of her seat, leaning forward eagerly. "And?"

"And I told him that I missed him." Despite being in her early –okay, mid, but she wasn't relinquishing her youth so easily– thirties, Sara felt like she was in her late teens again, discussing the minutiae of every interaction with every boy she'd ever met. "And he said he missed me too."

Unlike in her teens, neither she nor her bestie squealed after the confession was made. Instead, Gemma smiled broadly. "That's a good sign."

"Mmmhmm," Sara nodded. "Obviously, we've got a lot to talk through –a lot more than I would have originally thought– but...there's hope, right?"

"Definitely."

Another weight felt as though it had lifted from her shoulders at her friend's enthusiastic response. "Just...promise me one thing?"

Cocking her head to the side, Gemma asked, "What?"

"Can we not mention any of this in front of Beatrice just yet?" She wasn't deluded enough to think Beatrice wouldn't find out –either one of the woman's sons could tell her– but she hoped to be on better ground with Charlie by the time she did.

As her hazel eyes glinted with understanding, and just a smidgen of humour, Gemma nodded. "Good call."

* * *

Over wine and dinner a few nights later with Gemma, Brennan and Jeff, and knowing she couldn't side-step it any longer, Sara found herself divulging the entire story of her relationship with Charlie. They had promised her it was a safe space and, with Zoe visiting Marcus for a sleepover, she had no excuse not to.

"I know I lied about his identity and let you make whatever assumptions you needed to, but everything I told you about him was otherwise true," she prefaced, setting her glass down on the table. Picking up her knife and fork, she cut into the chicken breast which Jeff had cooked, running a bite sized piece through the excess of creamy sauce accompanying it. Her fork stalled at her mouth, and she lowered it. "So, I guess it started at Zoe's birthday..."

In between bites of food –damn, Jeff could cook– and more wine, she told them everything. Obviously, prior to that birthday party, she had never considered Charlie Rhodes boyfriend material before, but once he began sending her messages, how could she not start falling for him?

He was funny, charming when he wanted to be, and hot as hell. The accent was a bonus that she hadn't known she had an actual fetish for until he was saying all sorts of filthy things in that deep voice of his. The fact that they could converse effortlessly had surprised her. And the sex?

With her hands held a generous –and potentially exaggerated– distance apart, Sara whistled. "I mean, *fuuuuuuck* me, Gems, if you've got it even half as good as I had it? I *totally* get the crush on Mister Abtastico."

Gemma's cheeks pinked while Brennan pinched the bridge of his nose and repeated –not for the first time in this circle of friends– that he had no desire to learn anything about his kid sister's sex life. "As far as I'm concerned," he informed them pointedly as they all laughed at him, "Zoe's conception was immaculate."

Proving she'd had perhaps one too many glasses of the *fine* twenty-dollar wine her brother had procured, through lowered inhibitions Gemma snorted and offered the retort, "I don't know about immaculate, but it was in a bath."

Jeff howled with laughter as his fiancé choked and spluttered on a mouthful of his own drink.

Sara leaned over and high-fived her. She'd never gotten the full story –or *any* of the sexy details– from her usually reserved friend, so it was great to see her loosen up and finally dish some of the fun stuff. "I knew you weren't vanilla, babe."

"Stop it. Don't encourage her," Brennan begged, but he was smiling (well, partially grimacing) as he complained, "I don't want to know any more."

Gemma ignored her brother and grinned back at Sara. "All I'm saying is I have zero complaints in that department."

"I am so going to get the details out of you," Sara tipped her glass in her best friend's direction. "Let's see how different these brothers actually are, yeah?"

"Alright," Jeff intervened, shaking his head, "that's heading into creepy territory."

"Meh," Sara waved him off, "it's not like I'm suggesting we share or swing or whatever."

That was the point where Gemma broke. Disgusted, she leaned back in her chair, away from Sara. "Too far," she groused, "I'm out." Cocking her head to the side, she steered the conversation back towards Sara and Charlie's relationship. "So, you guys had chemistry on all levels...and when he went back to London you were obviously happy with whatever you were doing to stay in touch."

"Yeah," Sara's smile was tinged with melancholy. She put her glass back down on the table and ran a finger over the rim. "It was surprisingly fun." She shrugged in Gemma's direction. "I mean, after what you and Everett went through, I was worried we wouldn't be able to deal, but...we made it work. We talked a lot. Sent each other photos and stuff. It was hard not being able to hug or kiss, but it also built up this epic sense of anticipation, you know?"

"And then we—" Jeff waved his fork vaguely amongst the group "—convinced you that falling head over heels so early wasn't a bad thing."

Brennan nodded. "Which it wasn't, but knowing who you were talking about...well, your hesitance makes more sense now."

"That's what I said!" Gemma raised her glass in the air in salute to her brother, before turning her attention back to Sara. "Not that there's anything wrong with Charlie. He's a good match for you. A great one, actually."

"I mean..." Jeff cut back in, wincing as he tried to tactfully play Devil's Advocate, "y'know, aside from having completely different feelings about having kids and settling down and, oh yeah: *which country to live in.*"

Sara was mopping up leftover sauce on her plate with her dinner roll. She shrugged, bringing the delicious morsel to her mouth. "Mmmpphhm," she began attempting to speak while she ate, then swallowed, wiped the corners of her lips with her napkin and continued, "We never really spoke about any of that. It was always sort of a 'if we prove we can make it work, then we'll talk about the bigger picture' agreement."

"But you didn't give him a chance to talk about it," Gemma rose from her seat and started collecting their empty dinner plates. She eyed Sara pointedly as she reached for hers. "You just decided it was impossible and abandoned ship."

Holding her hands up in surrender, Sara defended herself. "I never said it was a smart move."

"You panicked," Jeff offered, addressing Sara while handing his plate across to Gemma without glancing her way. Gemma rolled her eyes and took it from him while he continued to pontificate. "You avoided the conversation with him in case it went badly and decided to end it before he could."

"Get out of my head!" Sara balled up her paper napkin and tossed it at him. It landed lamely between them on the table. She sighed. "You're actually not that far off, to be honest. I just…I got in my head about it. Convinced myself it wasn't going to work in the long run. *Someone,*" she gave a nod in Gemma's direction, "might have pointed out that I probably freaked out about my feelings, too. So, y'know, I made myself all angry and miserable and then…" She made exploding gestures with her hands and accompanied the motion with a matching sound.

"But you apologised the other night, right?" Gemma was ever the optimist. "And he misses you. You can fix this."

"Except…" Jeff was back to being the rational one, "you've still gotta go over all the big, scary stuff. It's even more important now."

Sara nodded. "I know. And I plan to. But I don't want to do it via Facetime. It needs to be face-to-face." Where neither one of them could 'accidentally' –or otherwise– terminate the call if it got too messy.

"Oh!" Gemma's exclamation –from where she was rinsing their dishes and then stacking them into the dishwasher– caused Sara to jump in her seat. "I've got it!" She yelled enthusiastically.

Sara wasn't certain she liked the dawning excitement on her best friend's face. Gemma was a hopeless romantic at heart and being with Everett had only made her more so. "What?" she asked with apprehension.

"Okay, so, I think I have a plan…"

As Sara listened –and the two men at the table also interjected their thoughts– she could feel her hopes increasing…along with the fear that if this went wrong, there would be no coming back from it.

"What do you think?" Gemma asked, her eyes wide and glistening with hope.

Sara licked her lips. It was go big or go home, right? "I'm in."

This time, Gemma did squeal.

179

* * *

"This is insane." Sara's hands were shaking as she clutched her ticket like a lifeline. She was standing outside the yellow Departures gate at Brisbane International Airport, wondering just how much wine she had actually had to drink when she'd agreed to this cockamamie idea roughly two months earlier.

Charlie had no idea that she was about to board a plane and interrupt his life. They'd exchanged a few more messages over the past couple of months, but nothing too deep or personal.

This was a huge leap to be taking, and it was very personal.

Gemma had obviously been inspired by Everett's similar action during their first few months together. Gemma had waxed poetic about how much she felt it had proved to her that he had desperately cared and needed to be with her. So, if Sara flew half-way across the world and deposited herself on Charlie's doorstep, it would prove the same, right?

God, I hope so.

"You're panicking over nothing," Gemma assured her, giving her a huge hug. "He's going to be happy to see you."

"And if not…" Jeff had also accompanied her, asserting that she needed the moral support, "you've got a hotel booked as backup. You can just enjoy a week-long holiday. Maybe find another sexy Brit and–*oomph*." He stopped and glared at his soon to be actual sister-in-law, who had elbowed him. "I'm just saying!"

"Well don't," Gemma huffed back at him, rolling her eyes. She turned back to Sara. "You've got this. It's going to be amazing." She shot a glare over her shoulder as if daring Jeff to argue with her.

"Is it too late to get one of you to come with me?" Sara was half joking, half serious.

As far as she was concerned, Charlie could think this was way too over the top –even for her– and reject her, leaving her to feel broken and humiliated. As it was currently, they were civil. Things were as they had been during the week following Zoe's birthday party, only somewhat more tentative. But if she did this, if she flew around the world to confront him on his home turf and he turned her away? There would be no way she could face him at any of their family gatherings ever again.

"Sarz, you'll be fine. Better than fine."

Her best friend's eternal optimism was not contagious, but Sara told herself that Gemma would have likely mentioned this crazy-ass scheme to her boyfriend. And, considering said boyfriend also happened to be Charlie's brother and –to Sara's knowledge– hadn't objected, it was a promising start.

Sara let out a deep breath. "Alright, well, I guess all that's left is for me to go board the plane."

"Technically you'll have to wait in the Departures lounge for a couple of hours first..." Jeff offered, chuckling as he dodged Gemma's elbow. "I saw it coming this ti–*hey!*" She'd smacked him lightly upside the head. He patted down his hair. "Never mess with the hair, Gems. Come on, now."

"Okay, that's my cue to leave," Sara laughed and shook her head. "Behave while I'm gone, children."

"You're spoiling my fun," Jeff informed her, but stepped forward to give her a hug. "Good luck."

Gemma waited her turn and then pulled Sara in for another hug, squeezing tightly. "I'm going to want details."

"Including any saucy ones?" Sara asked as she drew back, waggling her eyebrows suggestively.

With a put-upon sigh, Gemma shrugged. "I'm not going to be able to stop you if there are, am I?"

"Not a chance."

Gemma's expression softened out into something almost maternal. "As long as it means you're happy, I'll suffer through it."

"Okay, now get going," Jeff urged, checking his watch, "unless your goal is to not make it through Customs in time."

Sara planted a hand on her hip and arched an eyebrow. "I thought you said I'd be sitting in the lounge for hours?"

"I was exaggerating. Now get. Shoo. Vamoose." He made a shooing motion with his hands. He waited until Sara was on the descending escalator before he called after her, "Keep in touch! Tell us EVERYTHING!"

She nodded as they disappeared from view, silently hoping that 'everything' would be good news.

Chapter Twelve

"When are you going to stop moping and come out with us again?" Jim's question was one that Charlie had been fielding for weeks.

It was now mid-July; the days were longer and the climate warm. Or at least what most Londoners considered warm. After having experienced more than one Brisbane summer, Charlie didn't think his own summers were anything to write home about anymore.

Either way, his mates wanted to spend their Friday evenings out and about, but he still preferred to go home and nurse a pint in front of the telly.

It wasn't that he was miserable or moping like his friends thought, though. Charlie was just taking a bit of a break. He had been putting all his efforts into his career –and had made a few tough decisions in that regard lately– and didn't mind the peace and quiet of his little flat. He had even repainted his home recently, refusing to acknowledge to himself that the modern grey and white theme he'd chosen echoed the colour scheme of Sara's home. He'd just been due for a change, that was all. At least, that was the story he was sticking with, not that anyone else would have any idea about the inspiration for his apartment's new palette.

Sometimes, when he was feeling a little lonely, he shot Sara a message or two. They'd even had a few chats on the phone. He missed how close they'd been, and he certainly longed for the way they had once flirted and teased each other.

With every conversation they shared, things grew more comfortable between them again. He had hopes that, by his return to Brisbane for Zoe's next birthday in September, they might even have eliminated any awkwardness, altogether.

Perhaps then he could broach the subject of trying to date each other once more. Everett was still convinced that Sara loved Charlie, and Charlie assumed that notion was coming from Gemma these days, so he clung to hope like the lovesick fool he was.

"For the last time, I'm not moping," Charlie insisted, leaning against the door of his company pick-up truck. "I'm just buggered."

"Aye," one of the other lads ribbed Charlie as he strode past, his Northern accent thick, "busy abandonin' us."

"Not until this project's done," Charlie reminded him, smiling at the thought of the job offer he'd recently received. It had been a deal too good to pass up, even if it meant saying goodbye to his crew. "And I'm mostly in the office these days anyway. Admit it: once I'm gone, you lot'll forget all about me."

"Damn right we will!" Jim's retort was laced with humour. He gave Charlie's shoulder a light punch as he began to saunter away. "You get goin', then. I'm heading to the pub. Enjoy being a boring old man."

"I will," Charlie laughed and then climbed into his truck, turning the key in the ignition and enjoying the way it rumbled to life. He appreciated the fact that it was a company vehicle, but he'd miss it when he left the job. Maybe he'd get something similar of his own once he was settled into the new role.

The drive back to Putney wasn't too bad. He pulled into a park on the street a few hundred metres down from his flat. It was a nice, quiet residential area that had suited him well. He nodded at one of his neighbours walking their fluffy white dog, and absently mused that he might go for a jog along the riverfront, seeing as the evening air was still quite pleasant with not a hint of rain to be seen.

Charlie was so lost in his thoughts that, at first, he didn't see the woman sitting on the front steps to his building. Wearing jeans and a bright pink long-sleeved t-shirt, she stood out against the dark red brick, but that wasn't what had him pulling up short once he noticed her presence.

Gaping at her, Charlie inadvertently dropped the keys he'd earlier fished from his pocket as he neared home. They landed with a clatter on the footpath, but he made no move to pick them up.

"Sara?" he breathed, blinking rapidly, wondering if she was some sort of apparition. Maybe he had lost his mind after all.

She bit her lip and nodded, pushing herself to her feet and hopping down the few steps separating them before she came to an awkward stop in front of him. "Hi."

"What...how...why..." He couldn't form a sentence. He shook his head and tried again. "You're in London."

Very astute, Charles, he silently berated himself. *Idiot.*

"Yeah..." Sara tucked her hands into her back pockets and rocked back on her heels, "I am."

Charlie stooped to collect his keys. "Not that I'm complaining, love, but... this is somewhat unexpected."

She nodded again before tucking her long, dark hair behind her ears. "Yeah, uh, sorry about that. It was kind of a spur of the moment thing." Her cheeks turned pink. "I...I just wanted to see you. In person."

It finally dawned on him that they were having this conversation in the middle of the street. "Let's head inside," he gestured for her to follow him up the front steps. At the building's front door, he entered his security code, unlocking it in a daze. He then led the way up another set of stairs inside the building, which took them to his apartment on the second floor. He quickly unlocked the door and motioned for Sara to go in ahead of him. "Ladies first."

"Thanks," she murmured, hesitantly crossing the threshold.

He watched as she crossed the small living room and made her way to the glass door that led out onto his little balcony which faced the street. If you angled yourself to the right, you could *just* catch a glimpse of the Thames through the trees and other houses...if you were standing.

He couldn't believe she had travelled all that way to see him, and without warning. What would she have done if he hadn't come home? Given she didn't have any luggage with her, it was likely that she had accommodation sorted out somewhere else in the city, but how long had she been sitting there on his stoop? How much longer would she have waited?

Sara wrung her hands as she continued to silently take in the view. Her show of nerves further settled his own.

She was obviously anxious for his reaction to her presence in his home and in the country itself. Not that he could blame her. It was quite the leap of faith to travel halfway around the world as a surprise-slash-grand gesture when you were in a relationship. It was even more gutsy to do so when you weren't.

Naturally, his hopes for rekindling their romance had just risen exponentially. He was almost certain that Sara would not have orchestrated this with purely platonic intentions.

"I've missed you," he informed her, breaking the silence that had descended since they'd entered the apartment. "I'm happy you're here."

She turned away from the window to face him, relief and then joy lighting up her features. "Really?"

"Really," he replied, taking another step in her direction. He gestured to his lounge room, which could have used a vacuum and a bit of a spruce up, and said, "I apologise that it's so untidy, I wasn't expecting visi–*mmmph!*"

Charlie hadn't anticipated that Sara would throw herself into his arms, planting her lips on his, but he wasn't about to complain about that, either.

He hadn't kissed her since early January –the day before he'd flown back to the UK– but muscle memory was a magical thing. They fit together with the same ease as always, with their lips and tongues moving in unison. This was a slow kiss, but he thought he could feel her desperation and longing as badly as he felt his own.

When they finally separated for air, he continued to hold her close, looked her in the eye and confessed, "I love you." It wasn't blurted in a rush, but deliberately said. After that kiss, and after all they'd been through, he couldn't withhold it any longer.

Would it have been better if they were in a relationship? Yes. But whether they were together or not, he needed to tell her.

His spirits soared as she beamed back up at him and made no move to shift out of his arms. "I love you, too."

"I can't believe you're here."

Sara chuckled, shook her head, and shrugged. "Neither can I. You probably think I'm insane."

"Just a little," he acknowledged, "but I wouldn't have it any other way."

"Obviously. I wouldn't be here otherwise."

He didn't want to think about the alternatives to this situation. Not now that she was here, in his arms, having just kissed the life out of him. However, Charlie was determined to know exactly what her seemingly crazy decision to just turn up at his house without warning truly signified.

"What does this mean for us?" He knew he had to ask the question sooner rather than later. They had to restart everything on the same page. "Do we have a future together?"

She winced, and he felt guilty for phrasing it that way. But, seeing as those were the words that had ended their relationship the first time around, it was best to get the worst over with first.

"I want us to," she told him, pressing her cheek against his chest and snuggling into the worn material of his –actually rather filthy from a day at work– t-shirt. "I think we can have one. We just…we just need to be honest with each other. Right here, right now." She took a deep breath and pulled her head back again so she could look him in the eye. "I won't force you to have kids, and that's not something we have to decide on yet anyway, but…I mean, do you want a serious future with me?" She was working herself up into a ramble, which was out of character. "Will you consider moving to Brisbane? Not straight away, but eventually? Because I think…actually, no, I *know* I need that from you. I can't move away from my family. And if that's a deal-breaker–"

"Brennan offered me a job." It was the easiest way to end her anxious babble and drop the bomb he'd been holding onto for months now. Her eyes widened and her jaw dropped.

"He *what?*"

"Over Easter, actually." Charlie couldn't help the fact that he was enjoying this moment. Watching as she processed the information, likely plotting to kill her best friend's brother for keeping the revelation from her. "At the time, it was just a throwaway suggestion. But I thought about it –a lot– and, even though it didn't look as though you and I would work out, it meant being close to my family again. To Mum, and Zoe…and even Rhett, when he's not off gallivanting about the world." He shrugged. "I looked into the VISAs and the legalities of it and then went back to Brennan and told him I'd take it, if the offer was still on the table."

"When…" Sara's voice came out tight. She cleared her throat. "When was that?"

Charlie supposed she had every right to feel a little blindsided by the news. After all, he assumed that Brennan knew about her plan to drop everything and fly across the pond to hash things out once and for all. A little warning might have been nice for her.

"A couple of months back," he admitted, "just before we started talking again." And, alright, it might have behoved him to tell her himself. "I was going to tell you in September. Face to face." In fact, that was going to be his Hail Mary: *his* grand gesture to win her back. It was his turn to be a little sheepish now. "You stole my thunder and turned up here."

With her shock receding, she snorted. "What can I say? I know what I want, and I go for it." She paused, blushing a little. "But I'll admit, there's an irony in my saying that now, considering I should have done it back at Easter."

With a giant grin stretching across his face, and a small chuckle which dispelled the lingering awkwardness of her apologetic addendum, he dipped his head for another quick kiss. "Your determination is one of the many things I love about you."

"Hmm," she rested her forehead against his for a moment, then leaned back against his arms, running an index finger down his bicep and forearm. "I think maybe we should move this discussion somewhere more comfortable. I could definitely stand to hear more about what you love about me."

Not needing any additional encouragement, he took her by the hand and gave her a whirlwind tour of his little flat, starting through the little archway between the kitchen and the lounge room, down the hall and concluding it in his bedroom. The large windows in this room looked out towards the river proper, over the rooftops of houses and a stretch of park that filled the space in between.

It was now turning dusk, and lights were switching on, twinkling in the greying sky. When he'd moved in, he'd had the windows treated so that he could see out, but nobody could see in. It allowed him to let light in without sacrificing his privacy, and it was in this very moment that he applauded his decision the most.

Sara stood at the foot of the bed, backlit by the window. It gave her an ethereal glow. He considered pinching himself, astounded that she was here with him.

Not wanting to ruin the moment by talking –and because he had no idea what to say– Charlie closed the space between them and kissed her again. This time was soft and reverent, his amazement at having her with him infused in the way he pulled her close and threaded his fingers into her silky hair.

The elephant in the room was gone! Their relationship wouldn't be a secret from their loved ones. There would be no sneaking around, and she had been honest about what had truly been eating away at her.

Despite how well they'd communicated, and how bizarrely enjoyable their attempt at maintaining a long-distance relationship had been, Sara had wanted to know that he would eventually move to her. He didn't even bother questioning why he was the one expected to uproot his life. It just made sense. She had a family in Brisbane, a life she couldn't leave behind just for a lover. And he didn't have that in London. Not anymore. His family was there with her.

And yet she had obviously struggled with voicing those thoughts to him. Perhaps she'd worried that it was too soon to put that sort of pressure on their relationship? Or maybe she'd thought she was being unreasonable to demand he move to her when she was technically just as capable of moving halfway around the world to him?

But these were questions he'd ask later. In what he acknowledged had been a ridiculously short discussion, they had resolved their biggest hurdle, and that was enough for the moment.

For now, he was going to show Sara how terribly he'd missed her, and how deeply he loved her.

She had practically melted into the kiss, but his eyebrows drew together when he and Sara parted for air. He cupped her cheek with his free hand when he noticed a rogue tear trickling down her cheek. He brushed it away with his thumb. "You alright, love?" he asked quietly. "Is this too fast?"

As desperate as he was to reconnect with her, he'd understand if she wanted to wait. For all he knew, perhaps the magnitude of what she had done –flying across the world just to talk to him– was simply catching up to her.

"Fuck no," she replied fiercely. He snorted out a laugh. She brought her hand up to cover his against her cheek and squeezed. "I'm just so sorry I almost destroyed what we have together."

Charlie shook his head. "This is going to sound crazy," he told her while his thumb gently stroked her face, "but I think it was for the best." Her eyes widened. He hurried to explain, "I think, as well as we'd been communicating, we'd steered clear of the harder stuff –like how to make everything work in the long-term– for too long. This short break forced us both to re-evaluate what we honestly want from each other, right?" He smirked and kissed the tip of her ski-dip nose, adding, "And it got you to take a holiday. How long are you here for, anyway?"

Startled into laughter, she shrugged. "A week. I know it's not long, but–"

"It's a week more than I'd imagined we'd have together when I woke up this morning."

There was warmth and affection in her gaze, but her expression turned guilt-ridden again. "I know you have no reason to trust that I won't flip out again, but–"

"I'm willing to take that risk," he informed her seriously, and he meant it. Outside of her actions speaking louder than words, he wasn't going to turn her away based on the sheer possibility of their relationship taking a nosedive again. He loved her too much for that. "A moment with you is better than none."

"Naww," she was chuckling now, albeit a watery sound, "listen to you being all sappy."

"Only for you, love."

Charlie wasn't feeding her a line. He'd never been the romantic type before. No woman he had ever been with had inspired the emotions as Sara had. It was a little sad to think that, at his age, he'd never really been in love with anyone before. He had cared deeply for some of his ex-lovers, but never like this. Sara had wormed her way under his skin and into his heart. He was certain he'd never find anyone else quite like her even if he tried.

"I love you," she responded, as if overwhelmed by the same feelings he was experiencing. By her tone, he dared hope that she was.

"I love you." It was a thrill to repeat those words, to not be afraid that they were said too soon or that her declaration wasn't genuine. At this point, after what she'd just done, how could they not be?

They were kissing again, no longer as gentle and worshipful. The last vestiges of unpleasant emotional tension had dissolved. Now they were both on the same page, with a different –much more pleasurable– tension building between them.

Sara nipped at Charlie's bottom lip. She slid her hands down his sides, squeezing the globes of his ass playfully, pulling him as flush against her as she could. He grinned into the kiss, applying more pressure, wrestling her for control. As much as he wanted to lay her down and slowly make love to her, this first time would not be about that.

They had too much pent-up energy between them now. Too many months of tension to release. The last time they'd had sex together had been in December –seven months earlier– and following their breakup, Charlie had no interest in seeking out anyone in order to have sex for sex's sake.

With Sara's hands pushing his shirt up his chest, it was as though she had read his thoughts because she informed him, "Just so you know, there hasn't been anyone else."

He told himself he wouldn't have had the right to be upset if there had been. They hadn't been together, and she was her own person, after all. However, he couldn't help feeling relieved at her words. "Same here," he responded, assisting her in removing his shirt, tugging it over his head and tossing it towards the armchair in the corner of the room.

She grinned, seemingly equally reassured by his admission. Then her grin turned playful, and she swivelled her hips while his hands gravitated there. "Actually, I lie," she said coyly, "there was Bob."

"Ah, Bob," he acknowledged with a tilt of his head. "I can't blame you," he waggled his eyebrows, "I've seen him in action."

Her hands swept over his chest, down his abdomen and came to rest at his belt buckle. "He doesn't really compare to you, though."

"You know…" he began while he worked to coax her out of her own shirt. She allowed him to pull the clingy material up and over her head before he sent it flying towards his own. His eyes drank in the sight of her in her lacy red bra, "other parts of me could use stroking too, love, not just my ego."

Laughing, she unbuckled his belt and whipped it through the loops of his cargo shorts, tossing it aside. "I'm getting there."

"Get there faster."

"Impatient, are we?"

"Says the woman who flew around the world to see me because she couldn't wait until September."

With wide, dark brown eyes, she batted her lashes expectantly. Her hands stilled over the zip of his fly. "I hope you're not complaining about that."

"Never." Even though they were toying with each other, he meant it. He still couldn't quite believe that any of this was happening at all.

If this all turned out to be a dream, he'd be incredibly disappointed…and he would sign up for therapy immediately.

When Sara raised herself up on her toes to kiss him passionately, he knew he couldn't possibly imagine anything quite so vivid. As they kissed, they did their best to continue undressing until they fell onto the bed naked, laughing, and slightly breathless.

Their kissing slowed, until Sara wrapped her hand around his aching cock, pumping it a few times before she declared that she couldn't wait any longer. She threw one of her long legs over his hip, straddled him and sank down before his brain caught up to what was happening.

"Jesus Christ," he bit out, overwhelmed by how wet and tight and *amazing* she felt wrapped around his dick. He held his hands on her hips firmly. "Don't move." It felt absurd having to issue such a warning, as though he was all of sixteen and inexperienced, but it had been seven months with only his hand, and *fuck* she felt divine.

She gave him a moment, her eyes soft and understanding, and waited until he nodded at her. "You good?" she checked aloud. He nodded.

"Thanks."

It was one more thing to love about her. As much as they teased each other, she always knew where the boundaries were, and it just made being with her that much easier.

Case in point: she smirked and bucked her hips, causing him to groan and drop his head back against the mattress. "Good," she declared, full of cheek.

He took her by surprise by surging up from his prone position –never having thought that sit-ups would have prepared him for such a moment– and captured her lips with his, placing one hand on the mattress to steady himself with the other cupping the back of her head. She rocked her hips, riding him as they kissed. He moved with her as best he could, impeded as he was by the awkward way they were arranged.

When they broke from the kiss, she took pity on him by suggesting they move into a position more comfortable for him. He complained as she shifted away, hurriedly scooting back down the mattress until he was sitting on the edge, stabilised by his feet on the carpeted floor. Charlie gathered her back into his lap, having her straddle him once more, but this time with her long legs wrapped around his waist.

Sara crossed her wrists behind his neck, and he wrapped his arms around her back. They made similar sounds of relief as he slipped back inside her and kissed again, but more urgently, matching the pace he was setting as he bounced them on the edge of the mattress.

"Fuck," she muttered against his lips, grinding herself down into his upward movement, "fuck, fuck, fuck. Don't you dare stop."

He wasn't usually talkative in bed. Sara, however, liked to babble, with the habit only increasing the closer she got to orgasm. He couldn't help responding. "Wasn't planning on it," he whispered back, feeling her squeezing around his cock. "God, I've missed you. Missed this."

"Me too," Sara agreed. Her breathing hitched. "Oh, right there!"

She undulated her hips. He matched her rhythm while he watched her shut her eyes and tilt her head back, her long dark hair swaying behind her, the ends brushing his arms with her movement. He couldn't resist kissing the exposed column of her neck, guiding her to tilt her lithe body further back so he could travel lower and brush his lips over her breasts. She didn't protest, showing her trust in his strength, confident that he wouldn't allow her to fall backwards out of his hold. The only thing he lamented was that, with his hands behind her, he couldn't reach between them to give her the added friction he knew she craved.

"Touch yourself," he said, nudging one of her arms –currently stretched out as she gripped his shoulders– with his cheek. "I've got you."

Not needing to be told twice, she wound one hand into the hair at the back of his head, and the other slipped between them, rubbing firm circles over her clit.

Their pace picked up. It wasn't long before she was crying out. Charlie watched the euphoric expression on Sara's face as she clenched and fluttered around his cock. Though he wanted to draw this out and bring her to orgasm at least twice more, she ground down harder in his lap, chasing the last sparks of pleasure from her afterglow, and pulled him right over the edge with her.

He shut his eyes, coming hard, his hips jerking as white light exploded behind his eyelids. Sara rode him through it, slowing their pace as he caught his breath.

She kissed him gently.

"Much better than Bob," she informed him cheekily. Charlie swatted lightly at her backside.

"Mmm." His brain was still sluggishly trying to form words. "Glad to hear it."

She scrunched her nose as she finally extricated herself from his lap. "Shower?"

Looking himself over, Charlie grunted his approval, then finally managed the energy to respond verbally. "Wonderful idea." He jutted his head towards the hallway. There was only one bathroom in his little flat. "You get the water running, I'll get the towels."

"Who said you were invited?" she teased, giggling and sidestepping as he moved to swat at her butt again. She sashayed her hips as she sauntered to the doorway, heedless of her state of undress.

He watched her perfect ass shift from side to side and had to give himself a mental shake. *Shower. Yes.*

She smirked knowingly at him; he shrugged back shamelessly.

"Come on, tiger," Sara encouraged, crooking a finger his way, "let's complete the tour, hey?"

He laughed and followed, nabbing a couple of towels from the cupboard in the hall along the way. "I don't know that I've got energy for Round Two," he warned, leaning against the tiled wall of the bathroom as she stepped into the shower and played with the taps until the temperature was to her liking.

She turned back to face him, tilting her head back under the warm spray as she asked in a voice filled with faux innocence, "Who said anything about Round Two?"

His shower was small –almost too small for the two of them to share it– but he stepped inside with her, aware that his frame took up most of the space. She didn't seem at all bothered though, pressing herself up against his body under the guise of reaching for the shower gel on the shelf beside him.

While he mightn't have the refractory period that he'd had in his twenties, his body made a valiant attempt to flare back to life at her proximity.

Perhaps Round Two was on the cards after all.

* * *

"So," Charlie asked after their unsurprisingly extended shower, watching as Sara ran a comb –appropriated from his medicine cabinet– through her wet locks, "where are you staying?"

She bit her lip and named a hotel in the centre of London proper. "I didn't know what kind of reception I'd get when I turned up here," she confessed quietly, turning back to the mirror and grimacing as she fought a tangle, "so I left all my stuff there."

It turned out that she had flown in the night before and had slept most of the day, wanting to be at her best when she left the hotel to find him. He understood. Between the jet lag and her nerves, having a night and the better part of a full day to herself was a smart choice. He would have done the same.

An idea began to form in his brain.

"So…you've not seen much of the city, then?"

She gave a brief shake of her head and set the comb down on the basin before she dug into her hip pocket and pulled out an elastic band. "No," she replied, her long fingers now nimbly assembling her wet hair into a long plait, "I haven't been a very good tourist. I walked from the hotel to the tube station, and then caught the train here. That's about it."

"Why not make a weekend of it, then? No sense staying in this dingy flat when you've got a nice room booked, eh? I can show you around a bit, we can go out for dinner…like a proper little holiday."

The more Charlie spoke, the more excited *he* became about the prospect. In their time together, he'd never had the opportunity to take her out on an *actual* date. And, since Sara was in London, he wanted to show her some of his world while he still lived in it.

She tied off the end of her plait and turned around to face him with a warm smile. "I'd like that," she agreed, walking her index and middle finger up the front of his fresh polo shirt before she then toyed with the collar. "My own personal tour guide."

Feeling elated and silly, he gave a short bow. "At your service."

She laughed. "You should probably pack a bag, then, huh?"

"I don't know," he smirked, "we could just spend the weekend in bed. Clothing optional."

"Nope." She flicked her plait over her shoulder and strode past him, now a woman on a mission. "I was promised sights and dinner."

"I didn't say what kind of sights." He made his tone as suggestive as possible, feeling lighter and more playful than he could ever remember being. "And there's such a thing as room service."

Sara was her usual confident self as she made her way back into his bedroom, kicking aside their previously discarded towels on the way to his closet. "Nuh-uh, you said 'go out for dinner'. I'm holding you to that." She cast a playfully pointed glare over her shoulder. "And no jokes about how I can hold you."

"Alas," he played along, sitting down on the edge of his mattress, content to let her do as she wished, "foiled again."

She pulled a small suitcase out from the bottom of his cupboard and tossed it onto the bed, happily rifling through his clothes as though he had signed up to be her own personal Ken doll. "Are you going to stay with me the whole week?" she asked, holding up a forest green business shirt and examining it with a narrowed gaze, as though weighing its suitability. "Or just the weekend?"

"The whole week, if you'll have me."

There was no sense asking her why she wouldn't come back and stay here with him. Her room was paid for, and it was central to everything in the city. He was still scheduled to work –though he was actively considering calling out sick for a few days– and wouldn't be there to entertain her during the week itself. It would be a pain in the arse to travel to and from the middle of the city every day, but his answer had been a no-brainer.

Sara might not have let on that she was concerned about his response, but the surprise and joy which flashed across her features spoke volumes. She carefully set the shirt down on the bed –still on its hanger– and stepped into the space between his legs. With her arms loosely around his neck, she bent to kiss him chastely.

"Always," she murmured.

His heart soared.

* * *

The following evening, as promised, Charlie took Sara to dinner at a beautiful restaurant overlooking the Thames and St Paul's Cathedral. She marvelled over the famous vista, while he marvelled at *her*.

She was dressed to kill with pink, pouty lips, a figure-hugging pink cocktail dress, and colour coordinated stiletto heels. She stood out in the crowd of neutral colours, and as a bright point amongst London's typically industrial backdrop. She drew the eye and her effervescent personality had him utterly besotted.

He'd once mocked Rhett for being like this with Gemma, but now he understood.

Charlie didn't just love her; he was *in love* with her.

"What?" she asked him, turning away from the view and noticing his stare.

He was certain his smile would give his thoughts away, but he simply changed the subject, asking her, "Have you enjoyed the day?"

He'd done exactly as promised and taken her to many of the city's famous landmarks. She'd snapped photos with her phone –forcing him to join her in a multitude of selfies– and had proven herself a bit of a history fan, asking questions and Googling for additional information at every stop.

"It's been amazing," she nodded, turning back to gaze at the river in awe. "How did you get a booking here at such late notice?"

"I have connections," he shrugged.

Sara laughed. "Everett?"

"Actually," he reached for his glass of water, "no. Not this time, anyway." After taking a sip, he put it down and extrapolated, "We –that is, my company– have done a few projects for the owner and the head chef. I called in a favour, and they were happy to oblige." Alright, he'd begged a touch, but he wasn't admitting it.

"Amazing," she repeated with another shake of her head before turning back to him, "but I'd have been just as happy with McDonald's."

"I'll keep that in mind for tomorrow."

Any sassy response she'd planned was interrupted by a server bringing their drinks. Sara had ordered some monstrosity of a cocktail while he'd opted for a beer. As they drank and perused the menus, she offhandedly mentioned that Roger had preferred to order for her. This made Charlie see red.

Who did that? He couldn't quite imagine his fiery, independent lover standing for it, either, but he supposed she had liked the guy. Thank fuck that was over with, though.

"Well, I can barely make up my own mind for what I want," he tried to make light of the situation, while wondering at the tosser's gumption, "so you're on your own."

The edge of her lip curled upwards as she continued to read the menu. "However will I cope?"

Finally deciding on his own meal, he closed his menu, set it down, and reached for his beer. He lifted it in salute. "You're a big girl," he smirked, bringing the glass to his lips, "you'll be just fine."

Tilting her head in acknowledgement, she raised her cocktail back at him, and clinked their glasses together. "I'll drink to that."

Chapter Thirteen

❧

As she boarded her return plane, Sara had a greater appreciation for how Charlie felt whenever he left Brisbane. The last week had been better than she had hoped and leaving him was difficult. However, their relationship was in the best place it had ever been, and she was heading home feeling lighter and more confident than she had in a long while.

Over the course of the past few days, she and Charlie had properly reconnected, emotionally and physically. They had spoken more openly and honestly in the last week than they had in all the months prior –even though they'd never lied to each other, they'd held back– and any remaining doubts she had about whether they would work out had been silenced.

Once he moved to Brisbane, they would have some other issues to discuss, but they weren't insurmountable. She could see a future now, had caught a glimpse of it in their time spent exploring London together. Walking down streets and in stores hand-in-hand, going out to dinner, talking about the banalities of their days and making plans for once he was in Brisbane…it had all felt domestic, and easy, and *right*.

So much so that during her first conversation with him upon her return –Facetiming from her bed– she yawned and casually asked, "So, you'll be moving in with me, right?"

The magnitude of what she had asked him didn't hit her until he gaped back at her through her phone screen. "Is that what you want?"

"I mean, I don't want to pressure you if you think it's rushing things..."

Sara felt slightly embarrassed for having assumed. She supposed that, between his mother's little apartment and Gemma's place, he already had a wealth of options available to him if he hadn't been planning to buy or rent a place sight unseen.

Charlie could obviously sense the shift in her emotions because he shook his head and reached towards the camera, as if wanting to reassure her physically. "Darling..." the appellation had her eyes widening because he never used it, despite his mother and brother throwing it around with abandon. "I want nothing more than for us to live together. I just didn't want to presume..." he trailed off, chuckling. "We're as bad as each other."

Her heart gave a flutter. "A perfect match."

"Something like that."

Feeling as though she was back on solid ground, she smirked at him, "So... 'darling', huh?"

"Shut up," he cringed, playfully defensive as pink spots appeared on his cheeks, visible even on her little phone screen. "This is what you do to me, Carlisle. You have me channelling my mother. I hope you're proud of yourself."

"Extremely," she acknowledged, grinning back at him. She then waited a few additional moments before she teased, "Darling."

He groaned. "You're not half as amusing as you think you are." The fond smile on his face was incongruous with his words. "But, back to your original question...if you'll have me, yes, I'd like to move in with you."

She smiled, settling back into her nest of pillows. "And that's in November, yeah?"

"In time for the wedding, yes."

Brennan and Jeff were tying the knot in November, having picked a beautiful venue on the Gold Coast with their preferred dates available. Jeff had 'stolen' Gemma as his Maid of Honour and had asked Sara to be his other bridesmaid, while Brennan had asked Everett to be his best man. Zoe was to be flower girl. It was going to be a real family affair.

While she was excited for her friends, Sara was looking forward to being able to dance and flirt with Charlie for the night without a second thought. She had to admit, things were so much easier with their families knowing about their relationship.

She had obviously let Gemma and Jeff know in advance that she was coming back to Brisbane happy and very much in love, but they'd left it to her and Charlie to tell Beatrice. She and Charlie had done so via Facetime. Her would-be mother-in-law had been thrilled and supportive, to say the least.

A family group chat was also established –originally with the purpose of discussing the upcoming wedding– and she and Charlie had accepted their fair share of teasing through memes and gifs. Everett was the main perpetrator, admitting that he'd been taken completely by surprise by Charlie's initial disclosure of the relationship, but he followed that up by expressing his pleasure that they had sorted things out and were going to try to make the long-distance thing work.

Charlie was going to tell Everett and their mother in person, at Zoe's birthday in September, about his plans to relocate to Brisbane. In the meantime, it was their little secret (shared with Brennan). It was much easier to keep this one to themselves.

But her thoughts were getting off track.

"I can't wait to get you in that suit again," she told him, her voice low and full of sinful promises, "or, I should say, get you out of it."

With a Cheshire Cat grin of his own, he leaned forward, addressing the camera, "I'm counting on it, princess."

* * *

"I can't believe you're four!" Charlie tossed Zoe up into the air in Gemma and Everett's backyard and caught her with ease as she squealed and begged for more. "Soon you'll be all grown up!"

From her vantage point at the outdoor dining table, Sara watched the interaction, feeling her heart squeeze. She loved that kid, and she loved that kid's uncle. He was so good with Zoe. It made all the little maternal fireworks inside of her explode.

She'd once told Gemma that, as ovary-wielding types, they were wired to find hot men being adorable with children a turn on.

She hadn't been exaggerating.

Watching Charlie playing with his niece *–their* niece– made her want to grab him by the collar, drag him into the nearest private alcove and practice making a few kids of their own.

From the corner of her eye, she was aware of Beatrice watching her like a hawk.

Beatrice had always been lovely to her, but since she had returned from London and had admitted she was dating Beatrice's oldest son, the older woman had become even more maternal (if that was possible), attaching herself like a very sweet limpet. Gemma had warned her that it would happen, and, as she'd gone her entire adult life without her mother, Sara was honestly a little overwhelmed with all the additional motherly attention. It wasn't bad, but at times it was getting to be a little much.

Like right now.

"He's good with children, isn't he?" Beatrice asked in a manner that was too casual.

Sara arched an eyebrow but didn't turn away from watching Charlie and Zoe frolicking around on the lawn. "I'm on to you, lady," she replied, keeping her tone light, "and we've only really been together a few months." Not counting the original six.

"I know, I know," Beatrice sighed, "it's none of my business either way, really."

"You're good at this mum guilt stuff." Sara finally turned to smile at the other woman, who appeared completely unrepentant as she shrugged and reached for her glass of wine. Sara picked up her own and clinked their glasses together. "He's a good man, and he is *so* good with Zoe. I'll give you that."

"What are we talking about?" Charlie, stooped over with Zoe now clinging to his back like a monkey, interrupted their conversation. He was always just a little bit uneasy when she and his mum were left unattended with each other. While Sara found it amusing, she also wondered whether he was afraid that they would plot against him, or whether they would inevitably argue.

Jutting her chin upwards in light-hearted challenge, Sara replied honestly. "You."

"And me?" Zoe piped up, peering over one of her uncle's broad shoulders impishly.

"And you," Sara agreed, beaming at her niece.

Charlie's eyes narrowed at his mother, causing Sara to wonder what sorts of conversations they'd shared recently to inspire such suspicion in him. But, as the sliding door that led from inside opened, and Gemma and Everett appeared with platters of food, he was prevented from saying anything. Behind them, Brennan and Marcus carried in large bowls of salad. Jeff was unfortunately working but had been able to make it to the official birthday party earlier in the morning.

"Dinner!" Zoe cried, squirming until Charlie set her feet back on the floor.

"She's very food-motivated, eh?" he asked his brother, watching with amusement as the little girl scrambled into her seat at the table.

Everett laughed and shook his head. "No, she's excited for the second round of cake." He sent a pointed look towards his little female doppelganger. "Which she will only get after we've had dinner."

"Sound logic," Charlie acknowledged, walking around the table to sit at Sara's other side. He kissed her on the cheek; she smiled involuntarily. He caught Zoe's gaze as Gemma loaded up the little girl's plate. "I'm looking forward to a second helping of cake after supper, too."

"You gotta eat your veggies first," she told him firmly. He smirked across at Gemma because they could all hear her in the little girl's words.

"I swear I will."

The conversation flowed from there, and Sara felt that recurring fluttery, happy feeling fill her as Charlie's thigh pressed against hers under the table. This felt good. Natural. Effortless. Why had she been so convinced that it wouldn't be?

When Gemma returned with a small chocolate cake, bearing a candle in the shape of the number 4, they all sang another round of 'Happy Birthday' to Zoe. Charlie's singing voice –while not as polished as his brother's– was deep and pleasant, much like his speaking voice. Leaning into him while the cake was being cut, Sara complimented him on it, delighting in the blush spreading up his neck and over his cheeks.

"I don't sing, love," he informed her quietly.

She jabbed him lightly in the ribs. "You just did."

He rolled his eyes, but Zoe's little voice –thick with a mouth full of chocolate cake– declared, "Uncle Charlie says he's not gonna miss any more of me gettin' bigger."

"Is that so?" Beatrice asked with a curious lilt, while all eyes turned and landed on the man in question.

"Never trust a four-year-old with a secret," he muttered under his breath, causing Sara to snigger. Straightening his shoulders, he picked at the label on his beer bottle and aimed for nonchalance, "I was waiting until tomorrow to say something. You know, not wanting to take away from the little princess' big day," he gestured towards Zoe, who had lost interest and was too busy licking icing from her fingers, "but I've taken a job here in Brisbane, starting in the new year. So I'm moving over in November. Before this one's wedding." He tilted his head in Brennan's direction, reminding Sara that Brennan was technically Charlie's boss now.

His mother cheered, Marcus and Gemma congratulated him, and his brother's jaw dropped. "What?" Everett asked in surprise. "How long have you been plotting this, then?"

"Long enough," Charlie answered evasively, before he turned mildly sarcastic, "but thanks for your support, Rhett. Truly."

With a long-suffering sigh, Everett refuted, "I'm happy for you. I am. I'm just surprised that this is the first that I'm...that *we're*," he corrected himself, waving a hand over the gathering, "hearing about it."

Charlie snorted. "Kind of like that time Mum decided to move halfway around the world and neither of you told me for almost a year, eh?"

Sara placed a calming hand over his thigh under the table, empathising with him. His hand settled over hers and squeezed.

"Alright," his brother conceded, now a bit sheepish. He raised his beer apologetically. "That's a fair point." He cleared his throat, obviously eager to move the conversation back to a happier place. "So, tell us about this job, then."

Sara watched as Charlie's gaze slid over to Brennan and the other man nodded, taking a smug sip from his glass of wine. Charlie then turned back to his brother, but cocked his head in Brennan's direction as he spoke. "Well, turns out someone's business was expanding, and he needed a new Operations Manager to do site visits, oversee sales reps, assist with planning and logistics...that sort of thing."

This time it was Gemma's jaw that dropped as she leaned over to her brother to hit at his shoulder. "You couldn't have said something?"

"And miss this fun?" Brennan laughed and shook his head. "I don't think so, Gems."

His sister was not having it. She folded her arms and huffed. "You could have at least told Sara! I mean, after Easter and everything."

"No," Sara interrupted, defending Brennan, "he didn't, because he thought –rightly so– that Charlie should tell me himself."

"Ugh, I hate it when you people are all rational and logical." Gemma sighed, "You don't think Brennan saying something might have eased a bit of your conflict?"

Sara had considered this already. On the flight back from London, left alone with her thoughts and perhaps one too many glasses of wine, she had pondered the same question. Would knowing ahead of time –before she'd thrown caution to the wind and hopped on a flight to the other side of the world– settled any of her nerves?

She didn't think so. In fact, she would have been more conflicted, wanting to know why *Charlie* hadn't told her. Even if they were no longer together, it meant more to her to hear it directly from him. It had meant more knowing that *he* wanted to tell her.

Instead of relaying all of this to Gemma, though, she just offered a half-shrug and smiled. "Nope."

The two friends would discuss the matter at length later. Of that, she was certain.

"Well," Marcus shifted the conversation back again, raising his glass in the air, "I'm happy for everyone here. Brennan, to the success of your company. Charlie, to new adventures. And the rest of us, to family! Cheers!"

They followed suit, cheering and clinking glasses. Sara snuggled into Charlie's side as he and Brennan answered more questions about the plans for the business. The rumble of his voice was soothing, and she looked forward to this becoming their new normal after November. Mid-conversation, he caught her eye; she could tell he was thinking the same thing.

Or perhaps he was thinking about how easy it was going to be after dinner, to just say their goodbyes and return to her house to continue their own private celebrations, without the necessity to sneak around.

Later that evening, when she was on her way back from the bathroom and he pinned her up against Gemma and Everett's hallway wall and kissed her senseless, Sara considered the notion of perhaps still doing a little bit of sneaking around if it meant more moments like that.

...For old time's sake.

* * *

Naturally, Sara felt her luck slipping in October, when she found herself facing a whole new dilemma.

She suspected she was pregnant, and it sucked for a slew of reasons. Firstly, she and Charlie had really only been dating –with their family's knowledge and with most of their cards on the table– since July. Secondly, he was still in London, finalising the sale of his flat and tying up all the loose ends before he flew back over to Australia to start his new life in two weeks' time. There was no way she could talk this through with him via Facetime or Messenger. This was the sort of conversation to be had in person. Thirdly (and she felt awful for thinking this) she didn't want her relationship –her in-person, no longer long-distance relationship– to start the same way Gemma's had. She didn't want Charlie hanging around out of some sense of obligation.

She was scared and felt isolated in the same way she had back when she'd chosen to conceal her and Charlie's first attempt at a relationship.

She couldn't talk to anyone about this. Not even Gemma, whom she was certain would understand everything she was feeling right in that moment, seeing as she had lived it and whose situation had been against much greater odds.

There's no sense panicking until you know for sure, the voice of reason in her head told her as she scurried past the feminine hygiene products in the aisle at Woolworths. *Your period's been MIA before.*

And it had. Because of the implant in her arm, there were months when her body just seemed to skip it, and there had been other months when it felt as though the bleeding would never stop. But this time her boobs were sensitive –which was unusual for her– and she didn't know whether it was psychosomatic or whether she'd just been working too hard again, but she felt exhausted all the time.

God, what the hell was she going to do if she was pregnant? The subject of children hadn't been readdressed, not since she'd promised Charlie that it wasn't a deal-breaker if he didn't want them. It wasn't an issue she'd wanted to push him on.

And this was certainly not the way she had wanted to discuss it with him, either.

Just pick a freaking test, Carlisle. She stood in front of the shelf of boxes and sighed. She felt like an irresponsible teenager, instead of a woman in her mid-thirties.

Should have just nicked a couple of hCG strips from work. Which she hadn't done because the risk of Jeff, or Gemma, or any one of her gossipy colleagues catching her was too high.

After another moment of *umm*-ing and *ahh*-ing, with a trembling hand, she reached out and grabbed a pack of three rapid-response tests. She read the back, confirmed that the hCG sensitivity was acceptable enough for how far along she estimated she'd be, and stuffed the white and blue box with its bright pink label underneath the loaf of bread in her basket.

Sara's thoughts burned at the back of her mind for the short drive home, stretching the ten-minute trip into one which felt much longer. Despite her panic, her jumbled brain tried to get her to come to her senses. She reminded herself that the chances of being pregnant were slim.

But the implant's due to be changed out in January, the voice fuelling her concerns argued back. *What if it's not as effective anymore?* She had had it for almost three years. But doctors –medical professionals who she trusted implicitly– wouldn't say they needed to be replaced every three years if they lost effectiveness sooner than that, would they? No. Of course not.

But nothing is 100% effective, the voice returned. She groaned aloud, impatient for answers.

As soon as she got home, she raced into her ensuite bathroom, clutching her shopping bag like a lifeline.

Having guzzled at least a litre of water, it wasn't difficult to fill a sample cup (liberated from work) enough to dip all three of the tests in. She laid them all on her bathroom counter and watched with bated breath as the control line appeared on each one and remained alone.

All three tests held single lines.

Negative. She wasn't pregnant.

Negative.

Sara burst into tears.

They were not tears of relief. In fact, she was startled to realise that she had been hoping for a positive result. *When the hell had that happened?* It was a good thing she wasn't unexpectedly pregnant, wasn't it? Hadn't she *just* been panicking about the timing being wrong, and about not wanting to force Charlie into fatherhood?

Except those concerns hadn't had anything to do with whether she'd wanted a baby or not.

She sat heavily on the closed toilet seat with her head in her hands. God, she'd wanted that hypothetical baby.

Being completely honest with herself, she knew her biological clock had been ticking away ever since Gemma had popped Zoe out. Sara had always wanted kids, had always wanted to pass on the same unconditional love that her mother had given her. To nurture another life, and to have a connection that she couldn't possibly form with anyone else. And now she was dating a man who —as far as she was aware— didn't want children.

She had tried to convince herself that she could compromise. That she had Zoe as a niece, and that she adored her as though she was her own child. That there were as many pros to not having kids as there were cons. That she didn't need to have babies of her own to be fulfilled and happy in life.

There were many people who chose not to have kids, and they were extremely satisfied —travelling whenever they wanted, living in pristine houses free of toys and sticky handprints, not having the additional costs and stresses of raising children— and Sara had nothing against them. She had tried hard to assure herself that she could be one of them.

But her reaction to those tests turning negative proved otherwise.

This shook the confidence she had in her only recently repaired bond with Charlie.

She had just arranged for Charlie to move in with her. That was a huge step towards solidifying their relationship. It was supposed to be exciting, and proof they would make a future together work. But what would happen when she told him that she couldn't concede on the kid thing after all? She had no intentions on forcing him to compromise either. Charlie had known better than anyone what could happen if a father resented his children.

But how long should she let their relationship continue before she told him that she needed a partner who wanted kids as much as she did? Or, at the very least, wasn't reviled by the concept.

She loved Charlie. She was in love with Charlie. However, it wasn't fair on either of them for her to keep this from him. And if it was an insurmountable difference, it would be better to end things sooner rather than later.

At least he's not moving here for me, she mused, wiping at her eyes.

He had made the decision before they had repaired their relationship. He'd chosen to move here to be near his family. Being closer to her was a bonus, but she was glad it wasn't his sole motivating factor. Especially if they were going to break up, after all.

Sara realised that she was working herself into a state not dissimilar to the one she'd been in when she had sabotaged things between herself and

Charlie the first time around.

Biting back a sob, she tried to shake the negative thoughts off. Making assumptions hadn't worked out well for her last time, and they weren't going to help now, either.

Outside of a few short conversations very early on, she and Charlie hadn't discussed the bigger picture. Topics like children and marriage seemed too much too soon. Hell, just deciding to live together felt like a huge step in itself, but it had felt right. It still felt right.

After pushing herself back to her feet and tossing the used tests into the bin, she washed her hands and face and stared at her reflection in the mirror.

No matter what happened, this was something she felt strongly about.

She would just need to find the right time to discuss it with him, that was all.

How hard could that be?

* * *

Between sorting out the finer details of Charlie's move, Sara's job, her duties as a bridesmaid, and the last-minute preparations for the wedding, finding the right time to bring up her revelations actually turned out to be quite difficult. It was nice to have Charlie with her now, knowing that he wasn't on a time limit and that he was settling in for good, but she couldn't escape from feeling awkward.

While she smiled and told him to get comfortable, and to start considering the house his own, a little voice at the back of her mind told her not to get too used to his presence until she'd had time to talk to him properly. *Pretend it's just one of his trips,* she told herself, feeling guilty as she did. *Just until you know where you really stand.*

Thankfully, Charlie didn't seem to sense anything was amiss. He was cautious at first, behaving more like a guest than someone who lived in her home, so she gathered that this was probably all a shock to his system, as well. Which was yet another reason she put off talking to him about her pregnancy scare – he needed time to acclimate before she shook things up all over again.

Tick-tock, went the traitorous little voice in her head, *tick-tock*.

God, she wished it would just fuck off.

"I can't believe Brennan and Jeff are getting married tomorrow," she said as the two of them packed their bags in preparation of a couple of nights spent in a hotel on the Gold Coast. She would be staying with Jeff, Gemma, Zoe and Jeff's friend, Jack, for the night prior to the wedding, leaving Charlie in a room by himself for the night. She would join him in his suite after the wedding was over.

"You know you can always sneak away from your little slumber party and come have some fun with me tonight," Charlie waggled his eyebrows at her.

She rolled her eyes in the middle of folding a t-shirt. "I think you've proven you can live without me for a night." Her bridesmaid's dress was hanging carefully on the back of the wardrobe door in its garment bag, next to his suit which was also freshly dry cleaned. "But tomorrow night, I'm all yours."

"About that..." He chuckled awkwardly and scratched the back of his neck.

With a pair of denim shorts in hand, she paused and blinked at him. "What?"

"I know I should have consulted with you first..."

Sara was torn between amusement and concern. It wasn't often she watched Charlie squirm. "What did you do?"

He attempted to contort his expression into the pleading puppy dog one which his brother had perfected. "I...look, I may have told Rhett that we'll look after Zoe for the night of the wedding."

She could feel her eyebrows winging upwards. "Really?" Charlie was good with Zoe, so it made sense that he would make more of an effort to step up into his role as her uncle –especially after watching Uncles Brennan and Jeff in action– but to leap immediately into overnight babysitting took Sara by surprise.

"I'm sorry," he apologised, "I should have asked–"

Tick-tock. Her heart gave a tug at the thought of him offering to look after Zoe, and she swore her ovaries just about exploded.

"Don't be ridiculous," she cut him off, rounding the side of the bed to run her hands over his chest, "she's not just your niece, she's mine, too, and I think it's sweet that you're giving Everett and Gems a night off. I mean, he only flies back in tonight and won't even get to see Gems until the wedding, so..." she trailed off, shaking her head. "It's really thoughtful and kind of you. And that's hot as fuck."

The tension evident in his demeanour dissipated as his shoulders relaxed. He smirked back at her, once again his cocky self. "Want to tell me how hot you find it?"

Instead of answering, she sank to her knees in front of him and reached for his zippered fly. The voice in her head was thankfully silent, so she was able to enjoy the moment for what it was.

Later, they could make their apologies for their tardiness.

* * *

"Everett proposed!" Gemma cried over the phone, only a couple of hours after Sara had bid her best friend goodbye at the wedding reception and told her to take advantage of her night reconnecting with her boy toy.

The ceremony had been beautiful, and the party afterwards a whirlwind of dancing, drinking and laughter. She had even been a dutiful bridesmaid, running interference between Brennan's fame-hungry actor friend, Micah, and Everett, because the former had been behaving like an overzealous Labrador puppy when he'd recognised the Best Man. And to think that Gemma had been more concerned that Micah's sister, Rosie – an entertainment blogger– would be the one they had to watch out for.

It had all been fun, if exhausting, and she had sat down on the bed in her hotel room with a grateful groan mere minutes before her phone had rung.

"*What?!* Oh my God!" Casting a sideways glance in Charlie's direction and frowning as he grinned sheepishly and shrugged, Sara turned her attention back to the call, "Congratulations! When? *How?* Ugh, you need to tell me *everything!*"

Gemma laughed. "I will. Later. For now, we're phoning to check on Zoe." Sara pictured Gemma's expression being somewhere between loving and concerned as she asked, "Did everything go okay? She wasn't too bratty for you?"

"Nah." Sara's own smile softened, and she looked towards Charlie as she answered. "She fell asleep in Uncle Charlie's arms in the lift. We wrestled her into her PJs and now she's dead to the world on the futon."

Watching Charlie with Zoe always felt like a revelation in itself. He was far more paternal than he gave himself credit for. But tonight –armed with the additional feelings of desperate yearning which had been plaguing her since she'd stared at three solitary lines on three plastic testing wands– Sara's ovaries had practically ached while she'd watched him.

He had carried their niece with ease, her elfin face tucked into the crook of his neck as she snored lightly, her little hand wrapped up in the material of his shirt at his chest, while her long, pale legs dangled at his sides. An elderly couple in the elevator had smiled and complimented them on their 'handsome little family', and Sara supposed that, with Zoe's long dark hair so similar to her own, they did look the part. Instead of refuting the compliment, Charlie had only returned the smile and thanked them, and Sara had nodded mutely. She guessed it was easier than explaining the whole situation to these random strangers, but she had selfishly wondered if maybe he wouldn't hate the idea of them having their own child one day, after all.

When they'd made it into the room –the fold-out couch already set up into a bed– he had ever so carefully put Zoe down and shushed her gently when she'd roused during the process of getting her out of her dress and into her Disney Princess pyjamas. Then he'd smoothed his hand over her head and kissed her forehead as she drifted back off to sleep, the action setting off explosions of desire, love, and longing within Sara.

"Her hair's going to be a nightmare tomorrow," Sara added into the call with Gemma, "but I've got some detangling spray, so hopefully it'll help."

"Well, we'll aim to pick her up early, if you want a hand dealing with the tantrums."

Sara shook her head, even though her friend couldn't see her. "Don't be stupid, Gems," she stated, flopping backwards horizontally across the mattress as Charlie got up to go check on Zoe in the other room. "Celebrate being newly engaged and child-free. Do all the kinky shit you don't get a chance to do at home."

"Stop it," Gemma laughed again. "But what about you guys? I mean, your relationship is still pretty new...don't you want to enjoy the spoils of a hotel room together, too?"

Sara snorted. "There's nothing we can't do at home," she answered, thrilled to be able to call her house *their* home now, "because we don't have a small human demanding our time and attention." *Yet,* her traitorous mind added; she tried to brush the thought away. There were some pros to not having kids yet, Sara had to admit. "Ain't nobody gonna walk in on us –or interrupt us in any other way– is all I'm saying. Whereas, you don't usually have that luxury."

"No," Gemma sighed wistfully, "we don't. Not that I'd change it for anything, though."

Charlie returned from the other room and left the door open a crack with a soft look on his handsome face.

"No, I imagine you wouldn't," Sara agreed. "She's awesome, Gems. And she's fine. Take advantage of it. Sleep in. Have wild monkey sex–"

"Ugh," Charlie complained, his expression now contorting into one of disgust, "could do without those images, thanks."

Sara ignored him, stretching out like a cat, partially to watch his pupils dilate as she revealed a strip of skin beneath her tank top, "–*really* celebrate your engagement to Captain Abtastico and then we'll meet up for lunch or something and return your kid to you, unharmed."

There was a moment of silence before Gemma gave in, as Sara knew she would. "Alright, alright. As long as you're sure."

"I am."

"And if there are any dramas–"

"Goodnight, Gemma. Go, shoo, have fun. Give my congrats to Boy Wonder."

"But–"

Sara pressed the red button on her screen to terminate the call and dropped her phone carelessly on the mattress beside her. Her eyes landed on her lover as he loitered guiltily, and she sat back up quickly.

"How much did you know?" She demanded of Charlie, folding her arms across her chest.

"All of it?" He attempted the same apologetic puppy expression that he had when he'd told her about taking Zoe for the night. That particular decision now, of course, made much more sense. "I'm sorry. Rhett wanted to surprise her and swore me to secrecy."

Sara couldn't maintain her stern appearance. She laughed and shook her head, pushing to her feet before she took two steps to meet him in the middle of the room. She smoothed her hands over the silky-fine material of his shirt. He still looked damn hot in his suit, even with the jacket discarded on the back of one of the dining chairs in the other room. "It's fine. I wouldn't have been able to contain my excitement and then the jig would've been up."

He kissed the tip of her nose, his hands flexing at her hips. "Thank you for understanding."

"Mmm," she rose up on her tiptoes, chasing his lips. They shared a chaste kiss before she stepped back and allowed him to start readying himself for bed. She'd already changed out of her bridesmaid getup and into her summer pyjamas: a pair of short cotton boxer shorts and a loose tank top. "Zoe all good?"

Charlie nodded, the same warm look of affection stealing over his features again at the mention of their niece, once again causing Sara's ovaries to just about implode. He deftly undid the column of buttons on his shirt and slipped the material off his broad shoulders, throwing the garment to the side of the room. With his hands on his belt, he said, "Yeah. Out like a light."

Sara watched –now comfortably seated against the headboard in bed– as his pants followed his shirt. She felt ridiculous, aware that the prominent thought circling around inside her head was how badly she wanted this to be a discussion about their own little family. About their own baby. Ever since she'd thought she was pregnant it was like she'd developed a one-track mind about it. Trying to shake it off, she rallied by saying, "She's a good kid."

He was down to his boxer briefs now. "She really is," he replied, now climbing into bed beside her. "Rhett's a lucky man." He turned to face her in the dim light provided by the lamp on her bedside table. "I'm happy for them. Him and Gemma. I'm glad tonight went the way he'd hoped."

What Sara had planned to say was 'I'm glad, too,' but what came out was "I took a pregnancy test." Charlie's eyes widened, the look on his face now reminiscent of a deer in headlights. Her mouth kept running. "Well, three, actually."

"And...?" He finally managed to ask. She knew that tone: his measured, calm voice. It normally amused her to watch him struggle to maintain whatever outburst of emotion he was feeling –typically irritation, and normally with her or his brother– but in that moment it terrified her.

She hadn't meant to blurt out her confession. Not like that. And not there, not after the wedding, not when she'd had a bit too much wine and zero chance to brace herself emotionally. But it was likely the alcohol that had loosened her tongue to begin with.

"I'm not..." there was a lump in her throat so she attempted to clear it. "They were negative. I mean, with the implant, the chances are super slim that they wouldn't have been, but–"

"When?" he interrupted her rambling, frowning at her. Some part of her knew she should be pleased that he wasn't reacting with exaggerated relief, but the fact that she couldn't read him at all was more concerning.

"When what?"

"When did you think you might have been pregnant? Better yet, why didn't you tell me?"

She sighed. These were reasonable questions. "It...you were still in London, and I didn't want to tell you over the phone, but...I didn't want to wait to test, either."

Charlie exhaled and nodded slowly. "And after you took them–"

"I know. I know I should have told you." They had promised not to keep secrets from each other, and he knew her well enough to know that she would have felt some sort of emotional turmoil from the situation. She was certain, though, that he would never fully understand quite how much she'd felt after the fact. *She* hadn't even expected it. "I just...they were negative, you know? I didn't think it was worth putting you through that while you were on the other side of the planet."

"Jesus, Sara." He stared at the ceiling for a moment before looking back at her. "Why not tell me when I got here, then?"

"I…" There it was. The moment of truth. "I was scared, Charlie."

"Scared?" he echoed with obvious confusion. "Of my reaction?"

She shook her head. "Not exactly."

"Then of what?"

"I…Charlie, I took those tests, and I was panicking because the timing was shit, and I didn't want us to start the same way as Gems and Everett, and I didn't want you to resent me –us– or…well." She stopped short, not wanting to bring up his father's abandonment. She knew Charlie would already make that mental leap himself. "But when they were negative…" her lower lip quivered and her eyes watered; she couldn't look at him. Staring at her hands in her lap, which she was now wringing together, she explained, "I wanted that potential baby so much. Which is stupid, right? We've barely been together –in the same place– for a month at best, and I know you don't want kids, and I…"

"Sara…"

"No, I know. I know that the timing would have been terrible, okay? I do. I just…you're my person, Charlie." She forced herself to look at him now, feeling raw and terrified of whatever was going to happen next, but knowing she couldn't hide from it. "I love you. And I want a future with you. Including kids. I want it all with you, you know? Even if that sounds deranged because we've barely been dating a year, or six months, or wherever you want to start counting from. But…if…if you don't want that, I don't know if just carrying on as we are is enough for me, after all. Even though I know in July I said I didn't care…it turns out I do. I…" she sighed, "I really, really do."

He was silent for a long moment. She couldn't get a gauge on his thoughts, his face giving nothing away. "Are you done now?" he asked softly. "Can I talk?"

Sara nodded.

"I love you," he began, and she stifled a sob, because it felt like this was the beginning of the end. She was waiting for the 'but'. "Even if you're a stubborn twit sometimes." He reached out and grasped one of her hands, halting her fidgeting. "You should have told me, Sara. You shouldn't have had to deal with those thoughts alone."

"I—"

He squeezed her hand again. "Uh uh. My turn." When he was convinced that she wasn't about to repeat her explanation, he continued. "I'm forty-six. For most of my life, I've thought I was just fine on my own. Until I wasn't." He licked his lips, and there was a bit of uncertainty in his tone. "You asked me back at Easter whether I saw a future for us, and I lied to you."

"What?" she choked out, still waiting for the words that would confirm that their relationship had met its natural end.

"I imagined it," he told her with a rueful shake of his head. "A kid, a dog, a picket fence…the whole shebang. But, coward that I was, I kept that to myself. Didn't want to scare you off with how quickly my tune had changed," his lips curled upwards, "and you were already in the middle of dumping my sorry arse, so what was the point of putting myself out there like that?"

A bubble of inappropriate laughter escaped her, and she screwed her face up, trying to comprehend the words coming out of his mouth. "Wait…what?"

"I'm saying I'm in," he answered slowly, "kids and all. You're my person, too."

Still feeling overwhelmed with disbelief, Sara pushed, "You don't think it's too soon?"

"Love," Charlie sighed, pulling her closer to hold her against his bare chest. He rested his cheek atop her head. "Look at Rhett and Gemma. They did it all arse backwards, right? Still worked out for them. There's no reason to put some sort of arbitrary timeline on these things. I think you get to a point where you just know: if it's right, it's right."

Sara took a minute to process the words, but the steady beat of Charlie's heart under her palm –because her hands couldn't help gravitating over his deliciously firm chest– soothed her nerves. "You sound like your mother."

He chuckled. "I might have had a chat or two with her lately."

Given the conversations she had shared with Beatrice –who was very keen to see Charlie and Sara's relationship flourish– she had a pretty good idea what those talks had entailed. They had obviously helped him get his thoughts together, though, and for that she was eternally grateful.

"So…you're sure?" she asked for good measure, her own heart thumping away at a thousand miles per hour. Excitement simmered beneath her skin. Could it actually be this easy? "You want to have kids? With me?"

He pressed his lips to the top of her head before he shifted their position so he could look her directly in the eye. His green eyes were bright as they locked on hers. "I want it all with you, Carlisle."

Unable to form words to express the love and joy she felt in that moment, she kissed him deeply, pressing herself against him and losing herself in the action. She felt his hands glide under her tank top, slowly guiding the material up, until they had to part so she could pull it over her head.

He lay her back down on the bed, peppering kisses down her neck, over her chest and breasts, then down her abdomen, while his hands tugged her shorts and panties down. Usually, he'd tease her with his fingers and his tongue, but tonight he crawled back over her body after pausing to remove his underwear, and slotted in between her legs, which she gladly spread to accommodate him.

Mindful of the small child asleep in the next room, they kept as quiet as possible, kissing again as he ran his cock through her folds, teasing her clit with the tip. She clutched at his biceps, amazed that even this understated, hushed lovemaking could get her feeling so wet and needy for him. She mewled into his mouth as his tongue entwined with hers.

They'd had slow, gentle sessions before, but this felt a thousand times more intense. Sara wondered if their declarations just now had anything to do with that. It wasn't as though this was about immediately trying to get pregnant –she still had the implant in her arm, and there was a lot more to discuss than simply agreeing that they both wanted children together– but just the thought of him wanting to do that with her suffused her with feelings she couldn't quite describe. She hadn't anticipated this sort of reaction.

Charlie groaned quietly as he finally –*finally*– slid himself inside her. He stilled to give them both a moment to adjust. Sara still loved that first moment whenever she was with him. She was addicted to the way he stretched her, and the way his movements sent tiny jolts of pleasure skittering through her.

They moved in tandem, with her arching her back to meet his almost torturously slow thrusts. Their kissing matched their motions, intense and sensual, barely parting for air. As she felt herself nearing her peak, she panted against his lips, short of breath despite their actions being far removed from their usual frantic fare.

He hadn't even touched her clit. But with how closely they were holding each other, there was enough friction between them. She couldn't help but feel −sweat slicked and strung out as she was− that this was the most erotic moment they had ever shared. Or was that the wine talking again?

It didn't matter. He felt amazing. *They* felt amazing.

She came with an almost silent cry −a cut off squeak was the only noise she made− their heavy breathing providing the only other sounds in the room. He continued rocking into her, kissing whatever skin he could reach on her body, his pace increasing marginally as he chased down his own high.

Sara's lips found the shell of his ear, then her teeth found his earlobe, and she nibbled gently, still trying to catch her breath and calm the pounding of her heart. He swore into the crook of her neck, his hips losing their rhythm.

Shifting his weight onto his left arm, he slipped his right hand between them, his thumb finding the swollen, sensitive flesh of her clit with startling precision.

"Come again for me," he urged in a whisper, "I want to come with you."

If she wasn't already seeing stars, caught in just the right moment to take advantage of her lingering aftershocks, she would have accused him of being corny. But he knew just the right actions to take her back to the edge, and suddenly she needed to come again desperately.

"There," she breathed into his ear as he shifted his angle, pushing her ever closer to the precipice, "there. Don't stop." She was a quivering mess beneath him, desperate for this renewed tightening of energy inside her to snap and disperse. "I love you."

"I love you," he murmured against her cheek, "and whatever family we make together."

His jaw was tense, his movements faster and more erratic. As much as she loved the first few moments of their lovemaking, she loved these even more. When he began to lose his inhibitions, and his words poured forth in response to her own. It was half the reason she talked during sex. The honesty and connection in the moment was half the magic for her.

Her brain short-circuited while her breathing hitched, and her orgasm swept her up in its wave of pleasure and release before she'd even realised it was happening. Charlie followed suit, coming inside her convulsing walls, even as he continued pressing wet, urgent kisses into her skin and to her lips.

Moments later, while snuggling against him in the afterglow, the oxytocin dissipating, Sara's mind started to race. It should scare her how much she'd enjoyed the thought of them eventually making a baby together. But, she supposed, for someone who hadn't had any actual family since her teens, it made sense that her subconscious was driving the point home now. This was what she wanted. Badly, it seemed.

Dear God, she didn't have some sort of breeder kink that she wasn't previously aware of, did she?

No. No, this wasn't about the actual act of getting pregnant –of being bred (a term she was not at all a fan of, thanks)– it was about how deeply in love she was with this man. Further still, it was about how much she looked forward to building on that love, committing and creating an unbreakable bond through a child who they would both adore.

Back when she'd first met him, Sara never would have imagined that Charlie would be her perfect match. But, wrapped in his strong embrace, having just made some life changing promises to each other, she wouldn't change a damn thing.

This was her Happily Ever After, and she couldn't wait to start it with him.

Epilogue

The boat rocked gently in the deep blue waters off the coast of Hervey Bay. Almost two years to the day following his last visit, Charlie had returned. Unlike the first time, Charlie couldn't recall being as happy and carefree as he currently felt. The last two years had been a roller-coaster the likes his life had never experienced before.

Dating Sara in secret, breaking up, deciding to move half-way around the world, getting back together with her –thankfully without the secrecy– and then promising to start a family had been the first year. The second year had seen him settling into his new life with renewed enthusiasm.

Working with Brennan was a complete change of pace from his previous job. There was significantly less manual labour and more administration work. But he loved it, and under Charlie's management, Brennan's expansion had gone quite smoothly. Which was good, because they were essentially family now, with Everett and Gemma taking them all by surprise and eloping a few months after their engagement.

His mother had not been impressed that she'd missed the event, until a short, intimate, non-legally binding commitment ceremony was enacted for the family's benefit. Following this, Beatrice had made a point of sternly informing Charlie and Sara that, should they ever decide to marry, she wanted to be there for it. Marcus had quietly agreed.

So, between pretty much being Brennan's brother-in-law via Rhett, and his mother nagging him to spend more time with family, he'd also found himself spending a lot more time at Gemma and Everett's place than he had originally imagined he would. Even with his brother overseas, most weekends saw Charlie horsing around with Zoe and becoming even closer friends with his brother's wife. This had the additional benefit of pleasing Sara, given that her relationship with her best friend was as close as ever (though he often caught her glancing longingly at Gemma and Zoe when the pair were together).

In the months following Brennan and Jeff's wedding, Charlie and Sara had spoken in more detail about the baby she'd so desperately wanted. They had agreed to wait until the new year before she removed her implant and weren't going to pressure themselves into actively trying. After all, their relationship was still relatively new, and they were still settling into living together. Burdening themselves with the stress of deliberately getting pregnant was not worth the heartache.

That was what they'd agreed.

Of course, the new year had come and gone, and when June came along –six months of having completely unprotected sex delightfully frequently– and she still wasn't pregnant, it was obvious Sara was beginning to put that pressure on herself anyway. It pained him that he couldn't fix it.

Charlie had then secretly shuffled off for fertility testing, wondering if his *mildly* advanced age might be affecting their chances. It had been a huge relief to learn he was in perfect health, and so were his little swimmers. The doctor he'd seen had assured him that these things took time. Not everyone was as lucky (or unlucky, depending on one's perspective) as his brother had been, to create life so quickly or unexpectedly.

The doctor had also suggested that he and Sara take themselves on a holiday. Apparently, relaxing and taking their minds off how terribly they wanted to make a baby could potentially help to achieve that very goal. Sceptical though he was, Charlie set about enacting The Plan.

Every other weekend, he swept Sara up and took her somewhere special and new. She delighted in the surprise, and they definitely made use of whatever fancy facilities were at their disposal (the heated, private pool in the penthouse he'd rented in Noosa had been a favourite of his), but he could still sense her sadness every month when her period returned to remind her that their efforts had not yet been successful.

So, to commemorate their second anniversary –he was counting from the date of their first night together, and he didn't care if there had been a short break a few months later– Charlie had organised some time away on the Fraser Coast. It was the location where he'd first realised that he fancied her, and where he'd experienced a few other revelations that had led him down the path he'd taken with her. Besides, he had promised Sara that he would bring her back there one day.

He had booked a little beachside apartment in Hervey Bay for a few nights before they were to travel, by barge, across to Fraser Island, where he had splurged on four nights at one of the two large island resorts.

The weather was perfect; the skies were blue, the air was warm but not sickeningly hot, and the water was clear. It was the perfect location to relax and enjoy each other's company.

And to propose.

His hand travelled to the box safely concealed in the pocket of his cargo shorts. It had been so easy to assist Rhett in enacting his proposal plan, but Charlie felt at a loss with his own. He knew that he wanted to pop the question on this little holiday, but beyond that he'd planned nothing. He and Sara had always been the spontaneous sort –particularly when they were together– so it went to reason that inspiration would strike him when the timing was right.

But, two days in, he hadn't yet found the right moment.

Knowing Sara had wanted to see the whales, Charlie had booked the same charter that Everett had two years earlier. Luis, the Captain, had remembered him, shaking his hand and clapping him on the back as though they were old friends. The man was likely just being friendly because Charlie had parted with a good deal of money in order to book the posh catamaran just for Sara and himself, but it was a nice effort all the same.

So there they were, on a boat in the pristine waters off the coast of Hervey

Bay, watching whales frolic in the water a short distance away. Sara was rapt, her eyes wide, full of wonder and excitement, and Charlie could not tear his own from her if he tried.

Was this the moment? He couldn't think of a more romantic setting. Not with the sun bouncing from Sara's dark hair, giving her the illusion of a glowing halo – a goddess in the flesh.

"This is…wow," she told him, leaning over the railing with her back arched and arms thrown back, *Titanic*-style.

He chuckled. "If you go yelling you're the king of the world, we're turning this boat around."

Her laughter in return was bright and effervescent. "Spoilsport," she complained lightly, before closing her eyes and breathing in deeply. When she opened her eyes again, Charlie could see the sparkling water reflected in them. "I love it out here. It's magical."

"Yeah," he agreed softly, falling to one knee without any further thought, "it is."

He realised in that moment that so many things could go wrong with spontaneously proposing on a boat, the worst of which could be fumbling and dropping the ring overboard. But he pulled the box from his pocket anyway, opening it at the same moment she turned to ask him what the hell he was doing, the amusement on her face giving way to shock.

"Let's make it more magical, love," he declared, not caring that it was as cheesy a proposal as anyone might come up with. Not usually one to waffle –especially not with an audience– he dove straight into the big question. "Will you marry me?"

She squealed, tears leaking from the corners of her eyes, and dropped down to her knees. Charlie had just enough forethought to snap the ring box closed and clutch it tightly before Sara's arms were around his neck and she lunged at him, kissing him with fervour and joy. "Yes," she murmured against his mouth, "*fuck* yes."

He laughed, relieved that –even though he hadn't doubted for a second– she'd accepted his proposal. He kissed back while wrapping his arms around her, the box still secured in one fist.

"My knees hurt," Sara complained with a watery chuckle as they parted.

Charlie playfully rolled his eyes. "Nobody told you to join me down here, did they?"

She used the railing to pull herself back to her feet and he did the same. He re-extended the ring box towards her. "You didn't even look at the shiny thing," he teased.

"Oh, I'm so sorry that the love of my life proposing in the middle of the ocean was more exciting than a piece of...*ooooh*!" Charlie had opted for a delicate, feminine design: a platinum band with a large, central solitaire cut diamond and two diamond-encrusted twists – one down each side of the band. Sara held out her hand and he slid it onto her finger, where it stood out strikingly against the olive colour of her skin. She held it up, watching it sparkle. "It's beautiful."

He bit his tongue from saying anything cornier than he already had that morning. "I'm glad you like it."

"I love it." Her tone had softened, and there was a wealth of emotion in her gaze as she looked back at him, curling her hand over her abdomen, her ring glinting in the sunlight. "*We* love it."

"We...?" The penny dropped. Charlie's hand was covering hers within an instant. "Really?" He was overwhelmed by joy, choking up as Sara nodded. He hadn't expected to feel so intensely. "When? I mean, how far along?"

"Like four or five weeks, maybe? I only took the test this morning. I know I should have said something–"

"No." He attempted to clear his throat as he shook his head emphatically. "No. This is perfect. *You're* perfect."

Charlie had been thinking that the moment couldn't have been more magical if he'd tried, but he had been wrong. He was also secretly glad that he'd proposed when he did: there would be no doubt in her mind that he'd loved her with or without a baby in her belly.

A baby.

His baby.

His mind was blown. In the span of two years, he'd evolved from eternal bachelor to soon-to-be-father.

When he'd first met Sara Carlisle, he'd thought her a nuisance. An uptight pain in the arse whom he'd be forced to deal with for the rest of his life. And, to be fair, none of that had changed…too much. She was still a bit uptight, and still a pain in the arse at times, but she was *his* pain in the arse, and he loved her more than he could possibly begin to explain.

"Thank you," he told her, smoothing his palm over her still-flat abdomen, wondering if she had any inkling of the path his thoughts had taken. "You've changed my life for the better, Carlisle."

"Right back at you, Rhodes," she agreed, propping herself up on her tiptoes to rub their noses together in an Eskimo kiss. "I can't think of anyone else I'd rather do this with."

"Me either, love." Charlie kissed the tip of her nose, swallowing roughly over the lump in his throat. He didn't know what else the future would bring, but if the past two years were any indication, his future with her was going to be a damn sight better than any previously considered future he'd had without her. "Me either."

And when their son was born, squalling and daring to bear the same dark hair as Sara and his own brother, those feelings only intensified.

* * *

Thank you so much for reading *You Can't Hurry Love*. I really hope that you enjoyed it!

I'd love to hear what you thought of it at Goodreads or your preferred online retailer (**https://books2read.com/YouCantHurryLove**)

On the fence about leaving a review?

It's okay to leave a star rating and say nothing at all.

Thank you in advance for helping me out!

Happy Reading!

About the Author

Anita (A.N.) Verebes is a daydreamer and romance novelist. As a civil marriage celebrant, Anita makes a living telling other people's love stories and celebrating real romance! Also armed with a Bachelor of Education (Secondary), Anita is a qualified -but not practising- High School English teacher who loves to read anything she can get her hands on, including fanfiction. (And, yes, she's written her fair share of that, too.) Living directly between Queensland's sunny Gold and Sunshine coasts, Anita spends her days exploring the Great South East with her husband and their two rambunctious sons. When at home, she's also a slave to two cats and one very spoilt Great Dane X.

You can connect with me on:
🌐 https://anverebesauthor.wordpress.com
f https://www.facebook.com/ANVerebes

Subscribe to my newsletter:
✉ https://anverebesauthor.wordpress.com/newsletter_signup

Also by A.N. Verebes

A.N. Verebes writes Contemporary Romance. Light, feel-good, easy reads that scratch an itch…and turn up the heat!

Handle With Care

When Gemma Fox gets stuck in a lift with her celebrity crush, Everett Rhodes, she writes the whole encounter off as a fluke. However, life has other plans for both of them, and it changes everything.